A THRUST TO THE VITALS

A THRUST TO
THE VITALS

Geraldine Evans

This first world edition published in Great Britain 2007 by
SEVERN HOUSE PUBLISHERS LTD of
9–15 High Street, Sutton, Surrey SM1 1DF.
This first world edition published in the USA 2007 by
SEVERN HOUSE PUBLISHERS INC of
595 Madison Avenue, New York, N.Y. 10022.

British Library Cataloguing in Publication Data

Evans, Geraldine
    A thrust to the vitals. - (A Rafferty and Llewellyn mystery)
    1. Rafferty, Detective Inspector (Fictitious character) - Fiction
    2. Llewellyn, Sergeant (Fictitious character) - Fiction
    3. Police - Great Britain - Fiction
    4. Detective and mystery stories
    I. Title
    823.9'14 [F]

    ISBN-13: 978-0-7278-6479-6

Typeset by Palimpsest Book Production Ltd.,
Grangemouth, Stirlingshire, Scotland.
Printed and bound in Great Britain by
MPG Books Ltd., Bodmin, Cornwall.

Dedication

Auntie Berta – this one's for you. I thought it was about time that my greatest fan received a well-deserved dedication. Many thanks for your understanding and support: they've given me such encouragement.

Acknowledgements

To everyone at Severn House: your hard work and professional advice is much appreciated. Also to my previous editor, Hugo Cox, for his editorial efforts over the last few years. Good luck in your new career, Hugo. And especially to Vanessa, my agent, for her wise counsel.

One

It was just another day, yet another murder inquiry. And then Rafferty's mobile rang. It changed everything.

'JAR? That you?'

Detective Inspector Joseph Aloysius Rafferty immediately recognized his younger brother Mickey's voice, even though it sounded a bit strange. 'What do you want, Mickey? Now's not a good time.' Rafferty frowned as he watched the white-suited forensics team bustle busily around him at the scene, their practised routine ensuring they didn't get in one another's way even if *he* got in theirs.

It was one o'clock in the morning and he was having trouble keeping his eyes open. The last thing he needed right now was a phone call from a member of his family. A call at such an hour was unlikely to herald good news. But Mickey was his brother, so he relented and said, 'Come on, then. Spit it out. What can I do you for?' and then braced himself for trouble.

From the other end of the line came a swiftly indrawn breath. It made Rafferty's frown fiercer. These facial gymnastics attracted the interest of his sergeant, Dafyd Llewellyn. Rafferty turned away from this scrutiny as Mickey said, 'I just heard on the local radio that you're in charge of the Seward murder investigation.'

Bloody hell, Rafferty thought, the dead man's not even cold yet. Who let that cat out of the bag? But the suspects for this violent death were too numerous for him to even consider issuing reprimands right and left. News of the murder must have gone round the four-star, 100-bedroom Elmhurst Hotel and Conference Centre venue like nits round a nursery school. It was impossible to keep a clamp on the wagging tongues of so many.

His brother's voice interrupted the tail end of these thoughts and forced Rafferty from his wool-gathering.

'Sorry, Mickey. What did you say?'

'Christ, Joe. Can't you listen? This is important.'

'So's my murder investigation,' Rafferty retorted. 'And I'd quite like to get back to it.' Actually, what he'd rather do was go home and retire to bed with a nightcap. But chances were that wouldn't be on the cards for hours. Shoulders slumped, he leaned back against the nearest wall. Grumpily, he told his brother, 'Spit it out so I can get started organizing one more triumph for British justice, there's a good lad.'

'That's just it,' Mickey told him, his voice sounding increasingly tense, 'I'm scared this case might turn out to be yet another *in*justice. You asked me what you could do me for. I'm worried, once your inquiry gets started, that you might think you have reason to do me for something. That something being this murder.'

Aghast, Rafferty felt a deep foreboding followed by an unwillingness to delve any further. But Mickey's words gave him no choice and he demanded, 'What are you on about?' But before his brother could reply, Rafferty became conscious of the many listening ears surrounding him. Telling Mickey to hold on, he slipped from the murder scene in the plush penthouse suite of the Essex market town's Elmhurst Hotel. He found a quiet corner in the corridor where he could see and be forewarned of all the comings and goings before he put the mobile back to his ear. Then he said, in a harsh whisper, 'Christ, Mickey, don't tell me you were a guest at last night's civic reception for our esteemed prodigal, Sir Rufus bloody Seward?'

Please don't let him tell me that, Rafferty prayed to his long-ignored God. Fortunate it was that God chose not to ignore *him*, because his prayers were answered in the positive with an immediate and unexpected speed when Mickey said, 'No. I wasn't at the party.'

Rafferty brightened, but only for a moment, because his brother barely paused for breath before he rushed on to tell him, 'I know you won't believe this, but I got an invite from Seward himself. I didn't go. But, seeing as he was here in Elmhurst, I took the opportunity to go to see him late on in his hotel suite when the party was all but over.'

'You did *what*?' Rafferty realized he was shouting. Worse, he'd attracted odd looks from a couple of the uniformed officers guarding the outside door to the murder suite. They quickly averted their eyes when they caught sight of his scowling countenance. He was thankful to realize that his words sounded less incriminating than admonitory, as if he was giving some unfortunate a bollocking. Even so, he forced himself to calm down. He even managed to find a tight smile for Dr Sam Dally as he emerged from the lift, rolled in that familiar, bouncy way on the thickly carpeted hallway towards Rafferty and raised an eyebrow in greeting.

Rafferty told his brother to hang on again. He waited as Sam struggled to insert his generous body into his protective coveralls and disappeared into Seward's suite. It was too public here, he thought, to be having this conversation – too close to the police and forensic bustle that surrounded the discovery of recent, violent death. The thought made him even more uneasy. His uneasiness forced him to lower his voice again till it was all but inaudible. But his brother, with his fear-heightened senses, still managed to hear him. Rafferty hoped no one else could.

But never mind not having this conversation *here*; Rafferty thought it was undoubtedly a conversation he shouldn't be having at all.

'What on earth did you go and see Seward for?' Rafferty was becoming more seriously concerned for his brother as admission followed admission. 'It's not as if you were ever best buddies, is it? Even at school, you always hated his guts. And with good reason, as I recall.'

Rufus Seward had always been a bully. And Mickey, having never been tall or well built, had been a natural target for Seward's nastiness. Rafferty had protected his younger brother as much as he could, but bullies always found their moment and it wasn't as if he had been in a position to guard his brother all the time: they were different ages and therefore in different classes. Besides, Rafferty had been raised to stand up for himself, and part of him expected Mickey to be able to do likewise without help from him.

'I–I had something I wanted to discuss with him. A bit of business . . .'

Mickey sounded awkward and Rafferty wondered, even as his unease grew and developed love handles, why his little brother felt it necessary to lie. He'd never been any good at it; it was a trait they shared. What possible *business* could his brother, a poor carpenter, just like Jesus, have with Sir Rufus Seward, the local bad boy prodigal made good?

Sir Rufus Seward had returned to his hometown in triumph to receive Elmhurst Council's civic honours and acclamations by the bucketful after his knighthood in the New Year's Honours List.

This was the same Rufus Seward who, in his youth, had made Mickey's life – and those of so many others smaller and weaker than himself – a misery, until, fortunately for Mickey, Seward's other physical pursuits had caused him to be all but chased out of town by a posse of angry fathers of tearful teenage girls.

In the intervening years, Seward had made his pile. He had returned to Elmhurst in triumph only the day before, for the first time since his involuntary departure, to receive his hometown's accolades after his ennoblement.

Sir Rufus's civic honours had been awarded with all the dignity and pomp even his self-regard could desire. He had also received another, unanticipated honour: the attentions of a murderer who, unlike our own dear Queen with her gentle shoulder-tapping sword, had thrust a sharpened carpenter's quarter-inch wood chisel deeply and far from gently through Seward's back and into his heart.

A clammy hand seemed to clutch Rafferty's own heart. It gave it such a sharp squeeze that the organ paused in its beat for a few worrying seconds, before it resumed its *thud, thud, thud* again, but on its recommencement, it beat with a speed that was positively breathtaking.

As a carpenter, Mickey worked with such chisels. They were the daily tools of his trade. He also had reasons – several of them – to hate Rufus Seward. If Rafferty had been any other copper, after his brother's admission that he had been in Seward's suite on the evening of his murder he would have concluded Mickey had means, motive and opportunity in plenty and slap the cuffs on him. Fortunately for Mickey, if not for himself, as his brother had said, *Rafferty* was in charge of the investigation.

4

Last night's reception had, naturally, given Seward the fawning attentions such honours attracted, and had been attended not only by those who had peopled Seward's past, but also by the great and good who had peopled what had been his present. And, from what Rafferty had learned from uniformed's early questioning of the few guests who remained, Seward, during the party, had not hesitated to rub a number of his guests' noses in his success. It must, if the reported accounts concerning his behaviour from several of the more unguarded attendees were anything to go by, have left some of the party guests feeling the urge to plunge something sharp between Seward's meaty shoulders. For all his wealth and success, the man, like the boy, had been both a bully and a poor judge of people. Certain it was that he had badly misjudged someone, otherwise that someone wouldn't have given in to the plunging urge.

Rafferty could only pray that guilty someone *hadn't* been his little brother. Because he knew – who better? – how much rage Mickey nursed in his heart against his youthful perse-cutor. Mickey also had a temper; one he hadn't always managed to govern.

Now Rafferty, in an attempt to dispel his growing anxieties, did some confiding of his own. 'You're not the only family member with cause to be worried about Seward's murder,' he told Mickey. 'You'll never guess who else amongst our rela-tives received an invite. Only "dear" Nigel.'

'Not Slimy Nigel?'

'The very same.'

Nigel Blythe or Jerry Kelly, the name he had held before he had spurned it as being too common, was cousin to the Rafferty brothers, whom he considered himself a cut above.

'Trust him to slime himself an invite to such a swanky do.'

'Mmm. Muck, brass and Nigel always did form a natural, unholy trinity.'

In spite of his brother's worrying admission, Rafferty felt humour bubble up and he added, 'Bet he wishes he'd kept his distance from all that undoubtedly dodgy money for once. Even if he didn't kill Seward, with the number of crooked deals that estate agency of his goes in for, I imagine the last thing "dear" Nigel wants is the police having a reason to sniff around.'

'Especially if he's the one who topped the pompous prat.'

'True.' But although Rafferty tried hard, for Mickey's sake, he somehow couldn't see his devious cousin Nigel – who always had one eye on the main chance and the other on the exit in case a swift flit was required – committing this particular murder. It seemed too little thought through and spur of the moment for Nigel. If he had wanted to kill someone, unlike the less than cool-headed Mickey, he would bide his time and await his best chance of doing the deed without unpleasant repercussions. Like getting caught. Mickey, by contrast, could be a bit of a hothead. This was a worrying trait in view of his late night visit to the long-loathed victim, and the other, steadily accumulating list of circumstantial evidence potentially linking him to the crime.

Rafferty's lips thinned. And as his gaze followed the busy Scene of Crime team, he wondered if Mickey had left a trace of his presence behind. Anxiety over his brother's problem as well as the increasingly pressing need to get back to the murder scene made him curt and he asked, 'Where are you?'

'At home. Sweating.'

'Stay there,' Rafferty quietly instructed. 'I suppose you're on your home phone?'

Rafferty sighed as Mickey confirmed it. He wished his brother had had the nous to ring him from a public phone. If questions were asked at a later date, calls to his mobile from his brother's home at such a time would make it harder for him to deny either knowledge or complicity. 'Did anyone see you in Seward's suite?'

'The two security guards on the door and one of the guests,' Mickey confirmed.

'Did they get a good look at you?'

'Yes.'

Well, of course they had, Rafferty told himself. Stupid to ask, really.

Mickey's third confirmation was even more worrying than the previous two, as was his clearly reluctant admission that he had actually asked the guest where to find Seward. The fool had left a trail that even young Tim Smales could follow.

Conscious of time ticking away, Rafferty said, 'I've got to go. I'm still at the scene. There's no way I can leave yet – I probably won't be able to see you for hours, but I'll come to your flat as soon as I can get away. We need to put our heads together.' He would also need to separate the truth from the lies Mickey had already told him. The idea of his little brother having a 'bit of business' with the wealthy and successful Seward was about as likely as him reforming the band he had played guitar with in his youth and them having a smash hit. So why had Mickey lied? The question stirred even more uneasy feelings and yet more questions.

'In the meantime, stay where you are and keep out of sight. I'll try to think of somewhere I can stash you, since you clearly can't remain at the flat. Somebody's bound to recognize you when the witnesses' photofit is circulated.' He'd delay this as long as he could, but it would be only a short-term holding measure until he had time to organize moving Mickey somewhere safer and more low profile.

Although he missed her dreadfully, it was fortunate that Abra, his live-in girlfriend, was away on a hen party weekend in Dublin and wouldn't be around till late on Sunday night to notice his absence while he tried to sort Mickey out with the essential bolt-hole.

In spite of the promise he had made to Abra in October, only a couple of months back, about not keeping things from her, this was one secret he would have to keep to himself – certainly until he had had a chance to think of who was most likely to be able to supply him with a place to stash Mickey where he would, for the foreseeable future, at least, have the best chance of staying hidden.

Because Rafferty didn't relish the prospect of having to charge his brother with murder. Even less did he relish having to listen to what their ma would say if he did such a thing. But as neither possibility bore thinking about, he put both from his mind.

With a grimace, after warning Mickey not to panic and do anything they might both regret, he said goodbye to his brother, pocketed his mobile and returned to the scene of Seward's murder.

It was going to be a very long night.

Two

It had been after midnight when Rafferty, summoned from his bed by uniform, had arrived at the Elmhurst Hotel, following hard on the heels of his DS Dafyd Llewellyn and the Crime Scene Investigation team. Sam Dally, the pathologist, was the last to arrive as usual.

The hotel, situated to the northwest of Elmhurst, on Northgate near the River Tiffey and close to the site of the town's Romano-British ruins, was in all its four-star Christmas glitter when he arrived. Jonty Reynolds, the night manager, distraught and approaching hysteria at the thought of all the uniformed and forensic teams trooping through the front entrance during one of the hotel's biggest earning seasons of the year, had rung the station on learning of Seward's murder and pleaded with Bill Beard, the officer manning the desk, that they use the rear entrance for the sake of discretion. This message had been relayed to Rafferty as he was on his way to the scene and he had passed it on to the rest of the team. For what it was worth.

The discreet approach was holding up – for now, anyway. Rafferty couldn't help but wonder how long the manager imagined it would last.

Jonty Reynolds had made no objection to himself and Llewellyn in their civvies entering by the pretty route. But Rafferty, at least, as he stood and glanced around the foyer and took in the tall tree, rather thought he might have preferred the back entrance and the bins. The tree was what he imagined Lizzie Green, one of the younger uniformed officers, would have told him if she'd seen it was the height of fashion and style. Perhaps it would appeal to twenty-somethings like Lizzie, he thought, but he failed to appreciate how a sixteen foot, fake black Christmas tree could possibly encourage anyone to enter into a proper festive spirit.

This black Christmas theme, teamed with golden baubles to relieve the depressant effect, continued throughout the hotel, according to the manager, who seemed excessively proud of it. It was to be found in the hotel's four bars, its two ballrooms and its three restaurants. Rafferty hadn't enquired about the decor in the annexe. Talk about Christmas at Dracula's castle, he thought. Part of him half expected the count himself to appear from behind the thickly-branched black tree and set about adding to his problems. Such an appearance would do nothing for the anxieties of the hotel's night manager; Rafferty was already tiring of listening to the man's worries about the likely downturn in their profits once news of the murder spread. Besides, he thought the manager might be pleasantly surprised by the reaction of his clientele. In Rafferty's experience, there was nothing like murder for attracting the paying customers.

Rafferty was relieved that the late Sir Rufus Seward, when consulted by the manager about his preference in Christmas decor, had declined the fashionable nonsense of a funereal black Christmas tree in the suite hired by the local council for their reception, and had insisted on a traditional theme. Death black decor in the murder suite itself would be more than a tad macabre. Thankfully, the scent of the ten-foot-high Scottish pine he had instead selected brought with it the glorious waft of Highland mornings and was a welcome breath of fresh air for Rafferty after he and Llewellyn had left the lobby, been whisked up to the penthouse and first entered the murder scene. It had helped, too, to mask the unpleasant aroma of hate, envy, revenge or whatever other negative emotion had brought about Seward's murder, and which, like a spectre at the feast, had added its unwelcome ambience to the suite's atmosphere.

Uniform had been quick to organize the removal of the remaining guests from Seward's suite. They were now penned in another one, hastily opened up by the manager, and well away from the scene. Once installed there, Rafferty was told, they had grumbled, drunk the management's complimentary alcohol and grumbled some more, while they awaited Rafferty's arrival. But at least for now they were out of *his* hair. Rafferty, grown canny over the years, had no intention of subjecting himself to a barrage of questions from people by now more than well-watered and who were probably inclined to be disagreeably intemperate in their demands to be allowed to go home. He was already tired after a busy day, so he preferred to wait till they were relatively sober before he attempted to question them.

To this end, he had instructed the manager to remove all the complementary alcohol and bring copious quantities of black coffee instead. Clearly, judging by the reports that filtered back to him and the increased volume issuing from their gilded cage after this instruction was carried out, he was unlikely to be voted police officer of the month in any favourites contest amongst the VIP guest stragglers. Doubtless he'd get Superintendent Bradley at full throttle later in the day when the guests, who sounded a pretty self-important lot, made their assorted, vociferous and hung-over complaints. But that prospect, mercifully, was still some hours distant. It was the here and now he had to get through first.

It wasn't as if he was short of things to do while he waited for relative sobriety to kick in amongst the last remaining guests.

The hotel manager, on Rafferty's arrival and request for somewhere quiet to question Seward's assistant, Marcus Canthorpe, had offered the use of his office. Canthorpe quickly produced the requested guest list as well as Sir Rufus's address book and diary. Rafferty would take a close look at all of them shortly, but before he studied the scene, Rafferty questioned Seward's assistant closely.

Canthorpe, a thirty-something of middling height and slim build, was, thankfully, as sober as his dark suit. Rafferty was relieved to discover there was one party attendee able to coherently explain the evening's events.

But, although coherent, quietly articulate and impressively efficient given the circumstances, Rafferty surmised, as he took in the man's disordered, collar-length fair hair, that the subdued Marcus Canthorpe was worried about his future. His hair gave every appearance of the distracted Canthorpe spending the waiting time running his fingers through it. Rafferty, unused to such clear-headed competence from a person who found himself present at a murder scene, was surprised Canthorpe had been able to supply him with his late employer's diary and address book so promptly and had commented on it.

10

Canthorpe had given a weary shrug when questioned about it and explained, 'Sir Rufus does – did – business 24/7. He pays me well enough to be able to insist that I'm 24/7, too. And as his business interests are global, he needs to be able, at a moment's notice, to contact his various business associates around the world.' He paused, blinked, and then said, '*Did*, I suppose I mean.'

'I see.' Even the technophobic Rafferty knew there were such things as computerized diaries and address databases, so he asked why Sir Rufus's apparently more than capable seeming assistant had made do with such old-fashioned methods of record keeping.

Canthorpe smiled wanly. 'Of course we use modern methods as well – or rather, *I* do. But Sir Rufus is – *was* – surprisingly maladroit with technology. He preferred to have the means to get in touch with people himself, hence the old-fashioned diary and address book. He was a hands-on boss, who preferred to be hands-off with technology. That was my area of expertise.'

Rafferty nodded and thanked Canthorpe for the concise explanation, though he was a little put out at the discovery that he shared any trait, even an aversion to technology, with a man like Seward, whom he had known and disliked. They each even had their own tame computer geeks at their beck and call: Seward had Canthorpe and he, of course, had Llewellyn.

'I understand you found the body, Mr Canthorpe?' Rafferty questioned.

Canthorpe nodded.

This was always suspicious in Rafferty's book. Silently, as he studied Canthorpe's fair good looks, he mused on the possibility that this could be his first inquiry where the murderer dunnit from motives of sleep deprivation.

'Tell me,' Rafferty asked after this silent observation, 'is it normal for you to interrupt your boss when, from what you told the uniformed officers, he had retired to his bedroom for a brief space of privacy during a socially-demanding evening, and had presumably indicated that he didn't want to be disturbed?'

'Yes and no,' Canthorpe replied. 'Yes, in that if he was waiting for something urgent to be couriered over, he always instructed me to disturb him. Otherwise, no. But this evening was different. It was a very special occasion, of course, and I knew it meant a lot to him. Sir Rufus was very proud that his hometown had chosen to honour him in this way, especially in the same year he received his knighthood. Besides, Ivor Bignall was one of Sir Rufus's business partners. Not only that, he's the local councillor in charge of the evening's reception. And he and his wife wanted to say their goodbyes and go home. Mrs Bignall doesn't enjoy the best of health – I was surprised they stayed as late as they did. I simply didn't feel I could deny him access for the minute or two that would take and I didn't think my boss would be pleased with me if I did so. Which is the reason I intruded on him in his bedroom and found . . . and found—'

Rafferty raised a hand to stop Canthorpe's attempt to continue with this description. He'd already had this more than adequately described by the uniformed officers, who had been first on the scene and who had to provide such descriptions as part of their jobs. Besides, he and Llewellyn had already seen the body for themselves. He thanked the late Seward's assistant and added, 'You've made the sequence of events very clear.'

After a few more questions, he asked Llewellyn to escort Marcus Canthorpe back to the commandeered suite where the rest of the late-lingering guests were still sequestered. And after he had informed the hovering manager that he could have his office back, Rafferty headed back up to the penthouse murder scene to study it further himself.

From where Rafferty stood, with his sergeant, Dafyd Llewellyn, at the entrance to Rufus Seward's suite, it was clear the alcohol had flowed with a bacchanalian abandon at his celebratory civic reception. The Elmhurst Hotel's cleaning staff hadn't of course been allowed admittance and the debris left at the end of the extravagant spending of council taxpayers' funds indicated that a good, free-loading time had been had by all.

There were numerous bottles of what Rafferty learned were jeroboams of vintage champagne. Big buggers, anyway, thought a Rafferty unfamiliar with both the term and the extravagance. Stint me not on my big day, Sir Rufus must have said. And stint they hadn't.

Nice of them to be so generous with my money, thought the sober and begrudging council tax-paying Rafferty. Especially when police stations that had once been open all day and all night were now mostly restricted to office hours. That would be fine, of course, if criminals followed suit and adopted a nine to five working day.

Some of these big bugger bottles were lying on the floor like so many drunken sailors. If they'd had heels, they'd have kicked them up, for sure. The only wide and round thing that was no longer rolling around was Dr Sam Dally, who had departed after he had viewed the body, though the forensics team would be kept busy for some time yet.

Seward had been killed in the suite's main bedroom. Rafferty had, of course, already studied this bedroom and Seward's corpse while it had still been *in situ*. But, to give the forensics team room to move, he hadn't lingered longer than necessary to absorb the details, preferring to take in the suite as a whole.

The victim's bedroom was located down a short passageway lined with floor-to-ceiling closets near the entrance door to the suite. A large and ornate gilt mirror was on the wall opposite this corridor; Rafferty paused in front of it to tidy what he saw was thoroughly windswept hair. It seemed Seward had been seated at the desk the hotel provided in the largest of the three bedrooms, with his back to the door, when someone had crept up on him and plunged the chisel into his back. This creeping had certainly been made easier by the luxurious thickness of the carpet; the fact that Seward had, reportedly, been far from sober; and that the brief passageway that housed the en suite bathroom before it led into the bedroom itself would have absorbed any warning draught from the opened door.

Rafferty forced his concentration back to the scene in the main reception room. Several of the celebration's remaining buffet canapés of what looked like smoked salmon and caviar lay abandoned in the centre of vast silver platters, though by now these looked rather less appetizing than they must have been at the start of the evening. More bottles, mostly three quarters empty, were fixed into the optics behind the specially set up bar in the left-hand corner of the suite's main room. These bottles' earlier companions, now drunk dry, stood in crates stacked behind the bar, awaiting collection. There was a well-spread stain of what Rafferty assumed was red wine on the once crisp white cloth that covered the long buffet table facing the door. Someone had also crushed one of the canapés underfoot on the pricey looking carpet.

All in all, it looked much as Rafferty imagined a room must look the morning after one of those Roman orgies when the participants were all nursing sick headaches and saying, 'Never again, Nero.'

In his head, Rafferty could hear his ma tut-tutting in disapproval at the self-indulgent and careless antics of these new Romans. Of course they, like their ancient predecessors, could make as much mess as they liked, sure in the knowledge that some other, much poorer bugger was going to get the job of cleaning up their mess. It was ever thus.

But Rafferty, left with the job of cleaning up an even bigger, more bloody mess, was only too aware that he had no time to indulge in a bout of self-righteous moralizing. He didn't have time, either, to enjoy the Edwardian splendours of one of the more pricey of the Elmhurst Hotel's enormous suites, even though he felt like a round-eyed urchin with his nose pressed against the glass of an upmarket toy shop and with no hope, unless he was prepared to get himself hopelessly in debt, of ever playing with what was behind the glass.

The plush penthouse suite had, of course, been hired, at vast expense, by the local council for Seward's shindig, the usual town hall accommodation having been pre-booked for another, even higher status VIP. With its glittering Tiffany crystal chandeliers and its Sicilian Carrara marbled bathrooms with the Jacob Delafon bath ware and its giant-sized, carved African walnut beds, the suite gave a whole new meaning to the word 'ostentatious'.

Rafferty, who wouldn't have known a Tiffany chandelier if one had crashed down on his head, had gained this sophisticate's vocabulary after he had requested and been given one of the Elmhurst's promotional brochures by the manager on his arrival. It was from this slim but triumphalist piece of literature that he had learned of the hotel's self-proclaimed class and style. He had gained a knowledge of the hotel's prices, too, of course. They made him wince. Of course, such swank didn't come cheap: the quoted price for one night's stay had rendered him goggle-eyed in nose-pressed urchin mode. It had also sent up a warning signal to make sure he didn't take the brochure home with him in case Abra found it on her return from Dublin. It might give her ideas that would make his bank account, rather than his body, wince.

With the thought of the prices still at the forefront of his mind, Rafferty was moved to comment, 'I wonder what Elmhurst's council tax-payers would have to say about this extravagance if they ever got to know how much it must have cost – especially when they get their next inflation-plus increase on their bills.'

Dafyd Llewellyn, a sternly brought-up Welsh Methodist, gave a Puritan's sigh for such excess and told him, 'As I'm one of those council tax-payers, I'm sure I can provide you with enlightenment.'

Rafferty smiled tautly. 'Don't bother, Daff. I'm one as well, as you know. All this high on the hog stuff at our expense makes me sick. I've a good mind to write the Elmhurst equivalent of the "Disgusted of Tunbridge Wells" letter to the local rag – especially as our free-spending representatives have decided to put the tax up again next year.' He snorted. 'Probably need it to pay for the army of snoopers they're also planning to foist on us.'

'Mmm,' Llewellyn murmured. 'I can see that writing such a letter to the local newspaper might ease some of the pain, but I doubt it would be wise.'

Rafferty snorted – the effects of this snouts in trough business seemed to be spreading. 'Probably not. I'll have to wait till I retire before I can voice my protest at the way they spend my hard-earned money.'

'There's that too, of course, though I was thinking more of the fact that Superintendent Bradley was one of this reception's attendees.'

Rafferty turned and stared at Llewellyn. 'Old Snout-in-Trough-in-Chief? Now, why doesn't that surprise me?' Given Bradley's propensity for high-hoggery, this revelation wasn't that unexpected. Still, the thought of Bradley finding himself numbered amongst the murder suspects brought Rafferty a little shiver of delight. Then he protested as memory provided a reminder. 'But old Long Pockets wasn't on the guest list.'

'No, but I gather that's only because he had an earlier engagement this evening and said he would have to cry off on this one. It seems the other one ended sooner than he expected and he had kept his invitation to this reception just in case.'

'Trust Bradley to manage to get his snout in *two* troughs in one night.'

Although Llewellyn had no comment to make on his super-intendent's trough-seeking skills, he told Rafferty, 'I only know he was here because DS Mary Carmody overheard one of the guests mention his name as being present and she questioned the man about it. Although, I gather the superintendent and his wife weren't at this function for very long – an hour at most. They left shortly before Sir Rufus's body was discovered.'

Better and better, thought Rafferty.

'This particular guest, the local mayor, Idris Khan, seemed to think the presence of a heavyweight policeman like the superintendent would provide him with alibi enough.'

In spite of his rumbling stomach, the anticipated long night ahead and the worry about his brother, this information brought something approaching a grin to Rafferty's lips. 'Who knows? It might at that – especially if I'm able to prove our esteemed super was the chisel-wielder. After all, it wouldn't be un-precedented. He's shown plenty of previous form in plunging sharpened implements in backs. Even if it is more in the meta–meta—' Rafferty frowned and Llewellyn prompted, 'Metaphorical?'

Rafferty nodded. 'That's the bugger. Plenty of metaphorical knives in backs. Proves capability of the crime to my mind.'

'Mmm . . . You might like to know that several – more than several – of Seward's other guests are also reputed to have such a predilection.' Llewellyn gave a discreet cough. 'In fact, I noticed a certain Nigel Blythe was numbered amongst the guests. That wouldn't be the same Blythe—?'

Rafferty gave a weary nod. 'The very same.' Llewellyn, of course, remembered this Rafferty family cousin from a previous case.

16

Llewellyn wisely said no more on the subject.

Rafferty recalled himself to duty. Now, beckoning Llewellyn to follow, he walked back down the suite's chandeliered hallway to the main bedroom, the scene of the murder. He stood in the doorway, and, although Sir Rufus Seward's body had now been removed to the mortuary, the vivid picture of his fleshy-girthed and well-fed body slumped over the gilded desk in front of the curtained windows in the bedroom, the thin chisel thrust deep in his back, was unlikely to leave him any time soon. But then, neither were his worries about Mickey.

Rafferty recalled Dr Sam Dally's comment as he viewed and examined the corpse of the late Sir Rufus: 'At least you won't be short of suspects for this cadaver, Rafferty. From what I've heard of the man, he was one of those types who smarm all over those he regards as his social superiors – though, I suppose, since his knighthood, only royalty would be so regarded – and saves his bile for those not in a position to answer back. Not a likeable man, by all accounts.'

Rafferty had nodded. Even if he hadn't already been, from personal knowledge, well aware of that fact, he would have got a hint of Seward's reputation from the reported comments of the few guests who had chosen to linger long after the party was scheduled to finish and who had been herded from the scene once the police had arrived at Marcus Canthorpe's summons on finding the dead body of his employer. These guests had received the reward deserved by all such late-lingerers: nasty questions and unwanted invitations to linger even longer. Some of the replies, fortunately for the investigation, had been of the unguarded nature that copious quantities of alcohol invariably encourage.

Seward, like Rafferty and his two younger brothers after they had moved to Essex from their south London home, had attended the local RC secondary modern. But Seward, to give him his due, had been smart even then and had been destined for higher things. It had only been his early idleness that had caused him to attend the secondary modern in the first place, rather than the grammar school. But in his final year he had obtained a scholarship to St Oswald's, the nearby fee-paying boarding school with an excellent reputation.

He hadn't wasted the opportunity. Nor had he hesitated to

crow about it. Even now, twenty-five years later, Rafferty could recall his younger brother's resentment at Seward's boasting of his scholarship success and Mickey's relative 'failure', as Seward called it, in merely managing to get signed up to attend the local technical college. No, Seward had not been a nice man.

Rafferty, being a year older than both his brother Mickey and cousin Nigel, had seen less of Seward's youthful arrogance than had been displayed to his two relatives. And, as a teenager, Rafferty had been both taller than his younger brother and cousin and handy with his fists, so Seward had had the sense not to tangle with him in the way that he had so enjoyed tangling with those younger or smaller than himself – of whom, Mickey, of course, had been one.

But, while the grown-up Mickey might not have Seward's money or worldly success, he *did* have a craftsman's skills in carpentry, painstakingly acquired during the City & Guilds course he had taken at the local college during his apprenticeship. And even though his brother had managed to put himself in an extremely unfortunate position over Seward's violent murder and his self-evident failure to bring it to anyone's attention before he scarpered with the words 'chief suspect' inevitably trailing behind him, what Dally the pathologist had said about the number of people who would be glad to assist Seward to even greater, heavenly glory was true enough. It provided Rafferty with the only solace currently on offer.

Of course, he had yet to meet Seward's unwillingly lingering guests, though from all the reports he had so far heard, they sounded a pretty uncongenial lot.

OK, finding yourself involved in a murder scene when all you had expected to do was drink and stuff your face would be a shock to anyone. Still, given that Sir Rufus had known and associated with some characters who were, by repute, as unpleasant and ruthless as he was, Rafferty felt it wasn't unreasonable to hope that at least *one* of them would be revealed to have nursed a magnate-sized grudge against the dead man. It might yet let his idiot brother off the hook.

Three

After having a quick word with the rest of the team, Rafferty led Llewellyn away from Seward's suite. Outside, in the corridor, he found Reynolds, the hand-wringing night manager, hovering as close to the suite as the uniformed guardians of the door permitted. As soon as he emerged, Rafferty was met, once again, by the man's imploring, Bambi gaze, though what the manager imagined he could do to guarantee continued discretion on the murder front goodness only knew . . .

Jonty Reynolds was far from being a jaunty Jonty at the moment, as his hand-wringing testified. After his first, fraught few questions, he had asked little more. Probably afraid of the answers he would receive, as Rafferty presumed Mr Reynolds had managed, since they had last spoken, to conjure up for himself far more colourful examples of the publicity likely to spring from the murder of such a prominent guest than even a cynical policeman could have provided. Rafferty, fearing tears weren't far away, interrupted Reynolds' hand-wringing to remind him, 'You said we could use one of the ballrooms to question the reception's remaining guests. Perhaps we could see it now?'

In his late forties and clearly with fears of being 'let go' by his employers on his mind, Jonty Reynolds, his forehead beaded with the sweat of acute anxiety, nodded and led them into the even more impressive Edwardian splendours of the now deserted main ballroom. They found themselves surrounded by the detritus of some other party's long-since concluded festivities. The ballroom, like Seward's suite, was still awaiting the attentions of the cleaning staff, who, warned that the police would be using it for their interviews, had been told to keep out. The leftovers from the buffet and the bar were all around them, scattered on the floor and tables. The fiftieth wedding

19

anniversary congratulatory banners were still in place for Cyril and Cynthia.

Rafferty, wondering at the likelihood of current newlyweds staying the course over such a time and feeling the need to acknowledge such an achievement, from a nearby table plucked a glass still containing dregs of white wine and raised it towards the banner in a silent toast to the golden couple.

Llewellyn, the particular, seemed subdued by the abandoned and curling remains surrounding them. His nostrils faintly flared as if, even so far from the ground, he could detect the smell of bad drains.

Rafferty grinned to himself. He was only too aware that the Welshman could never abide such mess. Strange that he should choose such a mess-encountering career as the police in which to earn his living. Ironic, too, that he should have the far from tidy Rafferty as his senior officer.

Certainly, the mess didn't trouble Rafferty one jot – rather the reverse, in fact. He felt quite at home. Besides, by now he was absolutely ravenous and happy to help himself to the curling remnants of yet another celebratory party buffet in the hope this Oliver Twist act would spur the manager into offering them something to eat.

Thankfully, once the distraught night manager spotted how starving was his late-arriving and unexpected guest, he was obliging and wily enough to attempt some damage limitation – Rafferty had met him previously, during another murder investigation – and to temporarily put aside his handwringing and get on the right side of the investigating policeman.

He enquired as to Rafferty's food preferences and swiftly organized the late-night kitchen staff into rustling up a huge plateful of beef and horseradish sandwiches. These, fortunately, were of policeman preferred proportions rather than the hotel's normal, more dainty fare.

Rafferty wasted no time in getting himself outside most of these sandwiches before the guests still awaiting his questions had the opportunity to ruin his appetite.

In spite of Rafferty's enthusiastic encouragement that his partner follow the example of their freeloading boss and the rest of the party guests and 'fill his boots', as it was likely to be a long night and even longer day, Llewellyn seemed to have lost his appetite.

When Llewellyn still declined, Rafferty shrugged, said, 'Suit yourself,' and reached for another sandwich.

Once the guest list and Seward's address book had been photocopied so the rest of the team could make a start on contacting those named therein, Rafferty and Llewellyn settled down to a longer study of these documents. At the same time Rafferty didn't fail to address his attention to the very superior sandwiches.

By the time this study was concluded and the plate of sandwiches, but for a few crumbs, despatched, young Timothy Smales, the uniformed officer allocated the task of guarding the door where the late-staying guests were currently confined, passed along the message that they had now quietened considerably.

For Rafferty, this quietude provided a welcome indication that their over-tired and alcohol-stimulated belligerence had died a natural death. Perhaps now he would be able to get on and question them to some purpose. Maybe, Rafferty thought, he might be lucky and get a straight answer or two.

He had installed a couple of plain clothes officers in the newly-opened suite where the guests were sequestered. He hoped that Mary Carmody and her colleague DC Andrews had, before the alcohol influence totally abated, overheard something else to his advantage other than the revelation that Superintendent Bradley had been present for the latter part of the evening. Though given such a juicy piece of information, Rafferty couldn't believe he would be lucky enough to squeeze any more juice from the guests' overheard chit-chat.

Of course, once the removal of the alcohol had begun the sobering-up process and lessened the unwise confidences that it had encouraged, the presence of the two police officers had naturally inclined this revealing chatter to fade. But he couldn't have it both ways. Neither could he delay much longer the necessity of interviewing them all. By now they would all be tired, emotional and ready for their beds, so they might yet be encouraged to spill some more beans of the revelatory, or even incriminatory, sort.

But if he was honest with himself, Rafferty thought this

21

last unlikely: even those who had had no hand in Seward's early exit from the world would, once relatively sober, feel a guilty complicity in his violent demise and be keen to keep their mouths shut. Fortunately, in such circumstances, in Rafferty's experience, such wisdom usually came along too late. He was hopeful that one or more of these guests would, indeed, have blurted out something revealing in the interim.

Before Rafferty and Llewellyn left the ballroom to speak to the waiting guests, Jonty Reynolds had pleaded with them that they conduct their investigation with as much discretion as the circumstances allowed. Too late for that, was Rafferty's thought as he recalled his phone conversation with Mickey, which had revealed that news of the murder had already spread beyond the confines of the hotel itself. His reassurances sounded weak even to his own ears. Certainly, they must have sounded hollow to Jonty Reynolds, to judge by his drooping head as he slouched his way across the floor and out. Reynolds' body language acknowledged that the Elmhurst Hotel was, all too soon, likely to be besieged by the media – if it wasn't already. And, from the look of the manager, Rafferty could only surmise that the ladies and gentlemen of the Third Estate were hammering at the door – if they hadn't already battered it down in their usual Genghis Khan-like desire for the career trophies that the violent death of a VIP brought to the sufficiently quick off the mark to be in almost at the kill.

Constable Timothy Smales gave what he obviously presumed was a restrained, 'one professional to another' nod, as Rafferty arrived at the double doors leading to the suite holding the remaining guests, before he thrust open both the doors to the suite's main living area and invited the detective inspector, with a wide-flung arm, to enter the room.

Rafferty would have preferred a more discreet entrance less likely to induce excitement in the already over-emotional occupants, but young Smales, with his inherent feeling for drama, had ensured it was too late for that. Rafferty braced himself for the barrage as the remaining guests rushed forward in a body as if they were all still on an alcohol-fuelled high. And even if alcohol no longer greatly stimulated their bodies, the fumes were still evident on their breath as they demanded answers.

Rafferty had already been provided with the guests' names by Seward's efficient assistant, Marcus Canthorpe, before he had been requested to rejoin them.

Pushing himself to the fore was the imposing, grey haired, bristling and red of face Ivor Bignall. Rafferty recognized him from the local newspaper in which he often featured. As the councillor who had organized the reception in liaison with Canthorpe, Bignall evidently felt he must take command.

'You're Inspector Rafferty, I take it?' he began in a disconcertingly loud voice. 'Why have we been kept here for hours? It really is quite intolerable.'

Rafferty quietly apologized and explained the need to prioritize. And on a murder investigation the first priority was the victim and the scene of crime.

To his surprise, Bignall immediately subsided. He simply nodded his understanding. Presumably, Rafferty supposed, as both a councillor and a businessman, Bignall understood the importance of prioritizing one's workload. At any rate, he posed no more questions for the moment.

Rafferty also recognized his blonde, pale, though very attractive and much younger wife, Dorothea. She had elected to remain seated in the shadows beyond the suite's twinkling Tiffany chandeliers. She appeared subdued; hardly surprising in the circumstances, of course. Presumably she had concluded that it was pointless to attempt to pose any questions, her forceful husband, given time and opportunity, being more than capable of posing all the questions either of them could desire.

Surprisingly – or perhaps not so surprising given that the mayor must have the best part of fifteen years' advantage agewise – Bignall allowed himself to be edged aside by Idris Khan, the town's half-Welsh, half-Asian current mayoral incumbent. Khan was wearing his full regalia, which apparently included his much younger blonde wife, Mandy, who clung on to the back of his mayoral insignia like a limpet. Her pinpoint pupils indicated to Rafferty that she had recently been sniffing something that was rather more potent than snuff or her own mucus. Perhaps, between the drugs and the alcohol, she felt unsteady on her feet and required the support of the sturdy mayoral chain of office.

When Idris Khan spoke, it was clear he wasn't quite sure

whether the occasion demanded he be terribly British and pukka sahib about the whole thing or whether he would be more likely to coax the required responses if he played the minority card and let his Asian half predominate. Perhaps because he had spent most of his childhood in India, the latter won and he began to flail his arms about in a most excitable manner while directing a stream of sing-song sentences in Rafferty's direction.

'You must the inspector be,' he addressed Rafferty. 'This is very dreadful, dreadful thing to happen to poor Sir Seward. Very dreadful. My wife is over tired and wishes with a most strong desire, to go to her home now. As Mr Bignall said, we are waiting here these many hours and are most distressed. But let me assure you, most heartfeltly, my dear inspector, that poor dear Sir Seward's dreadful death has nothing what-soever at all to be doing with any of us and—'

He was interrupted by Bignall's big voice booming above his own. 'Be quiet a minute, won't you, Iddy? And don't be silly, my dear chap. Of course it must have been one of us who killed him. I don't know how you can even try to pretend otherwise. Who else could have done it?'

Clearly, Ivor Bignall wasn't one for trying the head in the sand approach. Of course, he had hit the nail squarely on its head. Who else *could* be responsible other than one of those present at the private reception, given that access to the suite had been policed by two of the hotel's own security guards throughout the evening, and that Dr Sam Dally estimated Seward had died but a short time before his own arrival – sometime between 11.00 p.m. and shortly after midnight?

'Inspector,' Bignall continued, 'I appreciate that as the investigating officer you have a job to do and will need to question us all as a matter of routine. But could you at least give us an idea of how soon we are likely to be able to go home? My wife doesn't feel well. She's very distressed – as are we all, of course,' he added as an afterthought. 'Poor Seward. The mayor's quite right. It *is* a dreadful thing to have happened. But—'

But life went on, Rafferty silently finished for him. He held up his hand before Bignall could continue or anyone else had a chance to get in on the act. 'Ladies and gentleman, if you

24

please. We will get through the preliminary interviews as speedily as possible so you can all go home. But we'll get done a lot quicker if you remain calm and quiet. Perhaps you will allow me to explain a few things so you all know the drill.' He paused. 'We shall require each of you, individually, to come along to the Boudicca Ballroom on this floor, where we shall be conducting the interviews. Unless any of you have anything of great moment to confide, I doubt any of these will take longer than a few minutes. Once you have been questioned, you may go home. Unless, of course,' he added on a sudden burst of optimism, 'one of you would like to confess now to Sir Rufus Seward's murder, and save us all a great deal of trouble?'

This brought a collective gasp, as well as a few uneasy sniggers, as he had known it would. But it was late, he was tired, they were tired, and, as Bignall had already pointed out, one of those present *must* have killed Seward. Who else was there, apart from Mickey? And Rafferty was as nearly certain as anyone could be that Mickey was no more capable of such a murder than he was himself.

If he had hoped that such a brisk suggestion might shock an admission out of one of them, he was disappointed. His quick sweep around the large reception room to check if there were any takers took in Marcus Canthorpe, the dead man's assistant, whom he had already briefly questioned, as well as Roy and Keith Farraday, thirty-eight-year-old identical twins whom he also had no trouble recognizing, as they had attended the same secondary school as Seward and Rafferty, as well as his brothers and cousin. Canthorpe had told him the twins had been taken on Sir Rufus's staff only a matter of months ago as general dogsbodies and gofers.

Rafferty wondered if the Farraday brothers still indulged their childhood hobby of snitching to teacher and spying out information they could sell for a profit. He was willing to bet this evening had brought a few unwise disclosures they must hope to use to their advantage. He was surprised a man of Rufus Seward's renowned acuity hadn't recognized them for what they were straight away. Or perhaps he had? Maybe he had had his own reasons for employing the pair . . .

Rafferty noticed his cousin, Nigel Blythe, hovering at the back

25

of the crowd as if hoping he wouldn't be noticed. Nigel proved unwilling to meet his eye. Bloody Nigel, Rafferty thought, annoyed all over again that his cousin should once more turn up in his life like the proverbial bad penny. His presence needlessly complicated an already complicated situation. As if the problem inherent in Mickey's brief but oh-so-traumatic attendance at the party wasn't causing Rafferty enough, yet to be resolved, grief!

Mickey had posed the question, how the hell had Nigel managed to wrangle an invitation to such a swanky do? It was a question that had already occurred to Rafferty. Its possible answer piqued his curiosity. He would make sure Nigel at least answered that one truthfully, whatever lies on other matters he might in the meantime have concocted and hope to get away with.

The two hotel staff – Randy Rawlins, the cocktail waiter cum barman, and Samantha Harman, the blonde and buxom waitress – who had been on duty in Seward's suite during the reception had clearly decided that the safer option in the circumstances was making sure they remained amongst the less suspect lower orders in Rafferty's mind. For they had adopted servile positions behind the bar, well away from the VIP guests. Randy Rawlins even retained a hold on one of the tools of his trade, tightly clutching a shiny metal cocktail shaker as if he thought his life depended upon it.

Rafferty had, of course, recognized Rawlins' name. It was curious that in Rawlins, Mickey, Nigel and several others, this evening's civic reception should have brought so many of his old, long since grown-up schoolmates together in the same room as the town's more elite inhabitants.

Randy Rawlins, in spite of the trendy diminutive that the manager had used when naming the staff on duty at Seward's reception and the barman's tight-fitting clothing, was none other than Randolph, the weedy kid that everyone – even the teachers – had picked on at school. Though the teachers, of course, had mostly had a far better developed instinct for picking out the weak than the majority of the kids.

After telling the guests what was next on the agenda and reminding them again that they would be questioned individually in the Boudicca Ballroom, Rafferty made his escape before any of the agitated suspects got a second wind. It was already late enough. They all wanted to get home, so he was keen to limit any further delays in the proceedings.

The first of the guests called to the Boudicca Ballroom for questioning was Ivor Bignall. Bignall was around fifty and although clearly still both tired and emotional, he carried his drink well. From his reddened face, it was apparent he got plenty of practise in this and, as a local councillor and prominent businessman, was presumably a frequent and far from unwilling participant in these free food and booze extravaganzas.

Still, given that the big man had been, according to Seward's assistant Marcus Canthorpe, a business associate and partner with the late Rufus Seward in various enterprises, as well as, presumably, a personal friend, he was far more reasonable than Rafferty had expected in such fraught circumstances, especially considering he had been forced to hang around for over an hour and a half.

By now, it was approaching two in the morning and the florid fifty-something undoubtedly wanted his bed. So did Rafferty, for that matter. But 'I've a Big'un', as Rafferty had already mentally dubbed Bignall – and given the size of the man's feet, he might well be so endowed – was undoubtedly to reach this refuge long before Rafferty, Llewellyn or any of the rest of the police team.

And, after Bignall outlined his experiences during the evening – his encounter in the hallway with the stranger, whom he readily described, who had enquired as to Seward's whereabouts and whom Rafferty had no trouble recognizing as Mickey – he professed himself unable to enlighten them any further. Once he, like the two security guards, had supplied a description of this late-arriving guest, Rafferty, conscious of the by-the-book Llewellyn hovering at his elbow, had told him he'd need to come to the station the following day to work with the police artist, then he let him go.

But this was purely a preliminary questioning. The meatier stuff would come later once further evidence had been discovered and sifted.

Next, they spoke to Bignall's beautiful wife, Dorothea,

though with so little result they might as well have not bothered. She did, however, blurt out one interesting piece of information: that she had attended St Oswald's, Seward's private boarding school, and had been in the same year as the dead man.

Dorothea Bignall, who told them she was thirty-eight to her husband's fifty-five, was slender and had a demeanour of such pale fragility it suggested her husband's claim that she wasn't well might be true. Though this could, of course, be down to the fact that she didn't carry her drink as well as her much larger husband.

Shortly after it became clear that Mrs Bignall was too tired to string a sentence together, never mind blurt out anything further that was interesting or revealing as to who might have killed the evening's honoured guest, they allowed her and her husband to go home. Both would, of course, be questioned again when a few more facts had emerged.

Next, Rafferty said he wanted to question the mayor, Idris Khan. The half-Welsh, half-Asian Khan seemed to have inherited the volubility of both his Celtic and Asian forebears. And although he had calmed down considerably from his earlier over-emotional state, he was clearly still highly charged.

Khan was a well-known local entrepreneur and fixer who, like Bignall, often featured in the local paper in the course of his duties. A skilled networker, he was said to know everyone who was anyone, which explained why he was the only one amongst the guests who had claimed to recognize Superintendent Bradley during his brief appearance at the evening's reception. He was more than happy to confirm this fact, which he had already confided to Mary Carmody.

This lack of recognition of Bradley by the rest of the guests was surprising in itself, given the super's fondness for getting his face on the telly and in the papers. But perhaps it was that Khan, like Llewellyn, was a teetotaller and, apart from Seward's soberly on-duty employees, was the only one amongst the official guests who had been both clear-headed and sufficiently astute to realize there might be mileage in mentioning Bradley's presence that evening.

Idris Khan and Mandy, his wife, had been amongst the early departing guests. Khan, as they had learned from the security guards posted at the entrance door to Seward's suite, had returned late in the evening, still trailing his wife, to retrieve something she had left behind.

Rafferty couldn't help but wonder if this 'something' that had been so urgently required by Mandy Khan had been the dainty tin containing cocaine that Constable Hanks had found in the suite's main bathroom. However, he decided to reserve this information for another time. He also resisted mentioning that he knew of their late return to the reception shortly before Seward's body was discovered. It was interesting that neither of the Khans mentioned the latter; maybe it would prove a useful bargaining tool further down the line.

Uptight and apparently in need of another little sniff of 'something', Mandy Khan seemed incapable of answering their questions with any degree of coherence. In fact, she seemed so spaced out and out of it that Rafferty quickly concluded he was wasting his time and there was no point in speaking to her further at the moment.

Marcus Canthorpe they had, of course, already spoken to. When formally interviewed along with the rest and asked about the late arriving visitor that was Mickey, he told them that he hadn't seen the man himself and had only learned about him from Ivor Bignall in the furore that had ensued after he had discovered his boss's murdered body.

It was Bignall, along with the two security guards, who had revealed the presence of this late visitor. All three would shortly contribute to the photofit description that would, in spite of Rafferty's intended delaying tactics, soon be winging its way to the media.

Questioned about the thankfully-still-unidentified Mickey's late night visit, Canthorpe became defensive, as if he felt his boss's murder was somehow his fault. Fretfully, he told them, 'According to the security guards, this man Mr Bignall described had an invitation. There was no reason not to let him in.'

Rafferty, desperate to cover all the bases for Mickey's sake, had earlier questioned the security guards on this very matter and asked them if they had got a good look at the man's invitation. Indignantly, they had both replied that they had and that it was genuine.

'And his name?' he had asked next, which was where their indignation slackened off and they confessed that they didn't actually read it. It was late, they had explained by way of mitigation for this failure. But as they had pointed out, his name would be on the guest list and it would simply be 'a process of elimination, wouldn't it?'

Rafferty had, of course, furtively checked for his brother's name at the earliest opportunity, but it hadn't been on the guest list. So how had he come to receive an invitation? He doubted the explanation his brother had proffered: that Sir Rufus Seward himself had sent it to him.

Questioned about this, Canthorpe shrugged and admitted he had no idea. 'I don't know how this stray, unknown guest managed to turn up with an invitation. Ivor Bignall and I were jointly responsible for the guest list, he for the council and me for Sir Rufus. I spoke to Mr Bignall earlier and, when he mentioned this late arriving guest and that he had asked to speak to Sir Rufus mere minutes before I found my boss's body, he told me he wasn't one of his invitees. He certainly wasn't one of *ours*, either. I don't have any idea who he could be.'

Rafferty thanked heaven for small mercies as Canthorpe shook his head unhappily. At first, Canthorpe said that he had no idea how the late arriving stranger could have got his hands on an invitation. But shortly after, he decided he might have the inkling of an idea.

'On Sir Rufus's behalf, I was responsible for the invitations *and* the guest list,' he reluctantly admitted. 'But my office in Sir Rufus's estate, which is a few miles north of Norwich, is pretty much a thoroughfare between the front door and Sir Rufus's office. It's possible that anyone passing through could have helped themselves to a blank invitation if they were so inclined.' He gave a weary shrug. 'Maybe we should have been more security conscious, but how could I, or any of us, have guessed that a violent maniac would conspire to get his hands on an invitation so he could kill Sir Rufus? It's the stuff of fiction.' He paused, then added, 'Or it was, before tonight.'

Somehow, Rafferty doubted that his brother would have had reason to visit Rufus Seward's estate or that he would have been likely to gain admission if he had made such a visit. But it was becoming increasingly clear that *someone* had wanted Mickey's presence at the evening's reception. But it was a conundrum to which he, for now, had no solution, and he had no option but to put it aside. It was evident that security over these party invitations hadn't been a big issue. Equally clearly, somehow Mickey had been in receipt of one of them. Rafferty could only hope his brother would be able to shed some light on the matter when he finally had a chance to question him more thoroughly.

'You said this late night visitor asked to speak to Sir Rufus as soon as he arrived?'

Canthorpe nodded. 'Though, as I said, I only learned this from Ivor Bignall later, after I found Sir Rufus's body. Mr Bignall told me the man seemed more than a little drunk. But such late visits weren't unusual. Sir Rufus often did private business at functions. I would barely have registered Mr Bignall's remark, but for—'

'Quite.'

By now they were all way past time being able to pose much in the way of useful questions or to have much hope of receiving useful answers from those they questioned, who mostly seemed out on their feet. More for the form than the expectation that they would gain any useful information, they questioned Roy and Keith Farraday, the identical twins who had been in the same school year as Mickey, Nigel, Randy Rawlins and Seward. Rafferty reminded himself that the twins had been the school sneaks: if it was a practice they still indulged in in their maturity, Rafferty intended to find out.

Like the rest, the Farradays proclaimed total ignorance of Seward's violent demise and refused to be shifted from this stance. The hotel staff on duty in Seward's suite – Randy Rawlins, the clearly now openly gay cocktail waiter and barman and Samantha Harman, the busty waitress – took a similar line. Even at this unsociable hour, the latter was apparently not too tired to flirt. But Rafferty, now too exhausted even for such a harmless diversion as flirting, sent them all off into the night. He was willing to give them the benefit of any doubt for now, but he was also willing to give them enough rope to implicate themselves if any of them had reason to nurse a guilty conscience.

It had become apparent, during his questioning of the guests, that Seward, as well as receiving his civic honours, had also taken the opportunity to revisit his past. And gloat about his success to the failures who littered it? From what Rafferty had so far discovered, he had treated the people who had populated that past and who had failed to shine in life – Rawlins, the Farraday twins, Rafferty's brother Mickey and cousin Nigel Blythe, who had all been in Seward's class at the local secondary modern prior to his gaining the scholarship to St Oswald's – with the same lack of civility as he had treated them in their youth. Had one of them decided it was payback time?

Rafferty saved the best till last. He felt he deserved a treat and had deliberately made his cousin wait till even the help had been questioned. Perhaps he was being petty, but given their past differences, he felt that he owed Nigel little in the way of consideration. Besides, there was nothing more likely to get his cousin's dander up and encourage him to blurt out things better left unsaid than making him wait until last to be questioned. And, anxious to prove his society credentials, Nigel might even tell him the truth about how *he* had got his name on the guest list.

Getting any kind of truth out of his devious cousin inclined Rafferty to make use of every weapon in his arsenal, petty or not. And if petty swung it by angering 'dear' Nigel, Rafferty wasn't too proud to stoop to that level.

Four

Nigel Blythe, Rafferty's sharp-suited estate agent cousin, strolled nonchalantly into the ballroom, gazed around at the party litter with a disinterested air that didn't fool Rafferty for a minute, and after making them wait a good ten seconds, finally condescended to saunter across the floor to the table where they had set up operations.

Nigel had yet to open his mouth, but never mind hoping to make his cousin's dander unwisely rise, Rafferty could feel his own equilibrium wobble. He was also discomfited by the calm presence of Llewellyn at his side. Ready to take notes, his sergeant was studying Nigel as if he were some rare anthropological specimen that he had not previously known existed. Rafferty envied him his scientific detachment.

When eventually he deigned to take a seat and be questioned about his presence at such a lavish, VIP function, Nigel languidly explained that he had met Sir Rufus at a house-warming party to which, as the selling agent, he had been invited by Sir Rufus's house-purchasing friends.

Nigel being Nigel, he would have made the most of the opportunity. Rafferty didn't doubt that his cousin had milked this potentially lucrative house-warming for all it was worth and then some. Almost as a reflex action, he would have left piles of his arty, oh-so-tastefully-produced literature, describing his determinedly up-market estate agent business, in the various rooms to which, as a guest, he had access, as well as a few that he most definitely *didn't*.

But Nigel had never believed in waiting for business to come to him. As Rafferty had learned when his cousin was placing his first, exploratory foot in the shark-infested waters of the estate agents' profession and had used him as both sounding board and potential sucker, Nigel's life philosophy was entirely proactive – it had had to be. 'Dear' Nigel would certainly have used his oily charm on the wives and partners of those present – women responded to Nigel, whereas men tended to regard his sharp suit and even sharper, calculating brain and overactive libido as a threat to them, their wallets and their wives.

However he'd managed it, 'dear' Nigel had wangled the invitation to Sir Rufus Seward's swish reception in order to mingle with rich potential house-buyers.

Rafferty stared across the table at his cousin. Untroubled on the surface at least, his cousin gazed back with his usual annoying confidence. Rafferty even thought he could detect the hint of a sneer in the angle of his cousin's lips. He immediately felt the familiar desire to remove it with his fist.

Instead, he acerbically enquired, 'And Sir Rufus was so charmed by your business methods that he felt his civic reception wouldn't be complete without your presence, is that it?'

'Exactly so, my dear cousin.' Nigel smirked and directed his sharp gaze around the vast, echoing ballroom and its assorted party detritus, as if concerned that eavesdroppers might be concealed in the wainscoting and be taking notes about his business methods.

His eye must, just then, have alighted on one of the celebratory banners at the end of the ballroom, for he froze, shuddered, and went quite pale. For a few revealing seconds, his accustomed confidence vanished to be replaced by an expression of dread.

Rafferty barely managed to suppress the grin this response drew in return. Finally divorced after an unhappy first marriage, Nigel had resolved to play the field and never again allow himself to be tied down. It was as if, in discovering that some married pair had manacled themselves to each other for half a century, Nigel had at last found something about this interview that *did* intimidate him. But he covered it well once he regained his poise.

'Oops,' he said, as he put a languid, well-manicured hand to his lips and hastily averted his gaze from the life sentence banner. 'I suppose, in the circumstances, that should be dear "inspector", shouldn't it?' Nigel crossed one expensively tailored leg over the other, admired the sheen from his Italian loafers, and remarked, 'How very astute of you to realize how Sir Rufus valued me and my professional skills.'

Rafferty's lips tightened to prevent the escape of an unwise response. He glanced briefly at Llewellyn, but his sergeant was wearing his poker face, so he couldn't hazard a guess as to his colleague's thoughts.

'Sir Rufus was interested in backing me in some property deals I had previously spoken to him about,' Nigel elaborated as he removed his hand from his mouth and studied his beautifully manicured fingernails. 'Very smart businessman, Sir Rufus. He's a sad loss. A sad loss.' Nigel's smoothly handsome face, beneath its equally smooth and sleekly styled hair, fell into suitably mournful lines at this.

A sad loss, certainly, to Nigel's ambitious aspirations, Rafferty guessed – if such they were, rather than the usual pack of ready lies that his cousin was so adept at pouring forth when cornered in an awkward spot.

'You're an observant fellow,' Rafferty remarked tonelessly. 'I imagine it must go with the *profession*.' He put such a lip-curling spin on the last word that he made it sound like he was talking about the *oldest* profession rather than merely one of the slickest and most treacherous for the innocent to negotiate.

Nigel's top lip did some curling of its own at this, but he volunteered no rancorous observations in response and Rafferty was forced to prompt him.

'So, tell me, Mr Blythe – Nigel – did you see anyone enter Seward's bedroom late on the evening of the party?' Rafferty found himself praying that Nigel hadn't spotted Mickey and was gratified at Nigel's reply.

'Me? No, certainly not. I didn't see anyone – me included, before you ask – enter *Sir Rufus's* bedroom, Inspector.'

Briefly pausing to wonder whether Nigel might actually be lying in order to gain some future financial advantage from keeping quiet about Mickey's presence, Rafferty was put on the back foot by this correction. Nigel, always looking for an edge over an adversary, hadn't failed to put him in the wrong by drawing attention to his failure to use Seward's recently acquired title. Of course his cousin adored such outmoded and mostly undeserved trappings of rank. Doubtless, he aspired to a similar or even superior prefix to his own name one day. Such things were important to Nigel. He felt a title added a certain – what was the word Nigel invariably used? – *cachet*, that was it.

Tonight, or rather this morning, Rafferty found himself even more irritated than usual by his cousin's cringe-worthy and snobbish airs and graces.

'You said you didn't go into his bedroom yourself? Not even to talk about your proposed property deal with him?'

'Certainly not.' Nigel put on an air of affront at this suggestion and for once in his life he was remarkably frank. 'I was busy networking for all I was worth, dear boy. Such occasions don't come along so often, even for me, that I wasn't going to make the most of it.

'As I said, Sir Rufus disappeared into his bedroom during the latter part of the evening, I presume to make a private phone call. If he had wanted a discreet word or two, he would have let me know. I can only assume he was still considering my business proposition. But good manners required that I wait until I was invited into such an intimate domain.' Effortlessly, for the second time in the course of a few seconds, Nigel managed to make Rafferty feel at a disadvantage, as he added, 'One doesn't simply barge into a fellow's private bedchamber, my dear Inspector.'

Oh doesn't one? Rafferty felt like saying. He restrained himself. Besides, beyond being made to feel as if he, rather than Nigel, was the investigatory prey, this baiting of Nigel was getting him nowhere. It wasn't as if his wretched cousin was likely to fall to his knees and confess even if he *had* murdered Seward. So, after posing a few more searching questions that brought similarly unsatisfying responses and with a reminder that he knew where Nigel lived, Rafferty let him go.

And as he watched his cousin saunter out of the ballroom with an even more aggravating nonchalance than he had entered it, Rafferty reflected that it wasn't as if he didn't have other pressing things to do with the rest of the morning. Like sorting out somewhere to stash Mickey.

The early part of the investigation was grinding along at the usual slow pace. By now, of course, if it hadn't been for the fact it was midwinter, it would have been approaching dawn. Everyone was tired and frustrated. The team hadn't been able to contact many of the bigwig party attendees, most of whom were far-flung and had hours since flung themselves and their partners back from whence they had come. And even when they were bigwigs of more local flavour, their business interests were often wide-spread, global and twenty-four-hour. Not for men such as they the luxury of falling into bed in a drunken stupor after a party. As Rafferty and his team had discovered during the hours after their arrival at the hotel, on telephoning the guests' homes, a large number of these guests had quickly inserted their weary bodies into chauffeured limos and been whisked off to the airport for flights abroad so they could attend yet more business meetings and drunken receptions.

So, for whatever reason, Rafferty and his team had thus far been unable to interview the vast majority of Seward's party guests. But at least the single virtue shared by all those who had left the party early when it was known the victim had still been alive was that they could be removed from the originally large and unwieldy list of suspects, though they still needed to be traced and questioned, of course. It was possible one or more had seen something that might yet provide a lead in the case.

As Rafferty had already discovered, Seward had made use of the security team supplied by the Elmhurst Hotel. These two men, Jake Arthur and Andy Watling, had both confirmed that, apart from the mayor, Idris Khan, and his wife, Mandy, whom they already knew about, none of the guests who had left the party while Seward's back was minus its chisel had returned to the suite.

The guest list had contained one hundred names; quite a small number, fortunately, by what Rafferty judged were the usual extravagant standards of such affairs. But the local council, who had funded the event with their usual wanton extravagance with other people's money, and who had been more than willing to push the boat out in terms of quality and quantity in the food and alcohol departments, had, according to Marcus Canthorpe, been more wary in terms of numbers. The local elections were coming up, of course, and they wouldn't have been keen for the electorate, who paid for their largesse, to have reason to express their anger at the ballot box by putting their voter's cross in the opposition's square, especially as they would be aware that the details of this reception would be written up in the *Elmhurst Echo* for all to read and splutter about over their cornflakes.

In the end, as Rafferty had learned from Canthorpe and Ivor Bignall, to both of whom Seward had grumbled about this restriction, he had been forced to accept the limited numbers – not least because a fair proportion of the invitees had, according to Canthorpe, apparently taken the trouble to write RSVP replies in vehement and purple-penned prose, in which they made all too plain the reasons for their refusal.

Which just went to show how many people had cause to dislike Seward intensely, and which, Rafferty realized with a droop, meant that his job was likely to be even more difficult than was usually the case, especially given the lack of security over the more than plentiful blank invitations, which Marcus Canthorpe had reluctantly told him about.

Sir Rufus had, he had discovered, insisted that the invitations were printed in a quantity sufficient to meet his original guest number specifications, confident that the council committee charged with liaising with Canthorpe would give way to his demands. Rafferty was surprised at the revelation that this confidence had been misplaced, as it seemed likely that Seward was a man used to getting his own way.

As was Superintendent Bradley, of course, he reminded himself – not that he needed such a reminder. After Mary Carmody's discovery of Bradley's late attendance at the event, Rafferty had realized he would have the unalloyed pleasure of questioning the super himself. And while he was aware that such questioning wouldn't be well received, he was hopeful that he might be able to wring some much needed amusement from this, though he doubted it would make Bradley love him any better.

Clearly the prominent write-up that the local newspaper had produced to proclaim the prodigal's return, in his pomp, to his hometown hadn't gone down too well in a number of quarters. But then, Sir Rufus Seward had been one of the Essex town's more celebrated and successful prodigal sons. And prodigals such as Seward invariably earned resentment, envy and spite, especially as the local boy had made it good – more than good.

The local paper hadn't stinted on the newsprint. Seward's return to Elmhurst had made a tremendous splash. It made good copy for the *Echo* and sold a lot of papers. But then, yet another recent discovery for Rafferty, Seward had owned Elmhurst's local rag, along with countless others up and down the country, and would be certain to ensure it gave him plentiful laudatory coverage.

But even this early in the inquiry, it was clear that not all of those newspaper purchasers had bought the paper and read the story with unalloyed pleasure at the thought that one of their own had done well and was now gaining his hard-earned glory.

If, along with the purple-penned RSVP party refuseniks, the ensuing letters sent to the paper's editor – spiked after orders from on high and retrieved by one of the team after an anonymous tip-off – were anything to go by, a number of these readers had learned of Seward's return with emotions stronger than mere resentment and envy.

Given Seward's violent death, it would seem that at least one of the paper's readers had harboured painful memories and had brooded over the pages with a party invitation in hand and murder in mind.

The reception must have struck one invitee, official or otherwise, as an opportunity not to be missed. Seward hadn't shown his face in Elmhurst once during the years after his involuntary and hurried departure from it. The civic reception in his honour might have been their murderer's only chance. He hadn't wasted it.

Certainly, *someone* had brought that sharpened chisel to the celebratory party, indicating more than a degree of premeditation, and had determinedly plunged it deeply between Seward's shoulder blades. And as Rafferty believed his younger brother was innocent of the crime, it was down to him to discover who else among those still at the party when Seward died could have done it or could have had reason to do it.

Rafferty, some hours later at last back at the police station after organizing the various strands at the start of yet another murder inquiry, stuck his head out of his office and looked left and right. Thankfully, the corridor was deserted. Most of the team had gone home for a well-earned rest and the uniforms' shift replacements were at morning prayers. But not for him the draw of bed and sleep; he would have to wait for both.

Gently, anxious not to make any noise and attract unwanted attention, he closed his office door behind him. Careful not to bump into any of the team who had yet to remember they had homes to go to, or to encourage unwelcome questions from any other stray, passing pig or piglet late in their attendance at duty allocation, he slipped down the rear stairs and out the back way. Even at such an ungodly hour, he was lucky enough to hail a passing taxi. It was a good omen, Rafferty told himself before he realized his fate-tempting faux pas, and hurriedly crossed his fingers to ward off trouble.

He sat back in the cab and as the car moved swiftly through the practically empty streets, he found his mind racing equally quickly through the options of what he could do with Mickey.

He'd have stashed him at Ma's, but although the fact she lived alone might have indicated her place would be ideal for his purposes, she really wasn't as alone as 'living alone' implied. Her home provided too much of an open house to all and sundry: an unguarded cough or sneeze would be enough to betray Mickey's presence. Besides, he thought harbouring Mickey might prove too much of a strain for her. She would be upset enough when she learned the news without him making her an accessory after the event.

Rafferty took a brief glance at his wristwatch as the cab passed under a streetlight. He must try not to be gone too long. With his car back in the car park he hoped, should anyone came to his office and discover he wasn't there, that they would assume he was still somewhere in the station, though it was possible that Llewellyn, with his bloodhound tendencies, might prove less easily put off the trail.

He must just hope that Llewellyn had already taken himself off home to Maureen as Rafferty had instructed. If, for a change, the fingers of fate were crossed in his favour and the ever-dutiful Llewellyn had done as he was told, he should manage to pass off his absence without raising any awkward questions.

Five

A s he paid off the taxi in the road where his brother lived and glanced around the dark street, empty but for the tail end of a milk float disappearing around the corner, Rafferty pulled his collar up to shield his face and tucked his chin into his chest. The last thing he needed was a neighbour with a crying child peering out of a bedroom window and spotting him. He was a frequent visitor to his brother's flat and his face was well known, so the fewer people able to identify him or reveal his presence here this morning, the better.

The early December day was, at just after six o'clock, still pitch black, with a chill wind that brought with it a feeling of foreboding. It had Rafferty shivering in his thin suit jacket. He had been forced, just in case he *had* met anyone in the station precincts, to leave his warm overcoat on its hook. If anyone had entered his office and noticed it was missing, it would be a sure pointer that he wasn't somewhere in the building at all, but had left the station.

Mickey must have been watching for him because as soon as Rafferty crossed the pavement and hurried down the path to the door of the terraced house that had long since been converted to flats, the door to the ground floor flat was quickly opened. Rafferty's no-longer-slender body was somehow, involuntarily and not without a degree of pain, roughly pulled and squeezed through the barely nine-inch opening that was all that his brother, in the circumstances, thought prudent.

Rafferty swallowed his protests along with the suspicion that such strange behaviour was more likely to draw the attention of any lurking watchers than a more bold approach. 'Discretion is us,' he murmured under his breath. With a sigh, he followed his brother down the narrow hall to the small, untidy living room at the rear, feeling, with each step, the

41

sinister breath of the Stazi chilling his shoulders through the inadequate jacket.

But, as he had previously suspected and could now see and smell for himself, Mickey was clearly beyond sober precaution; and as he caught sight of the nearly empty bottle and the amber liquid in the glass beside it on the small side table, his suspicions were confirmed. Clearly, his brother had been consoling himself with some calming alcohol while he awaited Rafferty's long-delayed arrival.

Rafferty breathed out on an even heavier sigh and he was hit with the realization that Mickey was again the kid brother with more mouth than nous. And it was up to Rafferty to look out for him. He was still unsure how he was to do this. Although he had taken the precautionary delaying tactic of locking the preliminary photofit picture of his brother in his desk drawer instead of immediately sending it out to the media, he had yet to come up with somewhere to hide Mickey. He needed someone discreet who owed him a favour and who would be willing to take Mickey in at such short notice without asking too many questions. Such people were not in plentiful supply, so for the moment, he let his subconscious worry away at this problem while he addressed himself to questioning Mickey.

It didn't take long for Rafferty to coax his brother's sorry story from him. The clumsy lies, too, were soon penetrated.

Mickey had gone to see Sir Rufus late, around eleven thirty on the Friday night and, as Rafferty had suspected, his visit had not been for the reasons of business that his brother had earlier claimed – not, as a trained detective or big brother, that he had ever been likely to believe *that* hastily constructed tale.

No, Mickey had gone to have a showdown with Seward and to tell him what he thought of him. Presumably, like the murderer, he had believed it might be the only chance he would get.

The party had been virtually over by the time Mickey had arrived, though, and once his invitation had got him past the bored security on the door, Mickey had felt at a loss. Intimidated by the suite's expensive grandeur, he had lingered in the entrance passageway for a minute. Until that was, a guest leaving the bathroom had pointed him in the direction of Seward's bedroom where, he was informed, his host was currently ensconced. This guest, they now knew, was Ivor Bignall, the local councillor. Just before this guest appeared, Mickey said he had heard loud voices coming from a partly open door down the hall directly in front of him.

'Did anyone else see you?' Rafferty asked.

Mickey shook his head.

'Not even cousin Nigel?'

Again Mickey shook his head.

'You're sure?' Rafferty persisted, wanting desperately to be certain.

'I told you – no,' Mickey told him sharply.

Relieved on this point, Rafferty continued to probe. 'So, what did Seward say when you tackled him?' he asked once he'd sat wearily down on his brother's sagging settee. He rubbed a hand across his face in an attempt to force himself to stay awake and get some answers; it would be useful if he could reduce the current approximate time of Seward's death. 'According to the security men on the door, you had an invitation. I gather they didn't trouble to tick you off on their guest list?'

Mickey shook his head.

Which was just as well as Mickey wasn't on it.

'Tell me about that. How did you get the invite?'

'It came through the post. Rufus Seward invited me himself.'

Rafferty's eyebrows rose in disbelief at this. He hadn't questioned the likelihood of this earlier as time had been too pressing to start an argument. But he did so now. 'Oh, come on. Don't take me for a fool. Not exactly likely, is it?'

Mickey bristled. 'Likely or not, I'm telling you that's what happened. He even enclosed a note with it.' Mickey paused as if his recollection had failed him, then he stumbled on. 'It said he had sent the invitation because he felt guilty about the way he'd treated me in the past when we were both youngsters and that since his knighthood he had come over all *noblesse oblige*, or something.' Mickey shrugged, and clearly in need of the alcohol, he picked up his glass and downed the remaining contents in one swallow. 'Anyway, he was keen for me to agree to let bygones be bygones.'

Rafferty – given Rufus Seward's character – thought the

last highly unlikely, but he managed not to raise his eyebrows again; it would only encourage Mickey's drunken truculence to increase even further. 'So where is this note?'

Mickey gestured towards the log fire, burning merrily to ward off the chill December morning. 'I threw it in the grate.'

Swallowing another sigh, Rafferty asked, 'When did you receive the invitation?'

'The day before the party.'

'It must have been a last-minute invitation,' Rafferty observed quietly, hoping to tone the proceedings down a little. 'All the other invitations went out weeks earlier.' But then, he supposed, the vast majority of the other attendees were VIPs whose engagements were always organized well in advance. Seward's diary already had dates pencilled in for the end of the next year. 'I checked the guest list. Your name doesn't appear on it.'

Apart from that of Superintendent Bradley, who had already said he was unlikely to make it, Mickey's was the only name not on the list. Even Nigel's made an appearance, which, to Rafferty's amazement, indicated that his cousin really must have been a bona fide guest after all.

Mickey shrugged. 'I don't know anything about that . . . But, thinking about it, it doesn't altogether surprise me. Seward would hardly be likely to shout about the fact he had sent me the invitation. His note might have claimed he wanted to apologize, but I didn't think it likely he would be keen to eat much humble pie. I can't see Seward becoming so humble no matter how sorry he might be. Anyway, I *had* an invitation. I showed it to one of the two security blokes on the door of Seward's suite, and he let me in.'

'From what I understand after questioning the security men and that guest you met in the hallway, you'd had a few drinks before you arrived.'

Mickey shrugged, but didn't trouble to deny that he'd needed the fuel of Dutch courage to get him there.

'You've admitted you went there to have a showdown with Seward. Did you relish the opportunity to hear him apologize and maybe make him grovel a bit?'

Mickey glared at him but made no other response. He didn't need to. Rafferty already knew that Seward had concocted some damaging lies in their youth, lies that had resulted in Mickey losing the young love of his life to Seward himself. 'For all the claims you said he made in his note, I don't suppose he was magnanimous enough to actually apologize? People like Rufus Seward rarely feel the need, in my experience.'

It was more likely that Seward had invited Mickey, as he had invited the other humble victims from his youth, merely to boast about his success and humiliate him all over again, though Rafferty found enough tact to keep this thought to himself.

Only Mickey had ruined the sport by turning up late when nearly all the guests had gone.

'You're right,' Mickey told him. 'He didn't apologize, but that was more a case of *couldn't* than wouldn't.'

Rafferty frowned as an unpleasant suspicion took wing. 'Don't tell me you're saying he was already dead when you went into his bedroom?'

'I won't then.'

'Don't play stupid games, Mickey. Was he dead or wasn't he?'

Mickey nodded. 'He was well dead. On the way to hell, I hope.'

Exasperated, Rafferty demanded, 'So why didn't you tell someone about it?' Clearly Mickey had not done so: if he had, he would scarcely have had the chance to leave the scene. The only plus factor was that his brother's identity was still unknown, though for how much longer that happy state of affairs would last . . . 'Did you touch him at all? Or anything in the room?'

Mickey shook his head. 'Only the doorknob. I was too shocked to think of wiping it.'

Rafferty supposed that was something. At least forensics wouldn't find Mickey's clothing fibres or DNA on the body. Not that they needed to in order to link him to the scene. Apart from the possibility he had shed a hair or two from his head and left fingerprints on the doorknob, three witnesses had already reported him as showing up drunk shortly before Canthorpe found the body, one of them, Ivor Bignall, with the additional, damning information that he had demanded to

45

speak to Seward. They had also provided pretty good descriptions; descriptions that were likely to be improved before the day was out and after the three had had the opportunity to work on them with the police artist.

It was suspicious, too, that Mickey should have left only minutes after arriving at the party. That he had left shortly before the body was found made Mickey's defence even more problematic. He had certainly done a damn good job of incriminating himself. As circumstantial evidence went, it was doubly damning.

More in sorrow than anger, Rafferty said, 'You realize that by running away, you lost your one chance to be quickly exonerated, your best chance to be proved innocent?'

His brother's already downcast face drooped some more. Mickey's brow was furrowed in lines of misery, the belligerence now nothing more than a fading memory. He told Rafferty, 'I suppose I panicked. You're right: I'd had a few drinks – more than a few – before I went to see him. I needed them. The bully who made my life a misery as a boy had become a man of substance. And although I had intended to have it out with him, I admit I felt a bit overawed, a bit out of my depth in such plush surroundings. A bit antagonistic, too, if you want the truth. Besides, don't you think I could see what it would look like, with him slumped over his desk, clearly dead and with a sharp implement like a carpenter's chisel imbedded in his back? Especially given our history of animosity . . .'

Clearly reluctant to make such a damning admission, even to his big, police inspector brother, Mickey's chin slumped several more notches as he quietly added, 'I even recognized the make: it's one I use.'

This was getting better and better, thought Rafferty grimly. Needing some reassurance himself, he asked again, 'Did anyone else at the party see you, other than the security men and this guest who directed you to Seward's bedroom?'

'No. I've already told you that once. How many more times? But all three got a good look at me. They're sure to recognize me again.'

Rafferty didn't trouble to contradict him. Mickey was right; the security men and Ivor Bignall *had* got a good look at him.

They had certainly provided a good description of Seward's late visitor. Even Rafferty, not the greatest ace at recognizing faces, would have felt a frisson of familiarity when he saw the first, hastily constructed photofit the police artist had worked up with Bignall and the others, even if he hadn't already been primed by Mickey about his presence at the scene. But without this prior knowledge, Rafferty suspected that the self-serving denial of a brain unwilling to cooperate would probably have obligingly worked its usual magic. The woeful inadequacy of such a denial would, of course, very quickly have been brought up against cold, hard reality; the sort he was now facing; the sort which he had to sort out. Somehow. For all their sakes.

'What are we going to do, JAR? You're in charge of the case. You've got to help me.'

His younger brother's voice, high-pitched and frightened into a too-late sobriety, brought Rafferty out of his reverie. As the eldest of six siblings, he had always taken the big brother approach when any of the younger ones were in trouble, so naturally he wanted to help Mickey. Of course he did. It was just that, for the moment, he couldn't for the life of either of them see how. The best he could do for the moment was get him out of harm's way, then hope that luck and inspiration came up with the rest. And, up till now, no likely help-mate in even this most basic of endeavours had occurred to him.

But desperation brings its own salvation. For, just as despair began to grip him by the throat, the identity of the person most likely to help him to a brief salvation at least came to Rafferty. 'Pack a bag,' he told Mickey. 'If we're to keep you away from the notice of other, less helpful policemen, you're going to have to do a vanishing act.' He took out his mobile. 'I know just the person who can help us stash you out of the way for a few days.'

'Who?'

'Algy Edwards.'

'That crook? Surely you can think of someone else who can put me up for a while?'

'I can't, as it happens. It's Algy or no one. Besides, while I admit that Algy might be a bit dodgy, his heart's in the right place.' Rafferty prayed he was right about that. He prayed, too, that Algy hadn't got rid of his limited property portfolio as they hadn't spoken for some time.

His third prayer was that a few days was all it would be. Or need to be.

While an increasingly agitated Mickey packed a bag as instructed, Rafferty phoned Algy, who was one of a group of the assorted, somewhat dodgy acquaintances of his long-lost youth. He was calling in a favour. He just hoped it was a call-in that he didn't come to regret.

Twenty minutes later, they drew up in Mickey's girlfriend's Renault at a caravan site further up the Essex coast. Mickey's girlfriend was someone else Rafferty knew he would have to square away, but she would wait as she was currently staying round the corner from the flat looking after her sick mother. He filed the thought away to think about later. Maybe by then he would have come up with some believable tale.

Fortunately, the site where the bitterly complaining at the early phone call, but eventually obliging Algy Edwards had a caravan wasn't one of those sites that catered for year-round caravan hire. Neither did it have any residents permanently on site. Rafferty had made sure to check on both points before settling on it.

From what they could see of it in the gloom, the place looked deserted – desolate, even. Which was just what Rafferty had been hoping for. At last, he thought, something was going right. He immediately cursed himself for a fool and crossed his fingers for the second time since he had been brought abreast of Mickey's situation.

In the raw, pre-dawn hours of the December morning, there was a forlorn air about the place. It reminded Rafferty of one of those old Wild West ghost towns that featured in so many of the cowboy films of his youth. It lacked only the wind-blown tumbleweed to complete the impression of a place long since abandoned by man. But what it might lack in tumbleweed it didn't lack in appropriate sound effects: somewhere close he could hear a creaking door that, presumably assisted by the rising wind, was spookily effective. It certainly sent a

48

shiver up *his* spine, so he could guess what it did to his already more than spooked little brother.

It was still too early for the sun to have struggled over the horizon. The only illumination was provided by the Renault's headlights. Between the lights all that could be seen were a shifting misty miasma coming off the sea – familiar to those with a nodding acquaintance with the chill, pre-dawn hour – and the caravans themselves, which seemed like huge, crouching beasts ready to spring on the unwary; the whole scene contained an atmosphere so eerie and filled with such hidden menace that it made the skin crawl.

Their arrival at this quiet, bottom-clenching, sometime sanctuary – not to mention the unsettling caravan monsters that had them surrounded – not surprisingly appeared to comfort Mickey not one jot. He hadn't once troubled to question Rafferty about their destination during the journey, presumably having questions of even greater magnitude to occupy him. But now, somehow, in the stygian gloom, light must have dawned, for Mickey spluttered, 'B–but you can't leave me *here!*'

The horrified quiver in his voice made it all too plain that he was aghast at the prospect. As Rafferty would have been, he admitted to himself, had their positions been reversed. But it wasn't as if either of them had a choice in the matter: time had been limited and options even more so. The dodgy Algy Edwards and his less than luxurious caravan was the best Rafferty could do in the circumstances.

Aware that he had to be tough for both their sakes, he just said bluntly, 'Quit moaning. At least it's quiet and out of the way.'

'So was Dracula's castle,' Mickey muttered, 'but I wouldn't want to stay there, either.'

Rafferty hardened his heart. 'You're staying. Get used to the idea. It's this or a cell in the police station. As long as you don't use a light or do anything else to draw attention to yourself, it's likely that no one will notice you're here.'

Reminded of the police cell alternative, Mickey shut up.

As they began hunting along the rows of caravans for the one belonging to Rafferty's sometime friend, they left the Renault's lights behind. Rafferty fumbled his way in the darkness, stubbed his toe on a gas canister and cursed. He finally persuaded the torch he had taken from the car to provide a half-hearted light. Flickering and inadequate as it was, with its begrudging assistance he squinted at each of the caravans' numbers, trying to find the one he sought so he could stash Mickey and get back to the station before someone started searching for him in earnest.

The torch's batteries were clearly running on empty and its light fluttered and died just as he at last located the right caravan. Plunged into the total darkness that is night-time in the country, he fumbled with the key, which they had collected en route, and managed to open the caravan door. Mickey followed him, stumbling up the steps and adding his own blue curses to Rafferty's.

From behind him, Rafferty heard his brother muttering to himself. 'If this is the best you can do—' The rest trailed off, presumably as Mickey, again considering the alternative that Rafferty had so bluntly pointed out, thought better of finishing the sentence.

Oh, wise little brother, Rafferty thought. He had begun to grin in perverse appreciation of their plight when he banged his nose on a cupboard. He swore again instead and decided he *would*, after all, comment on his brother's base ingratitude.

'Yes, actually, this *is* the best I can do. If you can do any better for yourself, feel free. What did you expect?' he demanded of the shadowy contours, which were all he could see of his brother. 'A top-notch hotel like the Elmhurst, smack in the centre of town and convenient for all amenities? I suggest you get real, bro. Surely you've grasped by now that you need to lie low? This, unfortunately, is what lying low means, whether you like it or not.'

The inescapable truth of this utterance must have suddenly struck Mickey with some force, for he fell silent and, feeling behind him in the gloom to ensure he didn't land on his arse on the floor, he slumped heavily on one of the caravan's side banquettes. With his head in his hands, he said, 'God, I sincerely hope it is only for the few days you said.'

So did Rafferty. Because Abra would be home by Sunday night and expecting him to have organized the romantic dinner he had promised her before she left for Dublin. Having finally plucked up the courage – with recourse to the Dutch stuff his brother had earlier so freely imbibed – Rafferty had proposed. Somewhat to his surprise, Abra had accepted. The girly weekend had been long-planned and un-getoutable-of, so, to make up for its interrupting their own celebrations, they had promised each other some quality time on Abra's return. Rafferty had been deputed to find the time to get this celebratory quality time organized.

Now, with this latest murder inquiry and the unwelcome complication of Mickey's involvement, Rafferty knew he would be hard-pressed to honour that promise and keep both Abra sweet and his brother safe. Especially if, as seemed only too likely given the many distractions, he failed to promptly put a name to the real murderer.

Maybe he would be able to find a restaurateur willing to provide them with a celebratory engagement meal at midnight? Their 'Cinderella' celebration, he could call it. Of course, Abra being Abra and sharing more than a smidgeon of her cousin Llewellyn's logic, would remind him that Cinders' perfect evening *ended* at midnight, rather than began then.

Rafferty felt a bout of hysterical laughter fighting to break free. But as he glanced again at his head-in-hands brother, the urge to laugh vanished as suddenly as it had come. He was beginning to feel that life had turned him into some kind of hydra-headed monster with all the heads striving to control the direction he took. He certainly felt he had no control over anything right now. The only thing he knew for sure was that each and every one of these heads was going to make increasingly unreasonable demands on him in the days and weeks to follow.

In need of some light relief from the doubts that he would be able to rise to any of the challenges the fates had thrown before him, Rafferty eased his weary bones on to the banquette opposite where Mickey was slumped. And as his brother seemed to have nothing further to say on *any* subject, he returned to contemplating his Cinders evening with Abra. He supposed that if Abra found fault with his logic he could always do his Blarney Stone spiel and say, 'Sure and begorra, and isn't it Oirish I am? And don't we always do things in a fey, charming and about-face way from all the other *eejits*?'

Abra would laugh. Hopefully. Though as a prompt, he might

first have to offer her the moon, the stars and a Caribbean honeymoon. Women could be so mercenary.

Thinking about women, Rafferty knew there was one other female in his life who would expect him to pull his finger out: Ma. But until he told her about Mickey's little problem, he would be safe from that pressure at least. Of course, Rafferty knew his and Mickey's ma was entitled to be told what had befallen one of her sons, and told at the earliest opportunity. He would never hear the end of it if he didn't soon break the unwelcome news. That was yet another little chore that stood between him and a few hours of much needed sleep.

Between the latest inquiry, his brother's current difficulty and the romantic dinner *à deux* with his new fiancée, Rafferty was beginning to wonder if he would ever see his bed again.

Six

In the course of a very busy Saturday morning, once he had hardened his heart and abandoned his brother to the chill, unwelcome embrace of a damp, out of season caravan and driven back to Elmhurst, Rafferty pushed his team hard. It was imperative, if they were to reduce the suspect list still further, that they speedily contact the rest of the elusive guests. Even if the early departure of so many of them from the party precluded their inclusion on the suspects' list as he had already concluded, it was possible that one or more of them had seen something during the evening that could provide them with a useful pointer to guilt.

While the team were occupied with this task and the second imperative of chasing up the rest of the entries in the dead man's contacts book, Rafferty again performed his will-o'-the-wisp act and sidled his way out to the car park, only too conscious that he had yet more discreet chores to perform. It was essential that he drive home, equip himself to make some anonymous purchases and get to the shops. The necessity of making these purchases had only dawned on him just before he had left the hotel after the initial questioning of the witnesses. Unbidden to his mind had come the recollection of the phone calls made several years earlier by the royal family that had been recorded by unscrupulous people, making him wary of leaving even details of the numbers he called open to scrutiny. Certainly, if questions were ever asked about his conduct, one would invariably be why he had found it necessary to call his elderly mother in the early hours when his telephone records would reveal he had never done so before.

No, he decided, it was better if he kept off the phone as much as possible. Anyway, even if he was prepared to risk making the phone call, his ma was entitled to hear the bad news about Mickey in person. He would have to find time later in the day to go round to her home to break the news; maybe, he thought hopefully, she could be persuaded to take on the task of breaking the news to Mickey's girlfriend. For certain it was that he didn't fancy coping with the likely ensuing hysteria. He would also have to explain that until he had organized some more secure means of communication, none of the family, including said Ma and girlfriend, was to attempt to contact Mickey on his mobile.

Rafferty cursed his stupidity as, too late, he acknowledged that he should have taken Mickey's mobile off him when he had the chance. Unfortunately, with so many other things weighing heavily on his mind, it hadn't occurred to him to do such a sensible thing. The idiot could, by now, have called all and sundry. And as Mickey used a mobile that didn't provide the useful anonymity of a pay-as-you-go phone, his calls could easily be traced. Even the latter weren't entirely without risk as, should the coils of his deceit start to be untangled, the traced location of any calls could only implicate him deeper. Once Mickey was identified from the photofit, his current mobile and any calls he might have made on it would provide a sure means for one of the brighter and more ambitious coppers on the team to track the call back to Mickey himself and the caravan where Rafferty had stashed him. From there it was but a short hop, skip and jump to Rafferty himself.

Yet Rafferty dare not call Mickey on his mobile and warn him of the danger – at least, not on any phone that could be traced back to him. If Mickey was quickly identified, his call to Rafferty's mobile would be sufficiently compromising, coming, as it had, when Rafferty was at the murder scene. And although he had deliberately delayed sending either the first or the second, greatly improved photofit of Mickey out to the media in order to postpone his identification, such a failure was also dangerously incriminating. Anyway, he didn't dare delay this much longer. He was surprised that Llewellyn hadn't already questioned him about it. Either way, the naming of Mickey couldn't be far off. Once he was identified, his home and phone records would be thoroughly searched. It was going to look very suspicious that Rafferty's brother, the main suspect in the investigation, had contacted him shortly after Seward's violent death. But, for now, a possible charge of conspiracy to pervert the course of justice was the least of Rafferty's problems. He just had to hope that he had the case sussed before it came to that, which was why pay-as-you-go mobiles was something else Rafferty had been forced to find time to organize. One conversation with an absconding suspect was bad enough: a whole series of them was something even *his* silver Blarney Stone tongue was beyond explaining.

But it was essential that he be able to speak to Mickey freely. And Mickey, frightened and alone in his chilly caravan, would need to hear at least one friendly, encouraging voice if despair and further unwise and impetuous actions – such as giving himself up and landing both of them even deeper in the brown stuff – weren't to follow.

So far, apart from not immediately reporting Seward's dead body when he'd had the chance, Mickey's instincts had been sound. At least he'd had the wit to ring his brother instead of taking off into the night and making himself the subject of a nationwide manhunt. Maybe his first instinct to keep quiet about Seward's violent death and leave before anyone other than the bored and careless security men and the half-sozzled Ivor Bignall had had a chance to clock his features hadn't been so foolish after all. Especially as the photofit and description they had concocted between them, although clearly Mickey to anyone who knew him, could also be any number of other men of his height, build and colouring and could apply to a sizeable chunk of the male population.

As Mickey had said, his and Seward's past history and the circumstances of Seward's death might well have conspired to force Rafferty – or his replacement, once – if – their relationship came to light – to arrest Mickey immediately they confirmed his identity. With a suspect in hand, as it were, another officer without the stake in the case that Rafferty had might not put in the requisite effort. Nor might he be as keen to check the guest list for other possible suspects as thoroughly as Rafferty intended to check there.

With his purchases made, Rafferty, his teeth grinding all the way, drove to his ma's house to break the news about Mickey. Ma, of course, was already up, dressed and ready for the day. Once he broke the news she was distressed, naturally, but life had made of her one of nature's stoics. After she had wiped the tears away and organized the essential hot, sweet tea, she sat back and said, 'So, what's to do, Joseph? Sure and Michael can't stay in that perishing caravan for long or it'll be the death of him. Not with *his* chest.'

'I'm working on it, Ma,' Rafferty reassured her.

Mickey had always been asthmatic and physically a bit puny, though with his daily carpentry, he had, over the years, developed a wiry strength that belied his slender physique. That was another worry. Although his physique was deceptive, Rafferty knew his brother's carpentry had strengthened his muscles; physically Mickey was more than capable of skewering a man as big as Seward.

His ma bent forward and her gaze, as it fixed on him, was troubled, as it had every right to be in the circumstances. 'He didn't do it, did he, Joseph?' she asked plaintively. 'I know that Rufus Seward bullied my Michael even though he would never admit it to me. Times enough I was up that school complaining to the headmaster about it, not that that fool ever did anything to put a stop to it. I'm thinking that Michael's always had a hot temper, even from a braw boy. But—'

Rafferty leant forward, took her work-coarsened hand and gave it a squeeze. As much to squash the similar doubts he was harbouring as to comfort his mother, he said firmly, 'No, Ma. He didn't do it.'

They continued their embrace for a few moments, giving and receiving mutual solace before Rafferty pulled away, took one of the three new pay-as-you-go mobile phones from his bag and gave it to her. Next, he handed over a slip of paper, which, he explained, contained the new mobile numbers of Mickey, Ma and himself.

'That's how we're to communicate. Pay-as-you-go mobiles. Untraceable.' Or as untraceable as anything was nowadays, he silently corrected himself. At least they were as long as none of their names came into the equation, by which time it would probably all be up anyway. 'Though, just in case, when you ring Michael, try to do so away from here. That way, in the event the location of any call is traced, it can't be traced back to you. I paid by cash in three separate shops, so no paper record can track the purchases back to me.' And with the precautions he'd taken, neither should any store security cameras or CCTV.

These precautions had taken precious time he couldn't really spare at such an early stage in an investigation, but they had been essential. Although he had little time to spend with Mickey to provide moral support, at least when he found time to drive to the caravan park further up the coast where he'd stashed Mickey and deliver his new mobile he would be able to talk to him freely whenever he needed to.

Rafferty had nipped home to find a change of clothes and a couple of baseball caps that his nephews had managed to leave behind after a visit. Between those and his late father's old spectacles, which he had found something of a mixed blessing in a previous case, he was hopeful that his appearance had varied sufficiently as he had made each purchase to render any connection unlikely. He didn't, if the investigation took such a turn, want any store video cameras or street CCTV easily picking him out as the oddball who had bought three separate mobiles in three different shops. Fortunately, most such surveillance gadgets produced fuzzy pictures, so he was hopeful no one would spot him in his various disguises.

'You'll be able to speak to him and reassure him, Ma,' Rafferty promised. 'Only, as I've yet to find time to take Mickey's mobile to him, you won't be able to speak to him till much later today. Don't, whatever you do, attempt to contact him on his usual mobile number. And warn his girl-friend and the rest of the family not to do so either.'

Ma blinked. 'And what exactly am I to tell them when I speak to them?' she asked.

In spite of her still lingering fondness for off-the-back-of-a-lorry bargains and preference for improving on an already told tale, Ma wasn't a liar. She was basically an honest woman and would find it difficult to attempt to deceive her family. Aware of this, Rafferty said, 'You'd better tell them the truth. We might need their help, after all. Just make sure you impress on them the need to keep their mouths shut.'

He paused for a few seconds to allow her to digest this, then he said, 'I'll ring you when I've delivered Mickey's new phone. But, as I said, I won't have a chance to get over to the caravan park where I've stowed him till later. I've already been missing for nearly two hours and must get back to the station and show my face before Dafyd sends out a search party.'

His ma nodded absently, clearly miles away – further up the coast with Mickey, probably. She was clearly so distracted that Rafferty was forced to repeat his instructions several times till he was sure she had grasped them.

'He'll need some provisions – bread, butter, ham – stuff that doesn't need heating,' Rafferty told her. 'If I give you some money, could you get a few bits in and I'll collect them tonight before I deliver his mobile?'

'Cold collations? For a son of mine?' Rafferty was relieved to see by this response that his ma had rallied. 'He'll have a flask with a filling, warming and meaty casserole. And another with some well-laced tea to help keep the cold out. My Michael won't go hungry, I'll make sure of that. There's an old sleeping bag somewhere in the house. I'll find it and give it a good airing and have the kettle ready when you arrive so I can fill a hot water bottle.'

Rafferty nodded. If concentrating on such basics helped her to cope with their predicament, he wasn't about to criticize.

'Only – only, Joseph, promise me you'll see to the rest?' His ma's determined bravado faltered.

Rafferty knew what she meant by 'the rest'. She meant it was up to him to get Mickey out of the mess his own foolishness and the murderer had got him into. Rafferty promised. What else could he do? It would break Ma's heart if one of her sons ended up going down for murder. Lucky it was for Ma that all her three daughters put together had never given a fraction of the worry that just one of her sons had caused her over the years. And although his mother didn't say it, in his head, Rafferty heard her frequent cry, 'Oh, what it is to be the mother of sons!'

It was a plaint he and his two younger brothers, Patrick Sean, as well as Mickey, had often caused their ma to express, and not just in their youth. It was fortunate that Rafferty, her far from secret favourite and the oldest of the six siblings, had always been able to detect the mother's pride behind the pain. He hoped, when his ma had got over the shock of this latest trauma, that he would still be able to detect that pride.

But Ma was getting older. She was now in her mid-sixties. How much longer would she have the stamina to cope with her trouble-bringing sons? One day, and that day no longer so distant, would one of her three braw boys be the death of her? It was a sobering thought for Rafferty, one of the braw boys who had caused Ma so much worry and heartache. So unwelcomingly, sobering a thought was it that Rafferty found his mind dwelling on the question of how much anaesthetizing Jameson's was left in the bottle at home.

Mickey, for once, must be doing as instructed, and keeping his head down and the caravan curtains firmly closed, for Rafferty had heard no reports of a man behaving suspiciously at the caravan park. But even if he managed to continue to do the sensible thing, Rafferty couldn't be sure his brother's identity wouldn't be revealed sooner rather than later. He reminded himself again that he had better look sharp about discovering the identity of the real killer.

Fortunately, so far at least no one had had the opportunity to put a name to the face in the photofit, though he couldn't believe this good fortune would last once it hit the street.

There again, it might, because none of his family – certainly neither of his brothers – had ever socialized with Rafferty in police circles. And even though Llewellyn *had* met Mickey once, it had been very briefly, for a matter of seconds only, at a Rafferty family wedding. Mickey had spent practically the entire evening at the bar, well away from the teetotal Llewellyn.

Another glimmer of hope was that Mickey, in spite of his sometimes hasty temper, was a well-liked man; generous with his time and his carpentry skills when his more inept DIY-er friends sought his assistance. The people with whom he socialized worked, like most of the Rafferty males themselves, in the building trade, as brickies, plumbers and so on. Only Rafferty himself and his cousin Nigel had branched out. Others of Mickey's friends worked as traders down the local street market. Building workers and market traders were renowned for having various nice little earners that operated in the black economy out of sight of both the law and the taxman. So, either from reasons of friendship, a desire not to bring themselves to the attention of the authorities or a mixture of the two, they were unlikely to turn Mickey in – certainly not for the sake of someone like Sir Rufus Seward, whom many of them would remember with dislike.

Which was just as well, because once – if – Superintendent Bradley realized that Seward's unidentified late night visitor and his investigating officer were brothers, Rafferty would be taken off the case so fast his heels would bring sparks, before he was sharply questioned about his ethics. Or worse.

The latter was a very good reason for Rafferty to press on with questioning the suspects as a matter of urgency. In fact, he thought, after he had given his ma another hug and finally managed to show his face back at the station, why not start with Superintendent Bradley, whom he had spotted through the stairwell window as he climbed to his second floor office, parking his car in the police rear yard? Rafferty congratulated himself on just getting back in the nick of time. He could do without the super having noticed his absence.

Temporarily brushing aside a questioning Llewellyn, who was champing at the bit outside his office and who had certainly noticed his absence *this* time, Rafferty hurried off up the corridor, with Llewellyn's plaintive voice and the word 'photofit' chasing after him.

Putting the super on the spot about his presence at a murder scene, never mind his failure to bring this to his attention the minute he heard news of Seward's murder on that morning's radio bulletin, would, Rafferty thought, bring some much-needed light relief in the circumstances.

Seven

'Ahem.' Superintendent Bradley cleared his throat with what was, to Rafferty, a pleasurable look of aggrieved embarrassment on his heavily-jowled features.

Rafferty, sitting in the visitor's chair in front of his boss's desk and aware he had his chief bang to rights, had just reported his progress thus far on the investigation. As a finale, he had, of course, lightly touched on the super's presence at the Elmhurst Hotel reception on the night of Seward's murder, as well, naturally, as the fact that his presence in Seward's suite had coincided with the approximate time of the murder, as provided by Sam Dally.

Well, it behoved a man to be thorough. This was something the super had always been at pains to drill into his troops, so it was good for Rafferty to be able to show that he had taken this instruction to heart. It was even more gratifying to witness the super's reaction, especially when, prior to Rafferty requesting this interview, his boss had failed to voluntarily reveal that he had been there on the night.

'Yes, well,' the super, having been rumbled, growled with visible reluctance, 'I had meant to mention to you before now, Rafferty, that I put in a brief appearance at Seward's reception. But I knew you had a lot on. I didn't want to waste your time with mere trivialities.'

'Very considerate of you, sir.'

Superintendent Bradley glowed pink with suppressed rage. Even he, as fond of flattery as anyone with the word 'super' in front of their names could be, was well able to recognize the laid on with a trowel variety when he heard it. Especially when it came from his least favourite detective inspector.

'Though it would be a help if you could give me some

times, sir,' Rafferty pointed out in a more than reasonable tone. 'Like when, precisely, you arrived and departed.'

'Of course, of course . . .' The super paused and frowned down at his large, imposing and paper-free desk as if searching for inspiration. Then his brow cleared. 'I remember now. Myself and my lady wife were there for about an hour. We arrived around ten thirty and left about an hour later. I heard the clock in the suite's main room chime the half hour as we retrieved our coats. I had an early booking on the golf course this morning,' he explained, 'which is why I didn't stay too long. Well, that and the fact that Sir Rufus was a little – how shall I say?'

'Tired and emotional?' Rafferty quickly suggested.

'That, certainly. And a tad belligerent but –' Bradley's heavy features formed into a ferocious scowl at the remembered indignity to his *amour-propre* before he continued – 'my wife and I had had a tiring evening, Rafferty, as we had attended an earlier function. I knew that our driver, too, must have been ready for his bed. So we said goodnight to the other guests and left. We didn't see Seward again to say goodbye to him.'

Rafferty studied the wall behind Bradley so as not to look at the super's expression in case a snigger at his chief's evident discomfiture escaped. Unfortunately, it was on this wall that Bradley displayed the egotistical photo collection that captured the super with various royal and political worthies. Like the rest of the office with its self-aggrandizing props to Bradley's greater glory, the wall was testimony to the man's self-importance.

Rafferty smiled inwardly at Bradley's expressed but unlikely concern for his driver's beauty sleep. Even if Rowbotham – Wrinkles to his friends – woke after a sleep of a hundred years, any beauty he might have started out with before becoming Bradley's driver had long since vanished into the increasing furrows.

'You say you didn't say goodnight to Seward himself?'

'Ah, no. Actually, Rafferty, by this time he'd retreated to his bedroom and remained there. It was some thirty minutes later when I and my wife were leaving that I caught a glimpse of some young blonde woman entering his room. Naturally, in the circumstances, I assumed Seward wouldn't welcome any interruption.'

Rafferty frowned. This was the first he had heard of any

young blonde woman entering Seward's bedroom. 'Do you know if anyone else saw this woman go into Seward's bedroom?' If they had, none had mentioned the fact – including that keen networker, his cousin Nigel.

'Er, no. They can't have. Apart from us, there was no one else in the hall at the time. Everyone else was still in the main reception room. I hadn't seen her earlier, which seems rather odd, now I think about it . . .'

'You said that you and your wife were leaving when you saw this woman. Didn't Mrs Bradley see this blonde?'

'No, I don't believe so.' Bradley's jowls gave a little jelly wobble, though his gaze was sharp as a stiletto when he was forced to deny the possibility. 'She was some yards behind me, while I was adjacent to the short hallway which I understand led directly to Seward's bedroom. Anyway, as I told you before, Rafferty, I only caught the briefest glimpse of this woman. One second she was there and the next she'd gone, passed into Seward's bedroom.'

It crossed Rafferty's mind to wonder whether the super might not be telling porkies for purposes of his own, such as inventing yet another suspect with more opportunity than Bradley himself to stick the blade in.

Still, if the super was telling the truth, it indicated that Seward's murderer was very daring to kill in the midst of a party with guests milling about – downright audacious, in fact. Strange that such a daring killer didn't feel it beneath him or her to kill in the cowardly, blade in the back way that Seward had been murdered.

'Did you recognize this young woman? Or know her name?'

Bradley shook his head. 'No. As I told you, I don't recall seeing her earlier in the evening, but I only saw the back of her head. She was wearing some sort of long raincoat. Came down to her ankles.' The super shrugged and added, 'The latest fashion, I suppose.' His lips thinned. 'We weren't introduced to anyone. Seward was singularly remiss in this regard – at least he was by the time my wife and I arrived.' To cover this humiliating affront to his dignity and to try to explain such an appalling offence, Bradley added, 'Of course, the party had already been going for some hours by the time we arrived. Most of the guests had already gone and the rest were well gone, if you get my drift. Not exactly up to making intelligent conversation. The alcohol had clearly been flowing liberally.'

Bradley, a real Yorkshire long pockets, clearly didn't approve of such liberality; certainly not when he had arrived too late in the proceedings to fully participate in this trough-fest. Rafferty also got the distinct impression that the super was decidedly miffed that his arrival hadn't been heralded by adulatory trumpets at the very least. Bradley took his rank seriously and expected everyone else, even civilians, to do the same. To be not even *introduced* must have been galling for a man of his sensitive ego.

'Actually, you know, now that I think about it, I don't recall seeing the young woman among the guests at all. She wasn't particularly tall, so, I suppose it's possible she could have been at the far end of the room from the bar where I was and was shielded from my line of sight by a larger guest. Unless she was another late arrival, a more intimate one than myself – which, I suppose, the fact she was wearing the coat would indicate – and she made straight for Seward's bedroom to offer her congratulations. Perhaps the security personnel will remember her?'

Rafferty nodded. If they did, they had yet to mention her to him. He wondered if Seward had ordered up a late night tart takeaway to divert himself from how disappointingly his civic reception had turned out, with so many of his guests departing with an insulting and early alacrity. It would explain why Bradley hadn't noticed the young woman earlier. If she had been there at all, of course, and wasn't just a convenient figment of Bradley's imagination. The hotel's security men would be used to such late night arrivals and had not thought to mention this one; they might even have ordered her up themselves, of course, and decided to keep quiet about it in case their willingness to oblige such guests' needs got them the sack. If, that was, Rafferty repeated to himself, she existed at all.

Now he changed tack. 'Did you know Seward well, sir? Was he in the habit of abandoning his guests for bedroom frolics?'

'I've no idea. I didn't know Seward at all. I, naturally, was invited by the council itself to represent the town because of my high profile in the area.'

Bradley took the trouble to preen a little and so soothe his bruised ego. 'It's my understanding, though, that this was the first time that Seward had returned to Elmhurst. Certainly, I'd never before met him at one of these junke— *functions*,' Bradley quickly corrected himself. 'And given that, like myself, he was a man of a certain prominence, I would have thought he would be sure to be invited, even if he was only an occasional returnee to the town. And as for his behaviour at the reception . . .' Bradley shrugged and did his best to summon up a Christian spirit of understanding and forgiveness. And though he produced the right words, it was clear his heart wasn't in it.

'He's a single man, I believe, and has no marital ties.' Bradley sniffed. 'I suppose that makes him a free agent in the romantic arena, even if it's a poor do that he should choose to abandon his guests while he indulged himself.'

If having three ex-wives and three divorces constituted any sort of 'freedom', Rafferty thought. The alimony alone must be far from 'free' for Seward.

That was a thought: Seward was reputedly an extremely wealthy man. And, as he had observed with regard to Nigel Blythe, where there's brass there's the possibility of further Nigels of either gender keen to get their hands on it. Maybe someone down to inherit a pile in Seward's will had decided they'd prefer to inherit the spoils sooner rather than later, and thus avoid the risk of the benefactor playing the rich man's favourite game of being tempted to scratch their name from the will. Given what he already knew of Seward's personality, Rafferty suspected this must have been a distinct possibility. For anyone with hopes of receiving an inheritance from Seward, life must have been like walking a tightrope with no safety net. It was yet another angle he would have to look into.

Till now, because of his brother's unfortunate dilemma, the ancient history Mickey shared with the dead man and the fact that Seward had been murdered on his belated and triumphant return to his hometown, Rafferty had been obsessed with the thought that someone with a grudge from Seward's *past* was the killer. But even this early in the investigation they had discovered that Seward still retained the uglier traits of his youth and had a well-deserved reputation for taking offending people to an art form. So it was possible that his killer was someone with a much more recent grudge than that of Rafferty's brother or one of the others amongst Seward's old playmates.

They would, at the earliest opportunity, have to check out Seward's assorted ex-wives and any others who might be down in the will to inherit a substantial amount. And even if one of these potential inheritors didn't turn out to be numbered amongst the party guests themselves, who was to say that one of the ruthless men present who made up Seward's many business acquaintances hadn't agreed to oblige a money-hungry damsel for a share of the spoils? From that angle, it might also be worth finding out if the finances of any of the business attendees' were less than sound.

While he had been following this interesting train of thought, Rafferty had tuned out Bradley's return to self-justification for his failure to mention his own presence on the night of the murder. But now, he tuned back in just as Bradley said, '. . . suppose Seward thought, that as it was his party, he was entitled to some fun instead of fulfilling his social duty of making conversation with his guests. Besides, I imagine he felt that as he was the star turn, he was entitled to behave like a prima donna, but . . .'

Rafferty bit down hard on his lip. It was clear that Seward, once the drink had started flowing in earnest, had downed his share and more, and with the night no longer young, had felt little interest in making conversation with the super, either. No wonder, ignored and un-introduced, a distinctly disgruntled Bradley had insisted he and his wife leave a mere hour after they'd arrived.

And unless they could trace this mystery blonde whom the security guards had failed to mention, and she and they confirmed what Bradley had just told him, the super had just placed himself nicely in the frame alongside Seward's staff, the barman Randy Rawlins, Samantha Harman the waitress, Ivor and Dorothea Bignall, Idris and Mandy Khan and Mickey himself.

Maybe, Rafferty thought, maybe there *is* a God.

After he had left the super, Rafferty returned to his own office. Thankfully, it was empty, Llewellyn presumably having postponed his attempt to retrieve the locked away photofit and make himself useful on another aspect of the case. Rafferty wanted some peace and quiet and thinking time to review the conversation he'd just had. Was it just his wish-fulfilling imagination, or had Bradley seemed decidedly shifty?

Of course, Bradley's odd behaviour might just be caused by embarrassment and the fear of potential humiliation once the media got hold of the fact of his involvement, however innocent it turned out to be. Bradley adored being a media darling and courted such attentions at every opportunity. He would loathe being minced up by them or being made to appear a fool that he hadn't detected a murder happening practically under his nose. He would also loathe the brass knowing about his predicament; he would, rightly, fear that the appearance of his name on the list of suspects would harm his future career prospects. And he would hate the teasing to which he would be subjected amongst his peers. For while Bradley, the bluff, gruff and some said 'professional' Yorkshireman might relish dishing it out, Rafferty had never seen him take it.

This thought prompted his brain to spring on him an astonishing possibility. He had earlier briefly considered, enjoyed and reluctantly dismissed the likelihood of Bradley being the murderer, believing it to be no more than the stuff of fantasy. But what if it wasn't? What if Bradley risked rather more than embarrassment and humiliation at the hands of the media and so on? OK, just as, given its MO, Rafferty found it difficult to consider his cousin Nigel Blythe as the murderer, he found it even more difficult to believe Bradley was the chisel-wielder. That didn't make either possibility *im*possible, though. Like Mickey, Bradley had a temper; unlike Mickey, the super had an ego that was a fine match for the temper. OK, the fact that Bradley had been ignored by his host was, even for the egocentric super, insufficient reason for chisel-plunging. But what if, in spite of Bradley's denials that he had known the dead man, they *had* shared a history, one that Bradley felt was deserving of the ultimate retribution?

According to a number of the guests, Seward had goatish tendencies where women were concerned and Bradley's wife was an attractive woman. What if the attractive blonde whom Bradley claimed to have seen disappearing into Seward's bedroom wasn't a tart takeaway at all, as he had surmised, but Bradley's *wife*? No. Rafferty shook his head. Why even mention it, if so?

But the thought was an intriguing one and Rafferty found it was not so easily dismissed. Because, if Bradley had reason to suspect sexual congress had happened before then the possibility of him indulging in some chisel-plunging moved up several notches. Bradley was a man who took himself, his ego and his pride very seriously. His wife, as an extension of himself, would be similarly regarded. If Seward had compounded his earlier rudeness by cuckolding Bradley, the Yorkshireman's temper might well descend into the red mist zone.

And even if Superintendent Bradley hadn't murdered Seward, he would hate his presence at the scene of a murder to get out, particularly as he had failed to observe anything untoward. Which gave Rafferty another idea. Of course, he had to investigate the possibility that his boss was the murderer – it was his *duty* as a police officer – but even if Bradley wasn't guilty of murder, he might yet still provide Rafferty with both consolation for himself and protection for Mickey in his current plight.

At the moment, the only people who were apparently aware of Bradley's identity and his presence at the reception were himself, DS Mary Carmody, Llewellyn, whom she had told, and Idris Khan, the guest who had first informed Carmody about it.

Neither of his sergeants were gossips, but he'd have a quiet word with both of them, just in case. Perhaps, too, if he had a quiet word with the mayor, Idris Khan, they might be able to agree to some mutual discretion – Rafferty about what he suspected might be the unfortunate cocaine habit of the mayor's wife, and Khan about Bradley's presence there that evening . . .

That left the other six well-sodden last-dreg party guests, as well as Marcus Canthorpe, the Farraday twins, the party help and the two security guards.

And as, according to Bradley, the sodden guests hadn't troubled to invite reciprocal introductions and clearly hadn't met the super before and the help had described Bradley as 'some pompous fat bloke', nameless and unrecognized; that left the security guards. How likely was it that the two ex-paras, as they had described themselves, would, by the time Bradley and his wife arrived, have bothered to take more than the briefest glance at the invitation?

According to Mickey, they had given his invitation only the most cursory of inspections. Which was a stroke of luck. They certainly hadn't troubled to mark his name off on any list of invitees, which, given that it wasn't listed, was just as well, as awkward questions might have ensued that would make them more likely to better recall not only his name but everything else about him.

Chances were they hadn't bothered to check their list when it came to Bradley and his wife, either. By the time these late guests had arrived the security men must have both been bored out of their minds and, after the briefest glance at the invitation, would have waved the couple through on the nod. With a bit of luck, no one else amongst the guests had recognized Bradley in the short time he had been present. And even if they had, the ones most likely to have been acquainted, like Ivor Bignall, the businessman and local councillor, must have suffered from a booze-bleary recall that would make them less likely to remember that Bradley had even been present.

Even Bradley, much as he usually loved self-publicity, would, given the unfortunate circumstances, be sure to keep his ugly mug off the TV screen and out of the newspapers for fear someone would recognize him.

No, Rafferty thought, if I can wangle that discreet little agreement with the mayor, I might just have a useful lever to use with Bradley on Mickey's behalf. A lever of the 'you keep a lid on any revelation of Bradley's presence there that night', to Idris Khan, 'and I'll do the same for your wife's cocaine habit', variety. With plenty of luck, and if Bradley's pride provided sufficient motivation for him to agree to play ball, that would place Bradley in his debt.

Of course, such a tactic wouldn't endear him to Bradley should it become necessary, for Mickey's sake, to make use of his insider knowledge, but then nothing was likely to do that. And Rafferty had never much fancied being clasped to the super's manly bosom, anyway.

But anything that kept Mickey's name out of the frame and gained Rafferty more time to check out the identity of the real murderer was OK in his book, even if it meant Mickey wheezing his lungs out in a damp caravan for the duration. But between their ma's goose-grease poultices, hot water bottles, well-laced flasks of tea and chunky casseroles, Mickey was likely to live better than he had since he'd left home. He could put up with a little damp. It had to be better than sharing an over-heated prison cell with some big, rough, bottom-bothering bruiser . . .

Rafferty still wondered if Superintendent Bradley might have reason to suspect Rufus Seward of playing him for a cuckold at the party or even before; his wife was an attractive woman and might find even a man like Seward light relief after years of being married to Bradley.

Even if that idea turned out to be a non-starter, there might be another reason for Bradley to be nursing a grudge. Why wouldn't he, when half the rest of the guests at the party seemed to? Just because he claimed never to have met Seward before didn't make it true. And even if it was true, it was possible that any grudge might have been earned at one remove. Rafferty had heard no whispers, but then Bradley was a big man and knew how to use his bulk to intimidate. If he wanted something hushed up, hushed up it would be.

But, Rafferty thought, there was one, infallible way of finding out . . .

Rafferty entered reception with a deceptively casual air and hailed Constable Bill Beard, who was propped behind the counter. Beard was something of an institution at the station. He had been there longer than anyone else on the strength. Luckily, he was an inveterate gossip. If anyone knew anything that Bradley would rather remain covered up, it was Bill.

'How's the crossword coming on?' Rafferty asked as he nodded towards the *Daily Mirror* that he knew would be hidden beneath the counter.

Beard raised his eyebrows. 'Since when were you interested in my intellectual pursuits?'

Wrong move, Rafferty. Beard had a natural antenna for sniffing out ulterior motives. Rafferty tried another tack. 'No reason,' he replied airily. 'Just looking for a bit of light relief from this murder inquiry. It's turning out to be the very devil. The murder victim, Rufus Seward, seems to have made enemies going back to the Flood and beyond.'

Beard nodded. 'So I heard. Isn't it your oppo Llewellyn who's fond of saying that the past is the only thing that smells sweet?' he asked.

'Yeah, tell me about it. His blasted quotations get on my nerves. And he knows it. But he and his dreary homilies couldn't be more wrong when it comes to Seward's past. It has the stench of the sewer about it.' So did his recent present, come to that. 'With three ex-wives and various girlfriends, Seward didn't stint himself in the bed-hopping department any more than he did so in his booze consumption or the making of mucho moolah. And to my mind, no one who didn't inherit money yet managed to get his mitts on as much of the stuff as Seward was reputed to have, did so without a few dodgy deals along the way.'

Rafferty certainly felt it unlikely that Seward's recent enno-blement had made of him a shiny bright knight fit for King Arthur's fabled round table.

Beard, clearly unable to resist the urge to show off his gossipy knowledge, leaned forward conspiratorially. 'This Seward had a major run-in with the super once,' he confided. 'Did you know?'

'I did hear something,' Rafferty untruthfully avowed, hoping such claimed knowledge would further loosen Bill's tongue. Even as he voiced the lie, Rafferty felt a painful twinge at the end of his nose. It felt like the growing pains he remembered from his youth, when he shot up all of a sudden. He rubbed the offending object and was relieved to find it had not grown. 'But I never knew the entire tale,' he confided encouragingly.

For once, the busy station reception was quiet and free of demanding customers. Rafferty doubted it would last, so he was eager for Beard to divulge all before they were inter-rupted. He gave a start as, briefly, he heard a few boisterous shouts on the stairs. But the voices faded and he guessed that, rather than coming through the reception area, the owners of the voices were heading towards the rear exit and the car park. He waited, gripped by the fear they would barge into recep-tion instead and put Bill off his gossip-sharing, until he heard the clatter of the rear door slamming shut. Then he relaxed and gazed enquiringly at his (hopefully) confidant.

With the departure of the boisterous brigade and with peace once again restored, Beard propped his bulk even further forward. 'Bradley came close to having to resign,' he told Rafferty in a stage whisper. 'Of course, this was years ago, before he rose so high. He's long since put it behind him.'

Had he, though? Rafferty silently wondered as he settled to hear the rest of the tale. Or had he brooded about it ever since?

Beard adjusted his stout body more comfortably on the counter and prepared to indulge himself. He lowered his voice even further and continued. 'It was all to do with an arrest Bradley made years ago when he was a lowly inspector like you.'

Not so much of the 'lowly', Rafferty thought indignantly. But, for the greater good, he let it pass and urged Bill to continue.

'He pursued the suspect like a rat up a drainpipe, even after the brass warned him off. My, but he must have had the bit between the teeth on that one because Bradley was never one to cross the bosses. He wasn't deterred, not even when the evidence went missing – deliberately missing, some said, including Bradley himself. There was a right carry on over it; shouting matches and all sorts, when Bradley refused to drop it.

'Anyway, this bloke that Bradley arrested – I forget his name – was a pal of this Seward who has just got himself murdered.'

Careful not to make plain that it was all news to him, by now, Rafferty's own antenna was all aquiver. 'As I said,' he airily confessed, 'I forget the details. Refresh my memory.'

Beard smiled a superior, knowing smile, but obliged Rafferty's request. 'Seward owned a big newspaper group. He used his editorials to kick up a right stink about this case involving his pal. This was before the brass got properly involved. It certainly concentrated their minds when Bradley's name and that of the Essex force were dragged through the editorial mud.

'Anyway, as I said, the brass ordered Bradley to drop the

case, or else. He got close to choosing the "or else" option, but came to his senses in time. Of course Seward was well in with the brass glitterati, even then. Men like that go in for all this networking malarkey. His contacts meant he was able to fix it for his pal. Bradley was hauled before the brass and told to drop the case before they suspended him. He saw sense just in time. Even so, he came close to losing his career over it. It doesn't do to go against the big boys. They have ways of getting their own back, as we know, when one of their own are threatened. Probably explains why, ever since, Bradley's been such an arse-licker.'

'Must be a bad memory for him,' Rafferty thoughtfully commented.

Beard nodded his grey head sagely. 'Especially as the rumour was that he was in the right of it and Seward had not only arranged for the evidence against his friend to go missing, but also pulled a few strings and passed a few backhanders to the superintendent of the time to make sure the case died.' Beard stared steadily at him. 'Rather a pity for you that the super wasn't one of the guests at that shindig where Seward was killed.'

'Isn't it?' Rafferty agreed. The fact that he and Bradley weren't bosom buddies was well-known. Still it was good to know that word of Bradley's attendance *hadn't* got out, not even to the usually all-knowing Beard. That information could well turn out to be Mickey's salvation. It would be foolhardy to squander it as a quid pro quo, even to the obligingly indiscreet Bill Beard.

'Certainly couldn't claim to lack a motive, the super, given his and Seward's mutual past. And it's not as if he's a man to forget a grudge. As I said, it's lucky for him he wasn't there as a guest, given his rank and his love of expensive shindigs. Though, given their past, I can't see him being willing to attend Seward's party. Most likely, he'd have sent someone else in his place.'

Rafferty nodded. That thought had occurred to him, too. So why hadn't he? he wondered. 'You've kept this business pretty close to your chest,' Rafferty observed, just avoiding turning it into an accusation.

'Have I?' Beard asked, clearly trying for the ingenuous and

missing by a country mile. Then he smiled. 'What is it they say?'

Rafferty shrugged. 'God knows – I don't. But I suppose *you* can tell me that as well?'

Beard beamed at him cherubically. But this Essex cherub then tapped his nose knowingly. 'Why, Lord love you, course I can. They say that knowledge is power, my old dear.' He gazed straight-faced over the counter at Rafferty as he levered his bulk off the propping counter. Then he winked. 'Just use it wisely, that's all. I want no unnecessary fallout. And,' Beard added, 'if anyone asks – you didn't get any of this stuff from me . . .'

Rafferty was thoughtful as he climbed the stairs to his office. As Beard had said, Seward had owned several chains of regional newspapers, including the *Elmhurst Echo*. He still owned them and more at the time of his death. No wonder his civic honour had received such extensive and fulsome coverage.

It was clear that Bradley had undergone several very unpleasant weeks at the time of the war of attrition from Seward and his pals amongst the brass. It seemed likely that he still nursed a hefty grudge that his desired upward thrust in his police career might have been damaged because of it.

This, to the ambitious, determinedly career-minded and hungry for *good* publicity Bradley would have been far worse than Rafferty's previously considered scenario of Seward possibly making a cuckold of him. It was certainly a treachery unlikely to be either forgiven or forgotten by Bradley.

Which made his attendance at the reception even more intriguing.

OK, it was well known that Bradley, as if he was a film star rather than a policeman, would have gone to the opening of the proverbial envelope, just to get his face in the papers. Given this propensity, it was possible that he had managed to swallow his grudge against Seward for a short while so as to indulge his ego. But even if that partly explained his presence, it didn't preclude the possibility that Bradley had indulged rather more than his ego that night.

Eight

After what he had learned from Bradley himself as well as what Bill Beard had confided, Rafferty was naturally curious to see if the two security men at the hotel would support Bradley's claims that a young blonde woman had arrived at Seward's suite. Or, indeed, if anyone else could back up his assertion about her entering Seward's bedroom late on the night he was murdered.

But, as with his questioning of both Bradley and Beard, these were conversations he preferred to remain confidential. So, before he left the station, Rafferty took the time to make sure that the now returned Llewellyn had a pile of statements to wrestle his way through and thus negate any possibility of him expecting to accompany Rafferty. He thought he'd got away with it, but Llewellyn stopped him just as he reached his office door.

'Is there something you're not telling me about this case?' he asked, so quietly that Rafferty almost didn't hear the question – he wished. But, tempted as he was to ignore it, Rafferty knew better than to do so. If he did, it would only encourage Llewellyn to believe he *was* being kept in the dark about something, which was the last thing Rafferty wanted. Especially as it was true.

Instead, Rafferty turned and directed his best questioning face towards his sergeant. 'Something I'm not telling you?' he queried. He warned himself to be careful not to overdo the air of injured innocence. Polite bafflement was the note to hit. 'How do you mean, exactly?'

Llewellyn gazed at him so steadily that Rafferty almost gave in to the need to indulge in some nervous fiddling – with his hair, his jacket, the change in his pocket. He restrained these only too revealing urges with difficulty and waited for Llewellyn to respond.

'It's just that I get the feeling you're shutting me out. And then there's the fact that you keep vanishing from the office. Each time I looked around the station but I couldn't find you anywhere.'

Rafferty tried a nonchalant laugh; it sounded strained even to his ears. 'You just didn't look hard enough, Daff. I was here. Where else would I be?'

'I don't know. Which is the reason I asked if you're keeping something from me.'

Nonchalance hadn't worked, so Rafferty tried bombast. 'Am I meant to be chained to my desk 24/7 on the off-chance that you might want to speak to me?' he demanded. 'Why didn't you try my mobile?'

'I did. It was switched off. I asked around and nobody else had seen you either.'

Rafferty shrugged. 'So, I locked myself in a cubicle in the bogs for a while. I had the trots.'

'For two hours? Perhaps you should see a doctor, though you certainly weren't in the toilets when I checked.'

Rafferty had had enough of this conversation. 'What is this,' he demanded, 'twenty questions?' He ignored the latter comment and addressed the one in the middle. 'And perhaps you should see a trick cyclist. You're getting paranoid, man.'

Llewellyn denied it. 'It's only paranoia when your delusions aren't true. When they are it's called realism. Or truth as opposed to fantasy.'

Rattled and cross, Rafferty opened the office door, threw a 'You're nuts' over his shoulder, and removed himself from the room as quickly as his size twelves would allow. God, he thought, as he headed along the corridor and made for the stairs at a run in case his questioner should decide to chase after him, Llewellyn thinking he was hiding something from him was all he needed. He had enough to deal with without having to head off his sergeant and his suspicions. What next, he wondered, Superintendent Bradley confessing all? He wished.

The two security guards, Jake Arthur and Andy Watling, both denied letting any mystery blonde visitor into the suite late on the evening of Seward's party. They were so vehement about the matter that they insisted Rafferty look at the security tapes.

Rafferty would have done this anyway as a matter of routine, as soon as possible. Conscious of his need to try to keep his super's presence at the party low-profile in the hope that he would be able to use the information should it become necessary to safeguard Mickey, Rafferty, who had picked up Hanks and Tim Smales on his quick breeze through the station and out, set them the task of checking through the hotel's earlier tapes of the evening. He checked the later ones; those that should feature the late-arriving Bradley and his wife, Mickey and the mysterious blonde that Bradley claimed to have seen.

It was some time later when Rafferty, in the security guards' subterranean lair in the hotel, sat back after having viewed the final security tape. It seemed the security men had been telling the truth, for when Rafferty and his two-man team had finally finished checking all the hotel's security tapes from the night of the murder, although all the guests could be roughly identified from the grainy tapes, of the late-arriving blonde that Bradley claimed to have seen, there wasn't a sign. Strangely, the only existence she seemed to have was in the super's imagination.

So why had he lied? What possible reason could he have to do so, and with a lie that was so easily revealed as such? Had he just panicked when Rafferty had questioned him and instinctively invented this blonde whom Rafferty would be forced to check out? It certainly seemed that way. Rafferty couldn't help but wonder just how much Bradley must be sweating at the certain knowledge that his deception would be discovered. Unless he had something else to sweat about than just being found out in a clumsy deception, such as murder. Was it possible that it had been the superintendent himself who had slipped his way into Seward's bedroom? Given what Rafferty now knew about Bradley's antipathy for Seward, the thought was an insidious one that refused to go away. Not that he tried *too* hard to make it do so.

After they had finished checking out the security tapes, Rafferty sent Hanks and Smales back to the station, but before he followed them, he asked the security men to direct him to the maintenance department. The wood chisel that had removed Sir Rufus Seward from his wealthy, comfortable life was a professional tool, as Mickey had said, rather than the cheap type available at DIY stores. The chisel hadn't looked new, either. It could have been stolen from any carpenter's workshop when the carpenter's back was turned. He thought it worth checking out if the Elmhurst's maintenance department was missing a chisel.

Unfortunately, this line of thought proved inconclusive as Des Carpenter, the aptly named man responsible for basic maintenance, turned out to be a man after his own heart. When he knocked and entered, Rafferty saw, as his hopes sank, that there were tools everywhere. The workshop looked even more chaotic than Rafferty's own office. But he asked anyway.

Des Carpenter, after Rafferty had introduced himself and asked if the man was missing a wood chisel, simply scratched his head, shrugged and said, 'Search me. I have people coming in here all the time when my back's turned and helping themselves to stuff.'

'Don't you keep the door locked?'

'I used to. But then I lost the key and had to force the door open. I've never got around to replacing the lock. Wouldn't make a lot of difference if I did as the other staff would only help themselves to the spare in the key cupboard.'

'Could you check anyway?' Rafferty asked.

But although Des did as he was bid, it was a half-hearted effort at best and confirmed nothing one way or the other.

Rafferty thanked the man and made his way out to the car park. Beneath overcast skies that matched his sombre mood, he made his way back to the station to pick up Llewellyn for the next round of interviews.

As he negotiated the busy roads filled with Christmas shoppers, who darted dangerously through the traffic as some must-have bargain on the other side of the street caught their eye, he pondered how he could best use the discovery about the super's deceit to the advantage of both Mickey and himself.

In one way, on top of his earlier failure to come forward about his presence at the party, to have caught the super out in a second deception could provide welcome additional ammunition should he need it. But he knew it would have to be handled carefully, very carefully, if it wasn't to blow up in his face.

*　　*　　*

It was fortunate from a time point of view that even if the three members of Seward's staff who had attended the reception had now returned to their late employer's estate north of Norwich, most of the remaining suspects lived in Elmhurst itself or very close by.

Samantha Harman, the party waitress, and Randy Rawlins, the cocktail waiter and barman, both lived in staff accommodation at the Elmhurst Hotel, so it seemed logical to Rafferty, as he pulled into the station yard and parked up, that they begin the next round of questioning with them. And even if neither of them had had anything to do with Seward's murder, it was possible they had noticed things, the significance of which they had perhaps not realized at the time. Hotel staff were trained to keep their eyes open and their wits about them, even if it was more to prevent petty pilfering by the guests rather than murder.

They spoke to Samantha Harman first. But beyond confirming that Seward had been rude to Rawlins, she was able to tell them little. Nor had she noticed anyone slip from the room in a helpfully furtive manner.

'I was kept very busy,' she explained. 'It might have been a buffet reception, but you'd be surprised how many of these bigwig types still demand table service. Too important and too used to being waited on hand and foot, some of them, to get off their fat behinds and serve themselves. I didn't even get a chance to visit the bathroom during the earlier part of the evening.'

'What about later? Say from 11 p.m. to when Sir Rufus's body was found – did you leave the main reception room at all then?'

She shook her head and supplied the names of several of the guests she thought would be able to back her up on this. Of course these had yet to be questioned again. One of these guests was the delicate looking Dorothea Bignall.

They thanked her and headed for Randy Rawlins' room. Rawlins, the weedy boy that Rafferty remembered from his youth and who had been everybody's victim, had become, if not any less weedy, then a lot less timid. Perhaps 'coming out' as gay had helped provide him with more confidence. Certainly, in Rafferty's estimation, he would have had to find some confidence to proclaim his sexuality, even in these days of Gay Pride.

In fact, Randolph Rawlins, in his spare time and out of the staff uniform of white shirt, black trousers and scarlet waist-coat, was, Rafferty discovered when he and Llewellyn went to his room to speak to him, quite the snappy dresser.

Although Rawlins' room was small, its limited space was dominated by clothes and clothes rails. They took up all of the area that wasn't occupied by the bed and its side table. There was even one rail crammed behind the door, as Rafferty found out once he'd squeezed through the small gap that was all this obstruction allowed. The necessity to squeeze himself through this gap gave him an unwelcome flashback to his early morning arrival at Mickey's flat after he had learned about his brother's visit to Seward. He felt a momentary panic flood his mind as he contemplated just how he was to extri-cate them both from the mess. He forced himself to stay calm. Just as long as Mickey had the sense to keep out of sight, at least during daylight hours when there were likely to be people about, and no one made a confirmed ID, they had a chance. A long-shot one, maybe, but a chance nonetheless.

Besides, he could do little or nothing to prevent Mickey behaving foolishly. He had to concentrate on the investiga-tion and the here and now if he was to have any chance of helping his brother.

And as he followed his own advice and concentrated on Rawlins, Rafferty acknowledged a certain surprise that the hotel didn't, on health and safety grounds if nothing else, demand their employee had a clear out.

One clothes rail, as Rafferty saw when he had finally nego-tiated his way through the limited door opening, contained nothing but shirts: plain, fancy, silk, satin and frilly. Every style and hue was there. The same with the trouser rail.

Rafferty couldn't help but wonder, after he and Llewellyn had fought their way past all the clutter and he had given Llewellyn the nod to begin the questioning, how the waiter could afford so many clothes. Most of them looked to be from the high gloss end of the designer trade.

From his perch on the radiator, a pillow beneath him to prevent scorch marks, Rafferty, only half listening to Randy Rawlins' monotone answers to Llewellyn's questions, took a swift inventory of the garments hanging from the rails and reckoned there must be several thousand pounds worth of schmutter there. He certainly liked quality, did Randy. Yet, as Rafferty knew, most workers in the hotel business earned low wages. Of course, he would get tips and he had no accommodation costs to find, but even so . . .

Rafferty told himself that how Randy Rawlins managed to afford such self-indulgence was none of his business. Not, that was, unless it had any connection to Seward's murder. This thought brought him back to Superintendent Bradley and why he had lied about seeing the blonde. Had Bradley lied to divert suspicion away from himself? But that didn't make any sense, because all he had succeeded in doing was the opposite. Surely Bradley of all people, even in a panic, would have the nous to realize that was what would happen?

Bradley admitted that he had visited the suite's main and only non-en suite bathroom, a bathroom situated close to the short corridor that led to Seward's bedroom. It would have been the work of mere moments to divert his footsteps and enter Seward's room, creep up on him as he sat at his desk with his back to the door, and stab him.

But would Bradley have brought a weapon with him on the off-chance that such an opportunity would present itself? Clearly, *someone* had. Why not Bradley as well as another?

They had found no fingerprints or DNA on the chisel. But the super, whatever else he might have done, would scarcely be so foolish as to leave any trace of himself on the murder weapon. But that wasn't necessarily a factor against him being the murderer. Most people with even half a brain now knew of the dangers of being convicted by DNA evidence and were equally careful.

In the super's favour was the fact that Rafferty found it hard to imagine the image-conscious Bradley so giving way to the need for revenge that he would risk endangering everything he had, particularly his precious career.

Still feeling the effects of sleep deprivation, Rafferty had instructed Llewellyn to conduct the interview with Rawlins. And while Rafferty might be using his time to think of other things, one part of his mind was monitoring the waiter's responses to Llewellyn's questions. So far, there had been nothing revealed that Rafferty, at least, hadn't learned since Seward's murder or recalled from their mutual schooldays.

But then, the sudden, awkward break in the rhythm of Rawlins' almost monosyllabic replies alerted him to the fact that Llewellyn had at last asked something of Rawlins that sparked more than boredom.

'So what if he was rude to me?' Rawlins demanded loudly. 'You'd be surprised how many guests are rude to the help. You get used to it. I really didn't take any notice.'

Rawlins' response held an underlying and surprising belligerence given his claimed tolerance for guests' lack of manners.

'It's more than my job's worth to dare to answer back to wealthy and important people like Sir Rufus Seward. Besides, I wasn't the only person he was rude to.'

'Yes, so I gather,' Llewellyn replied, 'but this was something rather more than rudeness, I understand. According to your colleague, Ms Harman, and the guests who attended the reception that evening, Sir Rufus sneered at your sexual orientation. Most people would, I think, find that extremely offensive and not something they would be prepared to tolerate. Especially coming from a man who – or so I have been told – had behaved in a similarly bullying manner back in their shared schooldays.'

Rawlins darted a resentful glance in Rafferty's direction. 'I suppose you're the one who supplied that information? I bet you've got me down as the worm that turned, haven't you?' He didn't wait for Rafferty to answer, but continued in a similarly resentful tone. 'I remember you and your two brothers. Right little Gang of Three at school, weren't you? I remember you sticking up for your brother Mickey, when Seward started bullying *him*.' Rawlins' voice developed a wistful wobble as he added, 'I often found myself wishing that I had a big brother to stand up for me.'

At Llewellyn's startled glance as he took in these revelations, Rafferty managed to smother the involuntary wince at the disclosure that he had known and shared Seward's schooldays. Anyway, he had suspected this wouldn't take long to come out. He had intended to bring this fact up himself, aware that his failure to mention it would look odd, but what with

82

one thing and another, he'd missed his chance. Thankfully, it was unlikely that Llewellyn would question him about the matter in Rawlins' presence, so he had a little time to come up with an excuse, however lame, that would explain his failure.

Anyway, that was of secondary importance. It was far more vital to keep the fact that his brother had been the late arriving guest quiet. It was fortunate that Mickey hadn't entered the suite's main room where he would have encountered Randy Rawlins, Nigel and one or two other old schoolmates, but had, instead, made straight for Seward's bedroom after meeting and questioning Ivor Bignall in the corridor. If he hadn't done so, Mickey would indeed be in a cell at the police station by now. And Rafferty would be off the case. As it was, the only people to have seen Mickey, apart from the reception staff, were the two bored and uninterested security guards and Bignall; none of whom had ever seen him before.

For a moment, as he dragged his attention back to their current interviewee, Rafferty thought Rawlins was about to make a return to his weedy past and the behaviour that had encouraged so many of the school bullies, and burst into tears. But maturity, not to mention dealing with the wealthy and demanding clientele of the hotel, had clearly toughened him, for no tears fell. Even the betraying wobble had gone from his voice as he told them, 'Nowadays, I fight my own battles. And yes, Sergeant, in answer to your question: I *did* find Seward's remarks offensive – of course I did. But they weren't any different from the things he used to taunt me about at school. Bullies, I've found, are remarkably unimaginative in their insults. I'd have given him the usual dumb insolence that none of them can bear, but I didn't even have to do that because Mr Bignall had a go at him. He told Seward to his face that he was a disgrace who wasn't fit to receive the enno-blement he had so recently been given.' Rawlins gave a mali-cious grin. 'Seward shut up after that. I think Mr Bignall made him see he was showing himself up.'

'So he didn't say anything further to you?'

'No, he didn't even ask me to get him a drink: he kept sending the Farraday twins over to the bar. By the end of the evening they'd made quite a few trips back and forth. He liked his tipple, did Sir Rufus. Must have made it easier for his killer to sneak up on him.' Rawlins gave another, even more malicious grin and it was clear the thought gave him pleasure.

Indeed it must, thought Rafferty ten minutes later, after Rawlins had denied knowing anything about his tormenter's murder, as he and Llewellyn squeezed their way back out past all the clothes racks.

'What do you think, Dafyd?' Rafferty asked as they walked back up the basement corridor that housed the staff quarters and climbed the concrete staircase leading to the marbled reception area and out to the car park.

'I'll tell you what I think, sir,' Llewellyn replied. 'I think it's very strange that you haven't once mentioned that you were at school with Sir Rufus Seward, Randolph Rawlins and the rest. I take it it's true?'

Reluctantly, Rafferty nodded. 'Are you sure I didn't mention it?'

'Quite sure.'

'Must be getting forgetful in my old age.' Quickly, Rafferty steered the conversation back to their interviewee and *his* behaviour. 'Reckon Randy Rawlins *has* learned to fight his own battles and decided to get his revenge on his old bully?'

'It's a possibility, certainly.' Llewellyn's response was cool, even as he added the observation, 'There would appear to be enough rage bottled up there to make him a viable suspect. Though I got the impression that if he decided to kill Seward he would prefer to do it in a way that would enable him to humiliate his victim as he had been humiliated.'

'Mmm.' Rafferty, keen to keep Llewellyn's mind on Rawlins and away from himself, said brightly, 'You may well be right about that. But it might be that Rawlins decided to forego that particular pleasure and seize the only chance he expected to have. It's not as if he could rely on Seward being likely to again come within his orbit any time soon. As we know, this was the first time Seward had ventured to return to his roots.'

Rafferty, bent on the further diversion of his sergeant, brought up the subject of their earlier interviewee. Samantha Harman had claimed she had not left the main reception room in the suite during the hour–hour and a half period during which Sam Dally estimated Seward had been killed. Rafferty suggested they might as well check out Samantha Harman's alibi. 'It might remove one person from our list at least. We'll try Dorothea Bignall first,' he announced.

To Rafferty's surprise, when they drew up in front of the Bignalls' substantial detached stone house just outside the busy market town of Habberstone, four miles to the west of Elmhurst, Ivor Bignall himself opened the door. He was in his shirt sleeves and looked remarkably relaxed considering he was a suspect in a murder investigation.

'Ah, Inspector,' he boomed, loudly enough to rouse several fat wood pigeons from their roosts in the surrounding trees – and to give his wife warning of their arrival. 'I wondered when we'd see you again. Do come in, both of you.'

He led the way down an enormous, square hall. It housed a giant Christmas tree with a mass of presents already piled underneath, even though Christmas Day was still a couple of weeks off.

Bignall must have noticed Rafferty's curious stare, for he said, just before he opened one of a pair of solid oak doors to the left, 'They're for the local children. We always host a children's party around this time.' There was a sad look in his eyes as he added, 'I had hopes for a brood of sons to take over the business, but it wasn't to be. My wife and I are child-less, so, lacking children of our own to spend our money on, we decided to treat those of other people.'

'Very generous of you, sir.' Rafferty looked again at the presents piled high and asked, 'How many children do you entertain, exactly?'

'Usually around forty.' Bignall laughed as he took in Rafferty's expression. 'I can see the idea horrifies you, Inspector, but it really is great fun. And I get to play Father Christmas.'

Rafferty, until he had heard how Ivor Bignall had stood up for Randy Rawlins, would never have thought the big man would have too many yo-ho-hos in him. It just showed how wrong one could be about people. And at least with his booming voice, he would be able to do the yo-ho-hoing justice.

Bignall led them into the drawing room. This was another generously proportioned room, full of original period features. A second, smaller Christmas tree stood in the corner, its decor a far more subtle silver and gold theme than that of the bril-liantly hued tree in the hall.

A fire roared in the generously sized white marble fireplace. Rafferty was glad of it. It was cold outside and his car heater was on the blink. He could almost hear Mickey's voice saying, 'Serve you right after the unheated hole you found to stash me.' Ungrateful git.

Dorothea Bignall gave them a wan smile from her seat by the fire. In spite of the great heat the fire threw out, she wore a thick jumper and an even thicker Shetland wool cardigan buttoned up to the neck. Even with his still unthawed chill, just looking at her brought Rafferty out in a sweat.

'Sit you down, gentlemen,' Bignall boomed from behind them, making Rafferty jump. Like the big man himself, Rafferty took care not to sit too near the fire. He was scared it might just send him to sleep before it slowly roasted him.

Their questions didn't take long. Dorothea Bignall was quick to confirm what Samantha Harman had told them.

'No, the waitress didn't leave the room during the time you said was of particular relevance, Inspector. I myself was there all the time. I found I couldn't take my eyes off her. I marvelled at her energy and the quick way she flitted around the room making sure each guest had what they needed. Time was—' she broke off with a barely perceptible break in her voice. It was quickly smothered by her husband's voice.

'I'm afraid my wife isn't a well woman, Inspector,' Bignall's hearty voice informed them. 'A trifle "delicate", as they used to say in the old days.'

Rafferty could imagine having a delicate – and permanent – sick headache if he had to listen to that loud and hearty voice every day. Mrs Bignall must be relieved when her husband went off on one of his business trips and she could give the painkillers a rest.

'Nothing serious, I hope?' he enquired.

'Women's troubles, Inspector,' Bignall boomed again.

Bignall's lack of delicacy made even Rafferty wince for his wife.

In contrast to her loud husband, Dorothea Bignall had a quiet little voice that had her husband saying, 'Speak up, my dear, speak up. I'm sure these gentlemen can't hear you.'

He was right, at that. Rafferty wondered if it was in an attempt to encourage greater volume in his wife that caused Bignall himself to boom so much.

But Ivor Bignall's hearty encouragement had the desired effect on his wife as she spoke up so Rafferty was at least able to hear her above the crackling of the logs in the grate, when, as well as backing up Samantha Harman's alibi, she confirmed what Randy Rawlins had said.

'I was very proud of Ivor when he spoke up for that poor barman. I must admit, I've always found Rufus Seward a dreadful bully. He was much the same at school.' For a second her voice faltered. Her husband came and stood behind her, placing a comforting hand on her shoulder.

'You shouldn't have allowed Seward to upset you so, Dotty. Those days are long behind you.'

From Dorothea's expression it didn't look as if she agreed with him.

'Anyway, as I said, he was bad enough when he was young, so I imagine he must be even worse now with all his wealth and power behind him.'

'You said you were at school with him?' Rafferty questioned. She had already said as much at the preliminary interview on the night of the murder, he now recalled. Doubtless Llewellyn, efficient as ever, had this fact neatly recorded in his notebook, even if it had slipped Rafferty's own tired brain.

Her pale skin flushed a healthy looking rose before just as suddenly reverting to its normal pallor. 'Yes, only for a short while – a year or two. He moved to my fee-paying school, St Oswald's, on a scholarship I believe, when he was about sixteen. He was there till he left at eighteen to go to university.'

Rafferty wondered about the reason for the blush. Had the young Dorothea and Rufus Seward had a teenage romance while they were both at St Oswald's? It seemed unlikely. He couldn't imagine either one being attracted to the other. But she had called Seward a bully; perhaps it hadn't only been same sex bullying the youthful Seward had indulged in. God knew there were plenty of City types not averse to reducing their female peers to tears from reasons of malice and sexual pressure. And Seward struck Rafferty as just the type who would get pleasure from such ungentlemanly behaviour.

'And were any of your other old schoolmates present on the evening of the reception?' Rafferty asked.

She shook her head. 'No – none whose names or faces I recognized, anyway, though I suppose there might have been some from the school he attended before he began at St Oswald's.'

There were several of these, as Rafferty already knew. He thanked them both for their time and stood up. 'I hope you enjoy your children's party.'

For the first time since they had entered the room, Dorothea Bignall looked animated. She sat up straight, her dull eyes brightened and there was the strength of real enthusiasm in her voice as she said, 'Oh, we certainly will, Inspector. I admit the children's party quite makes my year. I'm so looking forward to it.'

Bignall showed them out, on the doorstep cheerfully admitting that he wasn't as lucky as Samantha Harman in the alibi department.

'You'll find no one to vouch for me, I'm afraid, Inspector. I could easily have done for Seward. If I'd a mind to.'

From their discoveries so far, so could a number of the other party attendees. 'And had you a mind to, sir?' Rafferty asked.

Ivor Bignall laughed his booming laugh. Somehow, to Rafferty, this time it held a false air of jollity.

'Many a time, Inspector, many a time,' Bignall replied. 'Seward could be the most galling man. But not on this occasion. There was little enough time for us to have a falling out, anyway, as he had so many other guests who wanted to congratulate him on him hometown honour. Besides, a knife in the back is such a cowardly method of killing someone, don't you think, Inspector?' His gaze level, he asked, 'Was there anything else I can help you with?'

When Rafferty shook his head, Bignall simply said, 'Then I'll bid you both good day.'

The great front door shut behind them with a dull but resounding thump.

'Maybe he's got a point,' Rafferty commented as they climbed in the car and headed back up the drive. 'Perhaps it's those among the suspects with a yellow streak down their backs that we should concentrate our attention on.'

Nine

Samantha Harman, although grateful when Rafferty rang her to let her know that Dorothea Bignall's evidence had exonerated her from the inquiry and any suspicion that she might have killed Seward, was unable to reciprocate this service.

'I'm a man's woman, Inspector,' she told him with a flirtatious little giggle. 'To be honest, if I hadn't seen her watching me during the evening I'd have barely noticed this Mrs Bignall. She struck me as one of those little mice with nothing to say for themselves who vanish into the wallpaper on social occasions. It's not even as if she seemed to enjoy herself during the few times I noticed her at all. I didn't see her mingling with the other guests or anything. Still, thank her for me, won't you? And tell her I'm sorry I can't give her an alibi in return.'

As Rafferty said goodbye and replaced the receiver, he reflected that the flirty waitress's words indicated that Dorothea Bignall – 'one of those mice who vanish into the wallpaper' – could have skewered Seward at her leisure without the busty waitress or anyone else noticing she'd moved from her wallflower's position.

And if Mrs Bignall *had* left her mouse's corner, who was to vouch for Samantha herself? Apart from Mrs Bignall, none of the other guests whose names she had supplied had been able to confirm her claim that she hadn't left the main reception room at all during the hour–hour and a half before Seward's body was found.

As yet, they had found no connection between the pretty waitress and the dead tycoon. But the usual one – that of an attractive young woman and a wealthy older man – had more than proved itself down the years. The only difficulty with this scenario was, of course, that Seward hadn't set foot in Elmhurst since he was a young man. At least, that was what they had been given to understand and was, apparently, what Seward himself had told several of the guests. Whether it was true or not was anyone's guess, though what reason he might have had to lie about such a thing Rafferty couldn't fathom.

After he had finally managed to snatch some much needed but sadly insufficient hours of sleep, too soon for Rafferty's peace of mind, Sunday night arrived, and with it, Abra's return from Dublin. And although he was looking forward to seeing her, he was aware that her return would give him even more problems. How was he to explain his late night trips up the coast to keep Mickey provisioned without encouraging awkward questions? Abra was as curious as most females and would feel, now that he had proposed, that she had even more right to question his behaviour . . .

Once he had stopped off at the caravan after paying a flying visit to the police station to check on any progress, and dropped off yet more provisions for Mickey, who was getting increasingly stir-crazy, Rafferty drove straight to Stansted to pick up Abra.

He'd somehow, amongst all the other demands on his time, levered in a few precious minutes to practise a bit of bribery and corruption in order to get his and Abra's midnight feast organized, so at least one thing was going right.

Fortunately for his celebratory plans, Abra's plane was on time. She was perky after the short flight, having clearly enjoyed more than one drink from the in-flight trolley. Several of her hen party girlfriends had returned with her and had, equally obviously, enjoyed similar liquid refreshment. On her own, Abra was, as Rafferty had observed, perky, but the four young women together were pretty raucous.

'Oh dear, girls,' Abra confided with a swing of her thick, gleaming dark plait and a loud giggle to her girlfriends as Rafferty tried and failed to shush them, and then, as they were attracting several reproving glances, tried to pretend they weren't with him. 'My Josy's gone all posy on me. He's got his serious face on. Do you like him with his serious face on, girls?'

A loud and enthusiastic chorus of 'No!' followed.

Rafferty sighed and thanked his stars that most of Abra's girlfriends were already married. There were, at last reckoning, only one more friend, plus Abra herself, to be married off. And he had the latter in hand. But then, he supposed, the divorces would start and they'd have more hen parties for the second marriages. He smiled ruefully to himself and wondered if he *was* turning into a posy Josy, as Abra claimed, or if it was just that she was pissed and he was sober.

Rafferty, naturally, found himself coerced into volunteering to drive them all home. Fortunately, Marie, the soon-to-be-bride, and Abra herself, of course, lived in Elmhurst. The other two, Jules and Georgie, were on the way, so he dropped them off first and had to listen to another chorus, this one of protracted goodbyes.

But eventually Abra and he arrived home. They just had time for a quick shower and to change into something celebratory before they climbed into the taxi Rafferty had taken the precaution of ordering the day before: with all the December Christmas bookings at cab firms and restaurants, he had wanted to make sure of his transport.

Abra, far from being tired after her exhausting weekend of partying, was delighted that Rafferty had taken the trouble to welcome her back with a romantic midnight meal. She didn't even point out the illogicality of *starting* the Cinders celebration at midnight as he had expected her to.

Being so up against it with this latest inquiry, there was no way he could have fitted in a meal any earlier, and to get the restaurant of his choice to cooperate, he had been forced to offer bribes of large wads of cash to both the owner and his chef to encourage them to remain behind after the rest of the staff had finished for the night, the one to wait on them and the other to cook.

Although Abra's plane had been on time, the traffic in December always seemed more heavy and frantic than during the rest of the year so they were running late by the time they reached their flat. Rafferty had already been forced to stop and make several pleading phone calls on his mobile en route in order to get the increasingly surly restaurant owner to agree to remain open. Further large bribes had been demanded.

Rafferty was forced to agree to them. How could he not? he reasoned. He'd promised Abra this romantic, specially arranged meal before the murder of Seward and before she had flown off to Dublin. How could he tell her it was now off because he was unwilling to hand over his hard-earned cash?

In the end, in spite of Abra's frantic, almost sleep-free weekend, during their supposed to be romantic dinner *à deux* in the romantically situated Italian restaurant overlooking the river at the town's Northgate, it was Rafferty who started drooping over the flickering candlelight. Hardly surprising, as between the inquiry and his brother, he'd barely been able to grab more than a few hours' sleep all weekend.

'A fine Prince Charming *you* turned out to be,' Abra teased as she toyed with her wine at the table in the corner of the otherwise now empty restaurant. 'I don't suppose you remembered to bring the silver slipper, either?'

'*Au contraire*, Cinders.' Rafferty managed to open his sleepy eyes in response to this rebuke. 'Anyway, I suppose even the real McCoy Prince Charming would have felt a bit knackered after he went trailing around for hours trying to get the silver slipper to fit one of his many possibles.'

Rafferty wished he had as easy a task in his murder inquiry. How nice it would be to have a handy slipper to test on each of his suspects. 'The slipper fits, you're nicked' would be music to his ears. Alas, his once-upon-a-time story was a long way from the happy-ever-after ending.

But tonight was Abra's night, not the murderer's. Rafferty did his best to put thoughts of the investigation out of his mind as he told her, 'In fact, I have something with me that I hope you'll find a little more exciting than a silver slipper.'

This said, he whisked a small crimson jeweller's box from his pocket and opened it with a theatrical Irish flourish. A pretty – and pretty damned expensive – solitaire diamond ring nestled in the box. The candle flame sparked it into vibrant, sparkling life that had Abra oohing.

'Oh, Joe, is that what I think it is?'

'It certainly is. Do you like it? I can take it back if you don't and you can choose another one. Or we can choose it together, which I suppose is something I should have waited for and done with you.'

Rafferty had promised Abra they could go and choose her engagement ring when she returned from Dublin. But somehow he hadn't been able to contain himself. He wanted his ring on her finger. He had had his eye on this one for some days, so it hadn't even taken much valuable time from the murder inquiry. All it had involved was a quick in and out, taking a large chunk out of his credit card limit, and the deed was done.

Besides, he knew what would have happened if they had chosen the ring together: Abra would have hauled him from one end of the High Street to the other, not to mention trawling him through several malls in the surrounding towns, before she returned to the very first shop they'd visited. He had been there before over other purchases.

Luckily, Abra said, 'Don't you dare! It's perfect. Aren't you going to put it on?'

'I don't think it would fit my finger.'

'Idiot.'

Rafferty reached across the table and did as he was told; experience had taught him that, with the women in his life, it was by far the best idea.

He was rewarded by the sparkle in Abra's eyes outshining the glitter from the diamond. Behind him, the surly crashings and bangings that had accompanied most of their meal were silenced. In their place, he heard a heartfelt sigh and soon, Senor Fabio, the owner of this pseudo-Italian restaurant – otherwise known as Fred Ollins from Ongar – bustled over with two complementary glasses of Armagnac, something Rafferty felt he could well afford given the excessive bungs he had extracted for providing the after-hours meal.

Rafferty, naturally, soon spoiled the mood by telling Abra about the murder. Somehow, the news just slipped out past his tired mind and tongue. Resigned, he awaited the expected pouts from Abra, who, as his official fiancée, would, he surmised, expect to be the only belle of this particular ball. She would scarcely be likely to relish sharing the honours with the late Sir Rufus Seward and his murderer, never mind having the attention of her fiancé directed elsewhere during the long hours required during a murder investigation.

But Abra, still admiring her engagement ring, was, thankfully, for now at least, beyond pouts. With a shrug that dismissed the dead Seward as unimportant beside her new engagement ring, she commented uninterestedly, 'I caught the news of his murder briefly while I was in Dublin. I met him once,' she told him. 'I thought him a bit of an old goat. He even tried it on with me.'

'He didn't!'

'No need to sound so surprised,' Abra told him pertly, briefly raising her starry eyes from her engagement finger. 'I'm said to have *some* attractions, I believe.' Provocatively, she tossed the shining length of her plentiful hair. She had worn it loose tonight, in honour of their romantic dinner date. 'Certainly, Sir Goat thought so.'

'I'm sure he did. And so do *I*. Who knows? Maybe it was his goatish tendencies that got him killed.'

'I wouldn't be surprised. But,' Abra tapped his glass with the end of her fork, then was forced to wave away the romantically-minded Fred Ollins who had thought he had been summoned, and said, 'tonight isn't it *you* who's meant to praise my attractions in a pleasingly fulsome manner?'

Rafferty could only agree. Again. And, tired and worried about his brother as he was, he proceeded to do just that, until Abra was as happy in her beau as the original Cinders must have been in hers. He could only hope her happiness outlasted the duration of this latest murder investigation . . .

Ten

By Tuesday afternoon the team had succeeded in whittling the potential suspects on the one-hundred-strong party guest list down to ten, including the security guards. Although they had, as yet, been able to find nothing connecting either guard with the dead man, neither of them could be totally exonerated. They had had the opportunity to slip inside Seward's suite and murder him, which meant they couldn't yet be discounted from the investigation.

Still, such a reduction in the suspect list was a remarkable achievement, given that the murder had been discovered around midnight on Friday, the weekend had intervened and Rafferty's mind, body and spirit had been otherwise engaged for chunks of it. Weekends so often made busy people uncontactable. But then, Rafferty, newly engaged and with a brother in the worst sort of trouble, had ridden the team hard.

It was fortunate that Sir Rufus Seward himself had proved a great help to them in this suspect whittling. His determination to thoroughly enjoy the reception had caused him to imbibe too much of the free alcohol during the evening. This, in turn, had made him something of a party boor and had caused the bulk of his guests to depart earlier than they must have planned. Which meant the majority, at least, couldn't have been around at the appropriate time to provide a more plentiful cast list to the night's production of 'how to stick the knife in, in a far from metaphorical manner'.

All the guests whom Rafferty and the team spoke to said much the same: that Seward had troughed it up at the council-provided bar and buffet like a pig at a truffle party. He had, in fact, so heartily snorted down the liquid refreshment that his truculent personality hadn't, on this occasion, been reserved merely for his social inferiors and the help, as was apparently usually the case. Seward had himself *dis*honoured the honour the town had bestowed on him, much to the mortification of those council members present.

Even Idris Khan, the half-Welsh, half-Asian current incumbent of the post of town mayor, and Mandy, his blonde, possibly cocaine-snorting wife, had retreated in the face of Seward's increasingly truculent behaviour as the evening progressed.

They had already discovered from the security men on the door that Khan, with his wife in tow, had returned much later in the evening after their hasty departure to collect something that Mandy had left behind, though whether this was the small, cocaine-filled box that Constable Hanks had found in the main bathroom or the white cotton gloves discovered discarded amongst the buffet leavings, they had yet to ascertain. Khan himself had said nothing to them about his late return when first questioned and neither had his wife. Which, Rafferty reflected, might mean something or nothing.

But before Rafferty questioned Idris and Mandy Khan again or attempted to broach the benefits of mutually convenient discretion about Mandy Khan's suspected drug habit or Superintendent Bradley's presence that night with the mayor himself, there was something else that he needed to organize.

Time, he realized, was something he was desperately short of if he was to be in with a chance of finding the real murderer and freeing Mickey from his chilly, temporary bolt-hole before Santa started making his deliveries. Time was also essential if he was to stave off any complaints from his new fiancée. To this end, Rafferty had, since Abra's return from Dublin, decided he would have to mobilize the help of his family. It wasn't something he had been particularly keen on doing as it was often the case that the more people who knew a thing, the greater the chance of something getting out, but needs must, as they say. Besides, by now Ma had confirmed she had broken the news to the family. So he got on the phone and organized a rota for visits and provisioning. His other brother, Patrick Sean, and his sisters, Maggie, Katy and Neeve, her name Anglicized from the Gaelic Niamh, were all sworn to silence. Each promised to take time out from their busy, demanding lives, which a fast-approaching festive season made even more demanding, to spend time with an increasingly depressed Mickey and take turns keeping him company in his frigid metal cell.

One by one, by Thursday they had all reported back that Mickey was becoming increasingly despondent and was thinking of giving himself up. 'At least, in a police cell, I'd be warm' was, apparently, a recurring comment.

Yes, bro, Rafferty thought on learning this unwelcome news, but, once on remand, your arse is likely to be even warmer.

Mickey giving himself up was the last thing Rafferty wanted – and not just for his brother's sake. It would do his own career no favours at all if it got out – as it was bound to if Mickey followed through on his threat – what part he had played in his brother's disappearance.

As the senior sibling, Rafferty felt it was his duty to find time to go along and administer a kick up Mickey's skinny backside. Better that his brother's backside received attention from his boot than attention of another sort. Mickey would thank him for it later when all this was over and he had time to reflect on something other than his current misery.

But Rafferty found, when he arrived at the run-down and desolate caravan site that seemed to have been designed to leave it wide open to the nose-numbing wind that roared across the North Sea straight from the Siberian Steppes, that Mickey was far from being in a kick-receiving mood. This was perhaps not altogether surprising, because, as Rafferty looked round the caravan's ever seedier interior that his brother's careless habits had not improved, he discovered that one or several of the family visitors had brought bottles of seasonal cheer as consolation for his stint in solitary. The place stank like a distillery. Not, in other circumstances, an altogether unpleasing smell to Rafferty, but with Mickey in his current unpredictable mood, it was the last kind of aroma Rafferty wished to smell.

Spirits had always made Mickey belligerent. And Rafferty, belatedly appreciating that his little brother was no longer quite as little as he had always thought, came close to getting a kicking himself, almost upsetting and breaking the bottles in the process, which, given the solace they were clearly providing, really would have ensured a fraternal fracas.

Maybe he should have emptied the blasted things down the

sink, only his Irish soul hadn't quite been able to do it. But at least he had managed to persuade Mickey to go easy on the booze. As it was, he had arrived to hear the portable radio that must have been another family gift, blaring forth with more than enough volume to attract any stray nosy parkers who happened to be within a hundred yards of the van. It was fortunate that there had apparently been no creatures more naturally inquisitive than the whirling, argumentative seagulls to hear the racket. Mickey had been singing discordantly along with the music as if he hadn't a care in the world. He had evidently got himself outside the better part of several bottles since Rafferty had last seen him, and presumably the gentle art of alcoholic anaesthesia had worked its usual carefree magic and had helped him forget his problems.

Rafferty sighed as he acknowledged that the rest of his family were gong to have to be warned off providing Mickey with bottles of the hard stuff. As well as making him aggressive, the alcohol loosened Mickey's tongue.

Rafferty had tried for years, without success, to find out what exactly Rufus Seward had done to his brother in their youth. The only thing he *did* know was that the lies Seward had spread had caused Mickey to lose his childhood sweetheart.

Mickey's gaze was none too steady. The alcohol had had the expected effect, but Mickey was still able to take in the drab surroundings of the borrowed caravan. After Rafferty's stern lecture at his noisy lack of discretion, Mickey had become morose. But suddenly galvanized by self-pity and resentment, Mickey's anger at his predicament finally found voice once more.

'Bloody Rufus Seward!' he shouted, his promise to keep the noise down evidently forgotten. He ignored Rafferty's desperate shushings and ranted even louder. 'This is all his fault. If he hadn't been such a bastard when we were kids, I'd have had no reason to go to see him that night –' Mickey's lips pinched tight – 'no reason, if it wasn't for him, to be incarcerated in this miserable hole, either.'

Rafferty, by now more than a little fed-up himself and with his own store of resentment at the situation steadily growing, sat down opposite his brother and bluntly observed, 'It's a bit late for might-have-beens.'

'Ain't that the truth,' Mickey ground out between teeth that didn't look to have come into contact with a toothbrush since his hasty incarceration.

Couldn't even manage to pack himself a toothbrush, Rafferty sighed to himself. I suppose that's another job to add to the list. As he stared at the increasingly dishevelled Mickey, Rafferty felt his resentment grow a notch, then another, as his brother stared back at him with an unmistakably bellicose belligerence.

'And it's a pity you weren't there with your trite comments when Seward and his gang were sticking my head down the bog,' Mickey retorted.

'Is that what he did to you?' Rafferty asked, so appalled that his brassed-off feelings lost some of their indignant glow.

Mickey nodded, his expression now a strange mix of fury and shame. 'One of the things, only he made sure he'd deposited some turds in the bowl before my head went in.'

Rafferty winced at this and found his lips pursing tightly as, involuntarily, he found himself wondering what turds would taste like. The thought almost made him gag.

'The bastard even had his latest little tart and her cronies watch as he took my pants off and had one of his mates smear his shit all over my face and todger. Then he made me eat it – the shit that is, not my todger.' Mickey looked as if he was about to be sick at the memory. Or perhaps it was just from all the alcohol he had drunk.

Rafferty nodded in acknowledgement that even Rufus Seward at his nastiest couldn't achieve the physically impossible. He could find no words of comfort, instead, to his shame, he found himself on the brink of asking his brother to satisfy his earlier curiosity about the taste of such a culinary peculiarity and stopped himself just in time, certain such a question would not be well received. He'd heard of people drinking their own urine when in dire straits, but eating *someone else's* shit . . . Rafferty almost gagged again. But at least Mickey's alcohol-fuelled revelations had killed his resentment. They even almost encouraged Rafferty to pour his brother another drink so the booze could take away the remembered taste of the turds, but again wisdom prevailed and he stayed his hand.

After what his brother had told him, Rafferty wasn't sorry

that Rufus Seward was dead. In fact, he could have wished the sadistic swine had suffered rather more than one thrust of a sharpened chisel for his sins. But his death had been a quick one – too quick. To have Seward endure some of the suffering he'd happily doled out would have given Mickey some measure of consolation. Instead, even after his death Rufus Seward was still managing to make his brother's life a misery. Bloody Rufus Seward indeed.

There wasn't a lot more to say after Mickey's revelations. It was apparent from the shame on his face that Mickey regretted the confidence almost immediately the words had tumbled from his mouth.

Rafferty, aware that his presence only served as an unwelcome reminder of the indignities his brother had suffered, prepared to make his goodbyes and leave, but Mickey, exhausted by a combination of booze, shitty memories and shame, promptly fell into a drunken stupor before he could say anything. But at least with his brother slumped, snoring on the grimy orange banquette, Rafferty had the opportunity to look around him. His gaze alighted on Mickey's old mobile perched on the tiny, folding table between the twin banquettes, just visible beneath the pile of junk Mickey had managed to acquire from his various family visitors during his short time in the caravan. He'd forgotten to retrieve this during his previous visits, and now he slipped it in his pocket while he had the chance. No way did he want to risk a drunken Mickey using the wrong phone. It could prove to be a very costly mistake for both of them.

After Mickey's stomach-churning and quickly regretted revelations, Rafferty had reason to wonder what Seward and his loutish friends might have inflicted on others in his brother's year at school. What had he done to Randy Rawlins, for instance? He doubted Rawlins would tell him – certainly not if it was anything as humiliating as what Mickey had been put through, though he thought it likely the weedy no-mates Rawlins would have been subjected to even worse treatment. And as Seward couldn't tell him and Randy Rawlins probably wouldn't, Rafferty decided the only way he'd find out was to put the squeeze on one of Seward's old gang.

'Look, I'm not proud of what we did, but it was years ago, all over and forgotten. Most teenage boys go through a stage of being appalling thugs. We were no different.' Nick Marshall – a party guest who had been early exonerated – didn't seem to find it too hard to forgive himself his youthful excesses. His self-justifying bluster wasn't attractive.

'No different?' Rafferty managed to inject his comment with sufficient contempt to help conceal the fact that he had no idea what Seward, Marshall and their pals had done to the weedy Randolph Rawlins. It certainly seemed to convince Nick Marshall that he knew what he was talking about, because, in his attempts at self-justification, he immediately blurted it all out.

'Rufus Seward always swung both ways, even then, and little Randolph Rawlins was clearly effeminate. He was asking for it, or so Rufus claimed. OK, Rufus and a couple of the others took turns to bugger Rawlins, but I never did.'

Rafferty had already half-suspected that the young Rawlins had been subjected to gang rape, but, like his brother's turd encounter, it still didn't make Marshall's admission any easier to stomach. His voice flat with contempt, Rafferty asked, 'So how many times did it happen?'

Marshall shrugged as if it had been nothing to do with him. 'I'm not sure. I'd guess every week for a year till Rufus left to go to his posh school.'

Rafferty turned away quickly, before his disgusted fury made him do something even more unwise as far as his career was concerned than the cover-up in which he was currently engaged. He let himself out of Marshall's comfortable Elmhurst home without another word, but part of him hoped that Randy Rawlins *had* killed Seward. Part of him hoped, too, that he proved smart enough to get away with it. Though the trouble with that, of course, was that if Rawlins had murdered the tormentor from his schooldays and proved sufficiently canny to avoid leaving any trace of himself in the bedroom at the scene, it meant his brother would remain in the frame.

Idris Khan had elected to see Rafferty in his mayoral parlour in Elmhurst's Town Hall. This building was, like the Elmhurst

Hotel, another large, imposing Edwardian structure. Designed by the same architect, the Town Hall was in the heart of the town, on the corner of Market Street and the High Street.

The market town's mayors did rather well for themselves; from reading the local paper, Rafferty was aware that no expense had been spared in equipping the mayor to play host in considerable style, although, as he looked around the mayor's parlour, he decided that the councillors tasked with commissioning the building's embellishment were the sort of people who knew the price of everything but the value of nothing.

The town's heraldic device of three axes decorated the mahogany panels covering the walls. A high-end artist had been hired to make these emblems. Typically, as with the Princess Diana memorial in London's Hyde Park, there had been more reliance placed on the hype surrounding the artist's name than on discovering if he had the skill required to carry out the work.

The council certainly hadn't got their money's worth, was Rafferty's opinion as he studied the large room. The emblems had only been finished for two years, to his recollection, but already the red enamel the artist had used was flaking off the axes. This discovery made Rafferty cross all over again at the way his council tax money had been squandered at Seward's reception. There were any number of local craftsmen who could have done a better job and for a fraction of the price this hyped artist had cost, but their names didn't carry the prestige that the council seemed to consider their due.

The rest of the parlour followed the depressing and shoddy example of the flaking emblems. The carpet, another expensively commissioned item, this time from a fashionable Scottish weaver, was wearing thin in places, the red of the Essex axes in the weave already fading in the sunlight that flooded through the south-facing windows. The pity was that under the carpet was a glorious, golden parquet floor that Rafferty recalled from a previous, unofficial visit to the parlour.

He sighed and wondered whether his police career would weather the storm of emulating the brave pensioners who had endured a stint in jail rather than pay over-inflation council tax rises on their limited, fixed incomes. But he wasn't allowed to ponder the thought for long. Idris Khan, his mayoral chain once more resting on his shoulders prior to attending another official function, bustled in to meet his visitor. And when questioned, he wasn't long in emulating the self-justifying tones of Seward's school bully accomplice, Nick Marshall.

Clearly, Khan had decided that the more prudent, stiff upper lip, British half of his racial inheritance would serve him best, for his words and demeanour were both more reserved than during their previous conversations.

'In answer to your question, Inspector, and as I have already told you, I really have no idea who could have killed poor Sir Rufus. I saw no one enter his bedroom – *I* certainly didn't. As I told you, my wife and I left the party early and—'

Rafferty broke in. 'Yes, but you came back, didn't you, Mr Khan? A fact both you and your wife failed to reveal at your initial interviews.'

Idris Khan, now seated on his throne-like chair behind another enormous lump of mahogany, pursed his lips. Had he really expected to be able to conceal his late return to the party? Rafferty wondered. If they hadn't discovered it from the security men, they would still have had the evidence from the security camera. Perhaps he had thought his prominent position would preclude him from police suspicion and the investigation of his movements? It wouldn't be the first time that a VIP had required disillusioning in this regard.

When Khan said nothing, Rafferty asked, 'So what was it that made you return?'

Khan cleared his throat. 'My wife had managed to forget her evening bag.'

'Unusual for a woman to forget such an intimate item.'

'I'm sure that's true, for most women, but my wife doesn't habitually carry a handbag. She only tends to use one when she accompanies me on official mayoral functions.'

'You found the bag?'

'Indeed. It was in the main bathroom near the entrance, where she'd left it.'

'Your wife didn't return to the party?'

'As I imagine you already know, Inspector, she remained outside in the corridor while I went and looked for the bag. I only expected to be a short while, which, I recall, was all that it took – a minute or so, as I'm sure the security guards can verify.'

As it happened, the security guards had proved to be as lax in observation and timing as they had proved to be in checking the invitations of the later arrivals. The security camera, of course, had better recall and made a mockery of Idris Khan's claim that he had remained in the suite for only a 'minute or two'.

When Rafferty challenged him on this, the mayor flushed up sufficiently to blend in nicely with the red decor of his parlour.

'Very well, Inspector, since you are so insistent, I admit I may have been in the bathroom for slightly longer. I suffer from an unfortunate stomach problem,' he told Rafferty stiffly. 'Something akin to Irritable Bowel Syndrome. I found I had to make urgent use of the facilities.'

Rafferty gave an understanding nod. 'I see. And your GP will confirm this?'

Khan's flush faded to leave a strange, waxen pallor on his light brown skin. 'No,' he said, 'I have not consulted my GP. It is a recent problem only and one I have been treating myself, with over-the-counter remedies.'

Rafferty nodded again and, with his previously perfectly correct English in retreat, the mayor burst out, 'But surely you can't be suspecting me of this murder? What for would I do this thing? I have no reason to want to kill Sir Rufus – no reason at all.'

That remained to be seen, was Rafferty's unvoiced thought. 'Then I'm sure this investigation will exonerate you,' he told the mayor with a smoothness that was foreign to him.

But his words didn't altogether seem to reassure Idris Khan. Anxiety deepened the parallel furrows above his deep brown eyes. From somewhere in his red mayoral robes he found a set of beads which he proceeded to run through his fingers while staring with a fixed expression at Rafferty.

For a moment, Rafferty thought the mayor had pulled a rosary from his pocket, but then he realized his mistake. For whatever reason, Idris Khan was sufficiently rattled to need the comfort of worry beads.

But what reason would Idris Khan have to want Seward

dead? Rafferty mused as he stared at Khan and his fretful fingers. He was some years older than Seward, so clearly had not been one of the dead man's schoolboy victims. And his wife was some years Seward's junior, so the same reasoning applied in reverse in her case.

Had Seward somehow damaged one or more of Khan's many business interests? Or perhaps, given the dead man's goatish tendencies where women were concerned, it was possible the mayor had a more personal reason for wanting Seward dead?

But if he did, it had been plain during their conversation that he wasn't about to reveal it to Rafferty. And in view of his insistence that it was his wife's handbag rather than her cocaine tin for which they had returned to the party, it had become clear that a broaching of his back-scratching deal vis-à-vis keeping quiet about the superintendent's attendance at the reception wasn't an option at present.

Disgruntled that his hopes had been so prematurely dashed, after a few more questions that only gained answers of a non-revelatory nature, Rafferty said, 'I imagine I will need to speak to you again, sir. I'll see myself out.'

As he made his way to the car park at the rear of the town hall, Rafferty found himself musing on the interview with Idris Khan. The security guards, Jake Arthur and Andy Watling, had at least been able to agree with the tape's evidence: Mrs Khan hadn't re-entered Seward's suite. But for whatever reason, Idris Khan had been in the suite for long enough to both retrieve his wife's handbag and kill Seward. Neither act would have taken much time.

If he had killed Seward, it was unfortunate for him that Marcus Canthorpe had discovered his boss's dead body no more than ten seconds after Khan and his wife had said good-night to the security staff and begun to walk back down the corridor to the lift. They could hardly ignore the ensuing hubbub and return home. So, whether they had wanted to be or not, they were ushered back into Seward's suite by the surely no longer bored security guards and, along with the guests who had elected to remain at the party to the bitter end, were eventually persuaded into an empty suite to await the arrival of Rafferty and the rest of the team.

When he reached his car and climbed in, Rafferty sat brooding. He was disappointed that Idris Khan's insistence that it had been his wife's handbag rather than her tin of cocaine, as he had reason to suspect, that had forced their return to Seward's suite had made it difficult for him to broach the idea of some mutual discretion. The hope that he would be able, during this interview, to suggest that Khan might find it helpful to keep the super's presence under his hat, had meant that this had been yet another occasion when he had been forced to exclude Llewellyn. Needless to say, after his previous vanishing acts, this hadn't gone down too well.

As he turned out of the car park and drove himself back to the station to pick up his now suspicious and disgruntled sergeant so they could conduct the remainder of the day's interviews, he wondered if, on his return, he was to be subjected to another interrogation.

Eleven

Bested in his hope of discretion from Idris Khan about the super's attendance at the party, later that day Rafferty decided he ought to make a start on investigating one of the other possibilities in the case.

According to Marcus Canthorpe when Rafferty rang and questioned him on the subject, Sir Rufus Seward's solicitors, McCann, Doolittle and Steel, were near his Norfolk home rather than in London, as Rafferty had expected.

Canthorpe had put him straight when he had asked about it: 'He only uses the McCann firm for personal stuff. All the business legal work is done by a City firm, as you'd expect.'

'I see. So McCann, Doolittle and Steel would have written up Sir Rufus's will?'

Canthorpe agreed. 'He dealt with Philip Metcalfe, one of the partners.'

'If you could let me have their address and phone number, it would be helpful.'

'Of course.' Canthorpe rattled off the details immediately without having to check them.

Luckily, when Llewellyn rang McCann, Doolittle and Steel to make an appointment, it was to find that Philip Metcalfe, the partner who dealt with Seward's affairs, had had a cancellation for that very afternoon and if they could get themselves to the Norwich office around lunchtime, he would be free to see them.

After he had confided this information to Rafferty, Llewellyn, clearly still put out at being kept on the sidelines, commented, 'Unless, that is, this is yet another interview you would prefer to do solo?'

Hoping he wasn't going to have to endure Llewellyn's reserved and distant act during the long drive to Norwich, Rafferty tried to jolly him along. 'And why, my handsome

Welsh dresser, would I want to do that when you're being such a cheery soul?'

Clearly Llewellyn thought this comment undeserving of a reply.

The name of McCann, Doolittle and Steel might have sounded as dusty and Dickensian as Jarndyce and Jarndyce, but the solicitors' business premises were modern; a three-storey office building on the northern side of Norwich that could have been erected no more than a few years earlier.

Inside, it was sleek and streamlined and like no solicitor's office that Rafferty had ever seen. After he had introduced himself and Llewellyn to the receptionist and explained the reason for their visit, Rafferty, eager for some friendly chat after a mostly silent drive, commented on this to the middle-aged woman seated behind the black marble reception counter.

She smiled as she replaced the telephone receiver in its rest after alerting Philip Metcalfe's secretary of their arrival. 'I know what you mean, Inspector. I still miss the old building, even though it had four flights of stairs and the once-elegant rooms were partitioned off into cramped offices that meant you had to breathe in as you squeezed past a colleague. But even with all its drawbacks as a business premises, it was a beautiful building, Georgian and still with all its original features. For all its mod cons, this place is a bit soulless by comparison.'

Rafferty nodded. He, too, found the streamlined modern building pretty soulless, but then he felt this way about the majority of modern buildings: their architects had made no provision for the human being's need for beauty, for food for the spirit. 'Still, I suppose it's more comfortable here?'

'Yes. And it's certainly warmer, though the old place, being in the centre of Norwich, was much handier for the shops.' She nodded over Rafferty's shoulder. 'There's Claire, Mr Metcalfe's secretary, come to take you up.'

Rafferty thanked the receptionist. He and Llewellyn followed Claire into the lift and they were whisked up to the second floor. In no time at all they were seated in Philip Metcalfe's large, expensively appointed and book-lined office.

Seward's personal solicitor, from his gelled hair to his

beautifully manicured nails, looked as sleek as the firm's reception. Still, he was pleasant enough and proved helpful. He had even got his secretary to retrieve Seward's will from storage in the two hours that had elapsed between Llewellyn's telephone call and their arrival; a veritable feat of efficiency for a solicitor, in Rafferty's experience of the breed.

'Not that I really needed the document itself,' Metcalfe told them with a wry smile. 'I pretty much know the details by heart.'

'Really?' Rafferty was curious. 'Why's that?'

'Because I rewrote the wretched thing for Sir Rufus every few weeks. He liked to play the will game.'

'The will game?' Rafferty repeated. And although his repetition of Philip Metcalfe's phrase sounded suitably puzzled, he had already guessed what form this 'will game' might take before the solicitor responded.

'The "who will I disinherit this week" game was one of Sir Rufus's more frequently indulged hobbies,' Metcalfe told them with another wry smile that revealed teeth as gleaming and well cared for as the rest of him. 'Though I shouldn't complain. Keeping up with all Sir Rufus Seward's rewritten wills was what might be called a nice little earner. I must admit that I have reason to regret that his death brings this nice little earner to an end.'

'So you're saying that his heirs were disinherited regularly?'

'Oh yes.' Metcalfe nodded. 'I think I can agree with that statement.'

Rafferty found himself nodding in response. It was a possibility he remembered thinking likely himself. What curious ways the wealthy found to amuse themselves. 'I shall need details of his heirs,' he told the solicitor, 'and whether they're currently in or out as well as a copy of the will itself.'

'Certainly.' Metcalfe pressed the intercom that presumably went through to his secretary's office and asked Claire to come in. She appeared almost immediately and took the will off for photocopying.

'Perhaps, while we wait, Mr Metcalfe, you could give us the gist of the latest will and who's in and who's out?'

'Of course.' Philip Metcalfe leaned back in his black leather executive chair, closed his eyes and quoted from memory as Llewellyn took notes: 'To each of my three ex-wives, photographs of the luxurious foreign residences I've acquired since they left me and which they will never have the pleasure of visiting; to my sister Jennifer, the Caribbean house and three million pounds; to my nephew Garth, three million pounds and the apartment in New York; to my nephew Jason, three million pounds and the villa in Rome; to my nephew Rufus Junior, a photo of my Norfolk estate and an unmarked calendar for the current year.'

'Why a calendar?' Rafferty interrupted to ask.

Metcalfe opened his eyes and gazed at Rafferty. 'Because Sir Rufus, like a lot of wealthy men, liked his heirs to dance attendance on him. The empty calendar was a reminder to Rufus Junior that he'd failed to visit his uncle with the frequency expected of him.'

Rafferty's lips pursed in a silent whistle. 'A bit tough on Rufus Junior to miss out when the other nephews did so well.'

'Yes. For young Rufus, the timing of his uncle's death was unfortunate. Now, if it had happened this time last year, he would have been in and Garth out.'

'Why? Was Garth remiss on the visiting front at the time?'

'On the contrary. Garth got removed from the will because he showed his face *too* often. Even Sir Rufus found the extent of his sycophancy nauseating and told him so. His heirs had a finely judged balancing act to master, Inspector, in order to stay in his good books and his will.'

'What about his employees? Are they down to receive the usual bequests?'

'No. Sir Rufus always said his staff received salaries that were sufficient recompense for the workload. He didn't feel they were entitled to anything more on top. Not that he told *them* that. He always used to say that he got more work out of them when he dropped hints about benefits to come. He even used to send Marcus Canthorpe, his assistant, backwards and forwards with his latest instructions about his will and to collect copies for signature and so on. Claire, my secretary, joked he spent so much time here, often just hanging about waiting for the latest will to be typed up, that he should have his own office. I'm amazed he remained with Sir Rufus as he confided that he'd had several better offers.' He shrugged. 'But so many of these tycoons are the very devil to work for. I

110

suppose Marcus Canthorpe probably thought it was a case of better the devil you know.'

'And this latest will – when was it drawn up?'

'Two weeks ago. I remember I drafted it on the Monday morning and it went out in that afternoon's post, but it didn't come back with Sir Rufus's signature till the Friday as he was away on business.'

Claire returned with the original will and the photocopy which, at the nod from her boss, she handed to Rafferty before leaving the office.

'So who else stood to gain substantially?'

'I've given you the names of the principal heirs,' Metcalfe told them. 'The rest are mostly charitable bequests.'

The latter surprised Rafferty. Owing to the problems Seward's murder was causing himself and his brother, he had perhaps been rather too inclined to view the dead man as a thoroughly nasty piece of work, completely deserving of his brutal sudden death.

He rather regretted the necessity of revising this black opinion of the late Sir Rufus. Of course, no one's *all* bad; hadn't Old Nick himself once been one of God's heavenly angels before his attempted coup and subsequent demotion to the pit? 'Much of a charity giver, was he?' he asked the solicitor.

'Yes. You might be surprised. Sir Rufus donated some quite substantial sums to his favourite charities. He was a prominent and generous benefactor of several charities, both here in Norfolk where he had his main home and, more recently, since he first heard of the plan to honour him, in his hometown of Elmhurst.'

Rafferty nodded. He could understand why this honour bestowed on him by his hometown should spark a burst of generosity from Seward. It was good publicity for him. His newspapers had breezed over the hasty nature of his youthful departure from the town, the reasons for it and the fact that his status as benefactor to the place of his birth was a thing of very recent vintage. Instead, the editorial inches had waxed effusive about how deserving was his ennoblement and the ensuing hometown civic reception.

But, given what he knew of Rufus Seward's character, Rafferty couldn't help wondering just how much Seward had had to put into the government's coffers to 'earn' his ennoblement.

As Metcalfe expanded on the theme of Seward's generosity, reading between the lines, Rafferty got the impression that the solicitor shared his own view that Seward had made sure this generosity was widely broadcast. Perhaps with memories of his early days and those who had shared them with him and who hadn't done as well as he had in life to encourage him, Seward had also made donations to fund the education of Elmhurst's and the city of Norwich's talented but poorer sons and daughters. As Metcalfe told them, these donations were not revealed to the wider public in the way that the other charitable contributions were.

Perhaps, Rafferty thought, this was because they might have given his lowly origins an unwanted prominence, or perhaps they really had been given from a previously unsuspected fount of true generosity.

Whatever it was that had encouraged the latter benevolences, they were accepted more than gratefully by their recipients, several of whom had been invitees of the celebratory party, although, as their investigation had revealed, all had left early before Seward's alcohol intake had tarnished the gloss on his benevolent inclinations.

'Yes, Sir Rufus was pleased to regard himself as a philanthropist, both here in Norwich and in his hometown.'

Rafferty detected the tiniest tinge of irony in Metcalfe's reply. He couldn't stop himself from commenting, 'You didn't like him?' With his peripheral vision, Rafferty caught the sharp glance Llewellyn directed at him for his blunt question. Oops, he thought, another black mark. He ignored his sergeant's glance and waited to see if Metcalfe would answer.

Philip Metcalfe smiled, clearly amused rather than offended by the question. Rafferty could only surmise that the solicitor found such straight and to the point bluntness singularly refreshing after dealing every day with the tortuous and dusty verbiage of the legal profession.

'Is it that obvious?' the solicitor asked. 'No,' he shook his head, 'I didn't like him. I had too many dealings with him, you see. Not an easy man to work for, as I'm sure Marcus Canthorpe, the Farradays and the rest of his employees could tell you. I imagine that anyone who had much to do with Seward grew to dislike him intensely.' The skin at the corners of Metcalfe's clear, grey eyes crinkled. 'I suppose I should thank my lucky stars that I didn't get an invitation to that civic reception in his hometown. If I had, I imagine I might rank quite high on your suspect list.'

'You and half the guests, Mr Metcalfe,' Rafferty admitted, causing Llewellyn's lips to purse in disapproval. But then Llewellyn was always tight-lipped and had never grasped that even a policeman had to give a little if he expected to get something in return. It was fortunate for the guests that Seward had drunk too much of the celebratory alcohol that night; his behaviour had caused many of the guests to depart early and so, much, presumably to their own relief as well as Rafferty's, had nicely reduced the number of potential suspects.

'It seems,' Rafferty continued in revelatory mood, 'Sir Rufus Seward had another hobby in addition to changing his will: making enemies, some of years-long duration. A number of them attended the reception.'

'Sounds like he paid too much attention to that old adage about keeping one's enemies close.'

Rafferty nodded. And as he bade the solicitor goodbye, he mused that it certainly would have been far healthier for Seward if he'd kept his enemies at something farther than chisel-thrusting distance.

While they were in Norwich, Rafferty decided it would be a good idea to kill two birds with the one stone. He needed to further question Marcus Canthorpe and Roy and Keith Farraday anyway, so he might as well do it today and save the necessity of another four-hour round trip. Especially if Llewellyn's mood continued in its current uncongenial and unsociable Garbo-esque mode.

Once they'd left McCann, Doolittle and Steel's premises, Rafferty glanced at his watch. They'd get something to eat before they made for Seward's estate a few miles to the north of Norwich, he decided. He also wanted to pick up a local Norwich newspaper; you never knew, he might find it contained some juicy revelation that would prove useful to the case.

Marcus Canthorpe and the Farraday twins were all still

living and working at Seward's estate. As Canthorpe told them when Llewellyn rang through to check, Sir Rufus had left instructions in his will, instructions that had been passed on by Metcalfe, that his staff were all to remain in their posts until after his will was proved.

And why wouldn't they? Rafferty thought. Not only did they all have 'expectations', but, with their demanding boss dead, their continued employment was likely now to be more of a comfortable sinecure.

They left their car in the solicitors' car park – parking in any city was often a nightmare best avoided and Norwich was unlikely to be an exception to this rule. Rafferty hailed a passing taxi and gave instructions before climbing in the back with Llewellyn.

'I know just the place for a nice lunch,' he told his sergeant, hoping a good meal would melt the permafrost glinting from his colleague's countenance. 'Little pub by Norwich's market, called the Sir Garnet Wolseley. Run by a London couple. They do a nice selection of dishes and at very reasonable prices.'

It was a beautiful, bright day for December, the air fresh but not too brisk. And as the cabbie dropped them off, Rafferty glanced around with appreciation. With the flamboyant market stalls looking even more colourful under the beaming sunshine and with the shops adorned with their Christmas glad rags, Norwich had an air of being *en fête*. He had always loved open air markets. He supposed it was in his blood as his ma had worked in one for some years after she was widowed. He spotted a newsagent and after buying the local paper they headed for the pub.

A short while later they were seated at a table in the Sir Garnet Wolseley. Rafferty opted for the liver, bacon and onions with mashed potatoes and vegetables. It was one of his favourite dishes, one rarely found on the average pub menu. Llewellyn settled on the salmon and broccoli bake in dill sauce. While they waited for their meal Rafferty quickly scanned the headlines; but there was nothing that might help him. Apart from the usual burglaries and muggings there was a warning from the Norwich police that someone was dealing dangerously pure heroin in the city. Disappointed, he put the paper away.

They didn't have to wait long for their meal. And after Rafferty had taken the edge off his hunger and worked his way through two thirds of the tender lamb's liver, he slowed sufficiently to comment, 'It's interesting that Philip Metcalfe should have mentioned that Seward enjoyed disinheriting people. I bet his heirs would have promised Seward's solicitor a tidy sum in exchange for knowing when they featured winningly in the will.'

Llewellyn finished his salmon, replaced his cutlery neatly, dead centre on his plate, and commented coolly, 'Unethical, for a solicitor.'

Rafferty shrugged as he finished his own meal. 'I doubt many legal types have a great acquaintance with ethics – might get in the way of their income. Look at our members of parliament; more than a few ex-barristers amongst them, yet I certainly haven't seen much evidence of either ethics or morals amongst the governing fraternity.'

Llewellyn inclined his head to concede the point. 'So what are you saying? That you want Philip Metcalfe's finances investigated?'

Rafferty shook his head. 'What would be the point? If he's been tipping the wink to the would-be heirs, he's hardly going to leave evidence that he's on the take lying around for us to find. Anyway, I don't imagine the heirs would hand over the dosh before they knew they were going to get their mitts on the dibs.' He raised what remained of his pint of Adnam's bitter and drained the glass. 'No, all I'm saying is that even though none of Seward's heirs was at the reception where he died, it might be better for us if we don't discount them too readily. Any one of them could have found a partner for the murderous end of the enterprise amongst the guests; enough of them had reason to hate Seward. The temptation to murder him *and* receive a financial reward for the deed might well have encouraged one or two to stray from the "thou shalt not kill" part of the Commandments.'

Rafferty rose to pay the bill. 'But this is all speculation, of course. We'd better pay a courtesy visit to the local nick before we go and question Marcus Canthorpe and the Farraday twins again. Maybe one or both of the twins will, if they know anything, have decided to snitch to teacher by now.'

Twelve

After they'd had a brief chat about the case with a DI Apsley, Rafferty's opposite number at Norwich Police Station, and received directions to Sir Rufus Seward's estate, they got a taxi back to their car and drove northwards out of the city. The estate was, as Apsley had said, several miles outside Norwich, but it was a short journey as the traffic was surprisingly light.

On their arrival at their destination, even from the gate Rafferty could see Seward's estate was a sizeable place. 'The rewards of sin,' he remarked. 'For sure God's lot have never shown me much favour. Maybe I should give up on religion and the God-botherers altogether and sign up with Old Nick's crew instead?'

'I thought you already had,' Llewellyn snapped, before he got out and pressed the buzzer set into the brickwork at the side of the gate that connected to the house. He exchanged a few words and the gates swung back. Llewellyn returned to the driver's seat and they made their way up the lengthy drive.

Rafferty, irrepressible in spite of Llewellyn's best efforts, gazed about him as they drove past vast expanses of lawns that were still immaculate even in December. He was finding the wages of sin more attractive by the second. But, wary of encouraging a second snub, he kept his thoughts to himself.

Seward's house was a priceless gem enclosed within immaculate emerald lawns. It was stunning, an imposing, four-storey, seven-bay, late Georgian mansion, with its central doorway enclosed snugly in its own deep-set canopy. The ground's acreage surely extended well into double figures.

'Got to have a Grade One listing,' Rafferty murmured. He glanced at Llewellyn and tried a second rapprochement. 'Ever thought we might be in the wrong line of work, Daff?' He was surprised when Llewellyn met him halfway, and with more than a single, caustic sentence.

'No. Money has never been a major motivating factor for me. Besides, maintenance costs for a building of such a size and age must be prohibitive.'

'I never thought money was a motivating factor for me, either,' Rafferty commented as they reached the end of the long drive and parked in front of the house, 'but I could be persuaded otherwise.'

He was disconcerted to find that Rufus Seward should have chosen to live in such a beautiful house. Somehow, he had expected something more brash and modern.

Marcus Canthorpe, Llewellyn had reported, had been quite curt on the phone. He was no less so in the flesh once they had rung the bell and gained admission. Clearly, he wasn't pleased to see them.

Rafferty shrugged. Like Randy Rawlins, he could live with discourtesy, especially when he had the privilege of visiting such a place. And as Canthorpe led them through the house to the office accommodation at the rear, Rafferty's gaze took in, through an open door, a huge, elegant drawing room with a fabulous ornamental ceiling that, given the age and grandeur of the house (on which it was apparent that no expense had been spared), must surely have been designed by Robert Adam himself.

The ceiling was framed by an equally ornate cornice. Ahead, Rafferty just caught a glimpse of an enormous conservatory, which looked like a Victorian addition attached to the south-facing rear of the house, when Canthorpe opened the last in a run of handsome, panelled and pedimented doors off to the left of the hall and led them into a room that was clearly now used as his office.

Although Canthorpe's welcome had been far from effusive, once seated in the visitors' chairs in his office, it was easy to see why their interruption to his day was unwelcome, for his desk was piled high with files and papers.

Rafferty, thinking of the pile of paperwork doubtless awaiting him in his own office on his return, gave a sympathetic nod at these piles. 'It looks like you've got a lot of work on, Mr Canthorpe. We'll try not to keep you too long.'

Canthorpe's surly expression softened a bit at this. 'Since

Sir Rufus's death I've been swamped with paperwork. You've no idea what is entailed in winding up the different areas of the life of a man like him. And although his two solicitors, personal and business, are dealing with the bulk of his estate, there are still many aspects that fall to me to sort out.'

For a moment, the normally efficient Canthorpe looked all but overwhelmed by his workload, but then he smiled. 'But once this is sorted and I've got my legacy from Sir Rufus's will, I'll be off for some R and R on a hot sandy beach.'

'Legacy?' Rafferty queried, while doing his best not to catch Llewellyn's eye.

'Yes. Sir Rufus told me he was leaving me a generous legacy in his will.' Canthorpe's lips thinned. 'I've certainly earned it and I'll enjoy spending it.'

Rafferty wondered how much Marcus Canthorpe expected to receive in the promised legacy. Enough to kill for? And although the solicitor had confided the truth to him, still he questioned Canthorpe about the non-existent legacy. 'I hope it's a substantial one, sir.'

Canthorpe shrugged. 'As to the precise amount, I have no idea. Sir Rufus always insisted he opened and dealt with any correspondence to do with his will, including letters and redrafted wills that came from his solicitors. Such documents were easy enough to spot and put aside as they always carried the solicitors' logo on the envelopes.'

'What about the other staff, Mr Canthorpe? Sir Rufus's chauffeur, for instance?' Llewellyn asked. 'And the house-keepers at his various homes? And then there's Roy and Keith Farraday, too. Were they all to receive legacies also?'

'As to that, I've no idea, though I don't believe so. Although I can't say for sure, of course. As I said, Sir Rufus always kept such matters close to his chest. But from what my fellow employees have said, Sir Rufus seems to have given them the impression that he had remembered them in his will. Even if he did, I doubt any of them will receive much, as none of them had been in his employ for long.'

He spread a rueful smile between them. 'Sir Rufus didn't tend to keep his employees, you see. I've been with him for five years and during my time there's been a considerable turnover of staff.'

Rafferty nodded. 'Perhaps you could let me have a list?' Who knew where such presumably grudge-bearing and aggrieved ex-employees might have ended up? Working at the Elmhurst Hotel was certainly one possibility.

Canthorpe bit off a sigh at this request, but he rose to accommodate it. He opened one of an array of filing cabinets that lined the left wall of his office, and with an efficient hand, jotted down the details of Seward's past employees before, some fifteen minutes later, handing them over. Their personnel files tightly filled all of two drawers of a cabinet.

Rafferty thanked him.

Canthorpe shrugged. 'Not that I imagine it's likely to help your investigation. I saw none of those on my list at the Elmhurst Hotel the night Sir Rufus died. I would certainly have recognized any one of them.'

Rafferty nodded. 'You're probably right, but it's as well to check them out.' He paused and then remarked, 'I imagine, since you were with your late employer for five years, you would know a good deal about his life, his business dealings and any people who might have reason to bear him a grudge?'

A tiny smile curled its way round Canthorpe's lips. 'People with reason to bear him a grudge?' he repeated. The smile widened. 'It would probably be easier for me to tell you who *didn't* have reason to bear him a grudge. It wouldn't make a very long list.'

'Why did you remain in his employ for so long if he was an unpleasant man to work for?' Llewellyn asked.

Canthorpe shrugged. 'It's a good job and it's interesting. Oh, don't get me wrong; I've had offers – some very attractive job offers, as it happens – since I've been here. I was seriously tempted once or twice. But Sir Rufus was the kind of man who liked to keep the reins of power firmly in his own hands; he oversaw everything in his various businesses, which gave me learning opportunities not so readily available elsewhere. And I've learned a lot since I've been here – how the rich and powerful operate across a wide range of businesses, for instance. And while I might have earned far more elsewhere, it suited me to remain. You'd be amazed at what you can learn just by watching and listening to such people

119

as Sir Rufus and having the paperwork from their day-to-day affairs cross your desk.'

Rafferty didn't doubt it. He mused on what would be Canthorpe's likely reaction when he discovered he wasn't down to receive a legacy at all, never mind the substantial one for which he had such plans.

Rafferty glanced at Llewellyn to see if he had any further questions he wished to pose, and when Llewellyn gave a tiny shake of his head, Rafferty moved the interview forward. 'Have you remembered anything new about the night of the reception, sir?' he asked. 'Anything at all?'

Canthorpe frowned. He hesitated before he said doubtfully, 'There was one thing, but I'm not sure if it's of any significance. I doubt I'd have remembered it at all if it hadn't been for Sir Rufus dying like that, but I noticed that Ivor Bignall was distinctly cool towards him all evening. I don't know why or what it was about. And, apart from him remonstrating with my late boss when he was rude to the barman, it's not as if there was a big row or anything. I can't begin to explain what might have caused the frosty atmosphere between them, but it was there even before Sir Rufus started drinking heavily and picked on the barman, so it can't have been that which sparked it.'

'And this coolness you say was definitely evident *before* Mr Bignall spoke up for the barman that Sir Rufus insulted?'

'Yes. As I said, the coolness was evident immediately Mr and Mrs Bignall arrived.' He shrugged. 'Well, I've told you about it, for what it's worth. Maybe Bignall will explain the reason for it himself.'

As Canthorpe was able to tell them nothing more, Rafferty asked for the security tapes from the camera he had noticed mounted on one of the gateposts at the entrance to the estate. Although Canthorpe had already supplied them with a list of those who had visited the estate and who had opportunity to help themselves to a blank invitation or two, it was possible there might be some visitors he had forgotten about.

Canthorpe handed over half a dozen tapes before Rafferty asked to speak to the Farraday twins. He was directed to a cottage in the grounds. After a brief battle of wills, Rafferty, who was anyway feeling idle and replete after his filling lunch, handed the car keys to Llewellyn with barely a murmur. As

120

they made their way in the car to the twins' cottage, Rafferty glimpsed the blue water of a swimming pool through the glass of what appeared to be a remodelled stable block. 'How the other half live,' he muttered, overtaken with envy once again and unable to keep it to himself.

He felt Llewellyn glance at him before the Welshman, with all his upright Methodist morality to the fore, quietly remarked, 'Maybe, rather than dwelling on the late Sir Marcus Seward's wealth and property, you would do better to ponder what he had to do to acquire it all in the first place. From what we've learned of him, he didn't start out a rich man.'

As Seward had attended the same school as the decidedly unwealthy Rafferty brothers, this was undoubtedly true. Rafferty supposed Llewellyn was right. The cut-throat world of international business was ruthless and took no prisoners. He doubted his burdensome, demanding Catholic conscience would have provided him with much peace if he'd attempted such a life.

He smiled ruefully to himself at the realization that a lack of education and the requisite business nous had saved him from such a perilous existence. 'Thank you, God,' he murmured, with more than a touch of hypocrisy and even more base ingratitude in his heart.

The Farradays' shared cottage in the grounds was well away from the main house and concealed by tall trees, presumably so the rich man in the mansion didn't have his gaze soured by the poor people. Certainly, it had originally been designed as staff accommodation, probably for the male outdoor staff who, years ago when class distinctions were even more pronounced than now, were often housed separately from the indoor staff.

As Llewellyn pulled up and parked, Rafferty swept his gaze over the cottage. Plain and simple with a stable door, the cottage had none of the embellishments of Seward's mansion. Still, it looked comfortable enough from the outside.

One of the twins, Rafferty wasn't certain whether it was Keith or Roy, opened the door to Llewellyn's knock. Whichever twin he was, he looked even less pleased to see the two policemen again than had Marcus Canthorpe.

The identical twins whose schooldays had been devoted to

snitching to teacher and weaselling confidences from their schoolmates, hadn't improved with maturity, as Rafferty had had ample opportunity to discover when he had first re-made their acquaintance on questioning them immediately after Seward's murder.

They had both always been very thin, but, as he and Llewellyn followed whichever twin it was through to the living room where they found the second sibling, Rafferty noticed that now both had a brittleness about them that hadn't been evident in their youth. The reason for this brittleness became apparent as he studied them: their eyes had the pinpoint pupils and the unnatural glitter of those addicted to drugs. The discovery made him hope that the cocaine in the main bathroom of Seward's hotel suite didn't turn out to belong to them rather than Mandy Khan, as he still had faint, if fading, hopes in that direction. He could certainly do with such a lever to keep a lid on the superintendent's presence that night and so protect his brother by indulging in a little mutual backscratching with Idris Khan – and the superintendent himself, should it come to that. He still hadn't worked out how best to broach the subject with the mayor, or even if he dared broach it at all.

The Farradays' thin, weasel faces still had the sly air about them that Rafferty recalled from their shared schooldays and had noticed on the night of the murder. They had had that smug 'I know something you don't know' air even when young. You could be sure, when they were looking particularly smug, that someone was about to land in trouble with teacher.

After Seward's murder, they, like Marcus Canthorpe, had removed themselves back to Seward's Norfolk home. And although they had only worked for Sir Rufus for a matter of months, the cottage they shared was well-stuffed with attractive possessions and gave the impression of a residence of years' duration. It was plain that they both had squirrelling tendencies; every surface was crammed with collectable china and objets d'art. Neither twin had ever married, though perhaps, as they presented like an old married couple rather than brothers, they had no need of brides.

Their tastes were expensive, for although it seemed likely that most of the furniture came with the cottage, the other contents certainly didn't. Rafferty couldn't imagine Rufus Seward had been willing to adorn his workers' accommodation with modern artworks and other such extravagances.

'I see you're admiring our little collection, Inspector,' said the twin whose next comment proved him to be Keith Farraday. 'Roy and I like to consider ourselves connoisseurs of the art world, and fortunately, neither of us have wives or teenage children to spend our income. But do sit down, both of you. Make yourselves comfortable.'

Rather unwillingly, Rafferty sat down on an armchair when invited to do so. And although his seat was well padded, comfortable was far from what he was feeling; the twins had always induced a feeling of distaste. Although the place was spotless – the twins were nothing if not particular about their surroundings – he somehow felt reluctant to allow his body close contact with anything they used or sat on, perhaps with a superstitious dread that something of their personalities would be transferred to him in the process.

He was being fanciful, he knew, and did his best to dismiss the thought.

'So, what can my brother and I do for you, Inspector?' Keith asked as he perched his skinny bottom on a plumply cushioned Regency chair that Rafferty guessed must be one of their own. Certainly it and its partner at the other side of the hearth, on which Rafferty sat, were far from being in keeping with the rest of the furniture, which looked as if it had received some rough treatment over the years. Perhaps Sir Rufus's revolving door of employees had taken their displeasure with their boss out on his furniture.

Now Rafferty recalled that, as the older by some twenty minutes, Keith Farraday had always taken the lead. Roy had never quibbled about the arrangement and he didn't do so now. He simply sat, relaxed with his hands in his lap and let his twin do all the talking with that irritating, smug expression that, in their youth, had always given Rafferty the desire to hit him.

'We just wanted to put some follow-up questions to you both,' Rafferty told them as he forced a smile. 'See if time might have jogged your memory of the evening Sir Rufus died.'

The gazes from the twins' matching small green eyes met and held before both sets settled on Rafferty.

'It's been suggested to us that Mr Ivor Bignall behaved very coolly towards Sir Rufus on the evening of the reception. Can you confirm that?'

Both the twins shook their heads and Keith replied, 'We certainly never noticed anything like that, Inspector. Who can have said such a thing? And why, one has to wonder.'

Indeed one did, thought Rafferty, surprised they hadn't seized on what Canthorpe had said in order to shift his suspicions elsewhere. Then he told them, 'That's not relevant. But you're sure you never noticed any coolness?'

They both shook their heads again in unison.

With that question out of the way, Rafferty got on with the rest of the interview. At first, to his surprise, they were remarkably forthcoming, though all their confidences were of the unprovable, gossipy sort rather than anything more substantial. Perhaps they now regarded him as the teacher figure to whom they should pour forth their bile.

Certainly, it hadn't taken them long before they began to reveal tittle-tattle about their late boss's guests that they might have found more profitable to keep to themselves, if extracting a reward for their silence was indeed their usual habit. Or perhaps it was just that they had better, more damaging and even more lucrative sources of information and had judged it prudent to share the stuff they were unable to prove.

None of the twins' revelations showed Seward, several of his guests or the twins themselves, in an attractive light. Among other things, they confirmed that Mandy Khan *did* have a drug habit, though they informed Rafferty hers was a preference for heroin rather than the cocaine that Hanks had found in the main bathroom of Seward's suite. And as Rafferty had already noted from their own appearance, it seemed probable that they were well placed to recognize the signs of drug addiction in others. They must have some tidy little earners, Rafferty thought, if they were able to afford both their drug habit and an addiction to expensive collectibles.

The twins also revealed that Idris Khan had reason to hate Seward who had, according to the twins, seduced Khan's wife, even though he and the mayor were meant to have mutual business interests. Mandy, it seemed, had ambitions to move from her teetotal and somewhat repressive husband to the selfindulgent, international and far wealthier potential one that Seward had represented.

It was bad enough for Khan that Seward had bedded his wife and in his long-awaited and looked-forward-to mayoral year, too, but to have then learned that Seward thought her only good for sex rather than the permanent commitment she had sought must have been galling in the extreme. Especially as, to avoid scandal attaching to his mayoral name, Khan had felt obliged to take her back for the remainder of his term in office.

Certainly, as Keith told them, when Mandy had made her desire for a permanent union plain – 'within shouting distance of me and my brother while we waited in Marcus Canthorpe's office to report to the boss about some little bit of business he was engaged in' – Seward had laughed at her. According to Keith Farraday's version of events, if it could be believed, Seward had wasted no time in making clear she didn't have anything he wanted over the longer term.

'Is Marcus Canthorpe able to confirm this?' Llewellyn asked.

'No,' Keith told him. 'It was one of the occasions when he was away from his desk.'

Conveniently for their tittle-tattle – if that was all it was, thought Rafferty. Lucky for Mandy Khan that after such a humiliation she had remained outside Seward's suite when she and Idris Khan had returned late on the night of his murder to pick up her forgotten handbag and with the hotel security men and the security tape to back her up.

The twins looked remarkably pleased with themselves as their grubby secrets tumbled pell-mell from their fleshy lips. Their dark hair was still worn in the same old-fashioned style they had always sported, with the too-far-over side parting that looked as though it had been done using a ruler and a cut-throat razor and glued down with copious quantities of Brylcreem; no wonder each of their upholstered chairs sported a wide protective antimacassar.

Rafferty didn't know whether or not to believe what the twins had told them. Apart from their long attachment to tale-bearing, it was in their interest to foster suspicion elsewhere and so lessen any that might fall on them. Because for all Rafferty knew, the twins might also have had reason to bear a grudge against Seward. He had been their boss and Rafferty had already learned from several quarters that Seward hadn't been one of the most appreciative of employers. In the circumstances, it seemed more than possible that the twins could well have colluded in stabbing Seward themselves, waiting their chance till the evening of the reception when the finger of suspicion would have a wider selection of possible suspects to point at.

With this thought foremost in his mind, Rafferty questioned them even more closely. Unsurprisingly, when his questions veered round to themselves, they became markedly reticent.

He was interested in gaining confirmation about who could have had access to the party invitations. Marcus Canthorpe had told them that he had liaised with the council in organizing his boss's civic reception. But, as Canthorpe himself had admitted, he hadn't thought it necessary to lock the invitations away. They had been clearly visible on his desk for over a week, the blank ones and the rest. Any visitor, of which there were apparently a fair number, who passed through Canthorpe's office in order to reach Seward's inner sanctum could have seen them and helped themselves.

The twins confirmed what Canthorpe had said. They even admitted that Canthorpe had spent much time away from his desk, out on personal, confidential errands for Sir Rufus. This confirmation was not good news for Rafferty. He had hoped the person who had sent Mickey his unofficial invitation would be restricted to Seward himself and his staff. Clearly, that wasn't the case. The list of party attendees and possible murderer that also encompassed visitors to Seward's Norfolk home during the relevant time, included Idris Khan and Ivor Bignall, both of whom had shared business interests with the deceased in the past, as Keith Farraday now told them. Though why either of *them* should even know Mickey, much less try to implicate him in Seward's murder, was a moot point.

'Though I don't think either Idris Khan or Ivor Bignall talked about mutual business interests with Sir Rufus during their last meeting here – at least not *business* business, if you know what I mean,' Keith said.

Roy sniggered and made one of his first contributions to the conversation. 'No, bro. More like mucky business.'

The Farradays kept glancing at one another and exchanging furtive little smiles. It was getting on Rafferty's nerves. He couldn't help wondering what other secrets they had that they were keeping to themselves. He said with a stern edge to his voice, 'If either of you know anything else that might help us in our investigations, you would be wise to tell us about it now.'

The twins exchanged another secretive glance, then both shook their heads.

'I really can't think of anything else, Inspector,' Keith told him. 'Can you, Roy?'

'No, nothing at all. So sorry, Inspector. We really would like to help further, but—'

But if you *do* know something of value, you would rather it was of value to yourselves only rather than me, Rafferty guessed. These two weren't just squirrellers of objets d'art and paintings; they had always squirrelled away useful information, too. What valuable secrets had they learned during their employment with Rufus Seward? he wondered. A man like Seward would have had plenty of secrets, as would his wealthy business acquaintances.

'This isn't the schoolyard, you know,' Rafferty sharply reminded, 'where the worst you might suffer for causing someone grief was a beating. If either of you know anything more than idle tittle-tattle that might have relevance to Sir Rufus's murder, you should say so now. Whoever Seward's killer is, he's already murdered once,' he warned. 'I doubt he would have any compunction about adding another two people to his tally if he believed them to be a threat.'

'I don't know what you're trying to imply, Inspector,' Keith Farraday protested in tones of injured innocence, 'but there's really no cause to make such accusations. We've already told you all we know. We can't help you any further.'

Strange, Rafferty thought, that in spite of Keith's denials and his twin's nod of agreement, both their pasty faces had paled significantly at his warning. But they still chose to tell him nothing more.

If they *did* know something it was clear they were determined to keep it to themselves. It wasn't hard to gauge how they might have managed to acquire such expensive artworks while being on the limited incomes of unqualified gofers. If they elected to place themselves in danger by acquiring the secrets of others, it was their lookout. He had warned them. If they chose not to confide what they knew to him, he couldn't help them or keep them safe, as he told them on a parting warning shot as he and Llewellyn left.

Rafferty was relieved to get out into the fresh air and away from their cloying, over-furnished living room. Its over-powering scent of polish and air freshener had started to make him feel nauseous. Or perhaps that was more down to the twins?

Thirteen

Rafferty settled himself in the passenger seat for the journey back to Elmhurst while Llewellyn went through his pernickety pre-driving checks of repositioning the rear-view mirror, which hadn't been moved since they'd left Elmhurst, checking the wipers and windscreen wash bottle were working and generally being infuriating to the time-strapped Rafferty.

But as he had decided, as a sop, to allow Llewellyn to drive on the return journey, he didn't express these criticisms out loud. Instead, to distract himself, Rafferty asked, 'What do you reckon to Canthorpe and the Farraday brothers? They were all obligingly confiding today.'

'Mmm. They were certainly anxious to relocate our suspicions elsewhere.'

Rafferty nodded. 'Understandable, I suppose, in the circumstances. They've certainly, between them, managed to give us plenty to think about.' Too much, thought Rafferty, who felt he already had more than enough on his mind.

Llewellyn finally turned the key in the ignition. The engine purred quietly as he engaged the clutch. About time, was Rafferty's thought as, already regretting his decision to let his sergeant drive, he watched as Llewellyn at last moved the gear stick into first.

The camera on the gate swivelled towards them as they approached the end of the long drive. Canthorpe must have been watching for their departure, for the gates swung smoothly open to enable them to leave the estate. Rafferty raised a hand in a 'thank you' gesture to the camera as they swung through the gates and out on to the road.

'Interesting that Ivor Bignall was cool towards Seward. Wonder what that was about?' he murmured.

'There's one way to find out. But it's odd that no one but Canthorpe has mentioned this supposed coolness.'

'People aren't always that observant. Maybe Canthorpe told us about it in the hope of removing our suspicions from himself on the principle that when it comes to murder suspects we'd prefer to have one big bird like Bignall in the hand rather than several minnows like himself and the Farradays.'

'Possibly. Either Canthorpe is unusually perceptive and noticed the coolness when no one else did, or he's making it up for reasons best known to himself, though I suppose it's not necessarily suspicious that Canthorpe was the only person at the reception to notice Bignall's coolness towards Seward. You seem to have forgotten one important element in the others' forgetfulness: the lack of sobriety. Marcus Canthorpe was on duty and presumably expected to stay sober. It's scarcely surprising he was more observant of atmosphere and reactions. And I imagine he must have been very familiar with Bignall and his normal behaviour – rather more so than the Farraday twins, who must also have been expected to refrain from alcoholic overindulgence.'

'Mmm. I suppose so.' Llewellyn had a point, he knew. How was it that the abstemious Welshman had hit on the crux of the matter when he, who had plenty of first-hand experience of what alcohol did to your observational skills, had failed to consider it?

But there was one oddity that he *had* noticed and now he brought it to Llewellyn's attention. 'Marcus Canthorpe said he only discovered that Seward had been murdered because Ivor Bignall insisted on saying goodbye to his host. But—'

'But it seems unlikely that Bignall, after cold-shouldering Seward all evening – if, in fact, he did so and we've only Canthorpe's word for that – would be so anxious to observe a social nicety.'

I was going to say that, Rafferty felt like protesting, even though he knew it was a childish response. Instead, he asked, 'So what did he *really* want to do? Set the scene to make him look innocent of the murder? Who would draw attention to themselves in such a way if they were guilty, is the implied assumption.'

'A dangerous ploy,' Llewellyn murmured, dropping down

to a crawl after he allowed a slow-moving tractor out of a farm gate.

Rafferty's lips thinned. Does he do things like that deliberately, just to annoy me? he wondered. He kept his lips pressed firmly together to restrain the growing urge to criticize.

'It would have muddied the waters nicely if Seward's body hadn't been discovered till morning,' Llewellyn pointed out. 'Dr Dally's estimated time of death would have been much wider. Because the body was found so quickly the potential suspects are greatly reduced.'

'Perhaps, if Bignall killed Seward, he was prepared to risk it. He's a successful businessman; most such types have taken a chance or two in their careers. He could have thought such a calculated gamble worth the risk if he had a strong reason to want revenge on Seward.'

'Possibly. Mr Bignall's clearly an intelligent man, more than capable of making such a judgement. We've no forensics,' Llewellyn reminded him as they ambled along behind the tractor at a slow enough pace to admire the frost-crusted Norfolk fields stretching far into the distance on either side of the road. 'If he *did* kill him, if he keeps a cool head he could well get away with it.'

'Mmm, there's the rub: *if* he did it.'

The tractor driver, with a cheery wave, turned off and Rafferty breathed a sigh of relief as Llewellyn picked up speed. However, in Rafferty's opinion, he didn't pick up enough of it. Rafferty studied the speedometer and frowned. He forgot he was meant to be on a charm offensive and asked, 'Can't you at least match the speed limit, Dafyd? Go on, put your foot down, man. It's not as if the roads are busy. I'm keen to question Bignall about this alleged coolness of his towards Seward. But before we do that, and assuming we actually get back before I die of old age, we'll stop off at the station first. We've already been gone the best part of the day and I need to speak to the team as well and get up to speed on what's been happening while we've been away from the station before we do anything else.'

He sighed as the speedo edged up another couple of miles per hour; they were still five miles under the limit. But Llewellyn wasn't a man to be rushed so Rafferty decided it would be better to spend the travelling time to some purpose than to allow Llewellyn's careful driving style to irritate him.

'Interesting what the Farradays had to say about the impetuous, husband-hunting Mandy Khan. It's a wonder she and her husband haven't come to blows before. It's a big thing for an Asian man to find himself cuckolded. Even if Khan's only half-Asian, murders have been committed for much less in that culture.'

'Maybe his Welsh half is dominant on the matter of honour.'

Llewellyn pulled up at the traffic lights on the outskirts of Norwich just as they turned to amber.

Rafferty scowled, his good intentions forgotten. 'You could have gone through the lights. They'd only just changed.' They weren't even on red, thought Rafferty crossly.

'Not a good idea at a busy junction.'

Rafferty's lips thinned again, but although he directed a scowl towards Llewellyn's impervious profile, he refrained from making any further comment. As he sat drumming his fingers on his knee, he remembered it was his turn to visit Mickey this evening and take him more provisions. He checked his watch. It was already getting on for six o'clock. It would be after eight by the time they got back and were able to question Bignall again, always providing he was at home. He'd promised Ma he'd stop off at her house and collect the clothes she'd washed for Mickey. And then he'd have to visit a supermarket and get some bread and milk and buy Mickey a takeaway. God knew what time it would be when he got home.

But one thing he *did* know: he could expect a flea in his ear from his new fiancée when he finally got there.

Nothing new of any interest had turned up while they were in Norfolk. Soon they were back in the car and, with a brief phone call to confirm he was at home, on their way to see Ivor Bignall.

Bignall, since the murder, seemed to have become quite the house husband. As before, he led them through to the same attractive room. Again, Dorothea Bignall was seated by the fire. She greeted them warmly and once they had sat down at her invitation, she said, 'I didn't expect to see you again quite so soon, Inspector. How can we help you?'

The big man seemed more subdued this time than he had been on the last occasion they'd spoken to him. In contrast, his wife Dorothea seemed quite perky, as if she felt the need to compensate for the silence of her usually gregarious husband.

'Actually, Mrs Bignall,' Rafferty told her, 'it's your husband I wanted to speak to.'

Rafferty turned to Bignall who was standing, legs spread, with his back to the fire. 'We've been told that there was a distinct coolness between you and Rufus Seward during the evening of his civic reception, sir.'

Bignall raised his bushy eyebrows. 'A coolness, Inspector? Really, I don't know what you can mean.'

'Let me explain. It was described by someone in a position to notice that your manner to Seward was distinctly on the chilly side. I want you to tell me why that was.'

'Your informant was mistaken, Inspector, I can assure you. I was not cool towards Seward. I had no reason to be cool towards him. Admittedly, I didn't speak to him much. But as I believe I've already explained, that was because he had so many other guests who wanted to congratulate him on his hometown honour. I suppose it might, to some, look as if we had had a falling out, but I can assure you we hadn't.'

To Rafferty's surprise, Dorothea Bignall immediately contradicted her husband.

'For goodness' sake, Ivor, tell the inspector the truth. There's no need to lie. I know you think you're protecting me and defending my feelings, but I'm not quite the piece of Dresden you seem to believe me to be. I won't break, you know, if you tell them the truth. It really was all a very long time ago. But in case you don't believe I'm able to cope with the revelation and continue to lie for my sake, I'll tell the inspector all about it myself.'

Bignall frowned. Rafferty presumed he wasn't used to her contradicting him, and so forcefully. It was a surprise to both of them. Maybe Dorothea Bignall wasn't the timid mouse he had previously assumed her to be, and maybe it wasn't his wife Bignall was trying to protect . . .

Dorothea Bignall turned to Rafferty. 'I was upset on the day of Rufus Seward's civic reception. Ivor found me in tears in our bedroom.' She paused, gulped in a lungful of air and then continued. 'We'd been trying since a year or so after our marriage to have children. But I never once conceived in all the years that followed. I thought I knew why, but Ivor had no reason to suspect. He forced the truth from me when he found me in tears for no apparent reason.'

Her eyes were glistening with unshed tears now as if her memory had forced a reconstruction of the events, but she continued determinedly on in a room now silent but for her low voice and the crackle of the logs burning in the grate. 'You remember I told you that Rufus Seward and I both attended St Oswald's, the fee-paying boarding school?' she asked Rafferty.

He nodded. Given the revelations he had so far heard about Rufus Seward and his behaviour, he was beginning to get a suspicion of where this was going. He stole a glance at Bignall. The big man's face was a frozen mask, whatever he was feeling well concealed behind it.

'While I was at the school, Rufus Seward raped me and I fell pregnant. My parents insisted on an abortion. Unfortunately, the abortion was botched and I got an infection. It damaged me rather badly. Much later, I was told that the damage the infection had caused made it almost impossible for me to have children. The day Ivor found me in tears was the anniversary of the day I murdered my child and removed any possibility of being able to give my husband the large family he wanted. I hadn't been well that day and I suppose the anniversary combined with my ill-health to make me weepy.'

'And you learned this, as your wife said, on the day of Seward's reception?' Rafferty asked Bignall.

Bignall nodded at this as if he no longer trusted his voice.

Rafferty found it strange that the forceful Bignall had shown such restraint at the reception and had limited himself merely to a display of coolness towards Seward. If it had been me, Rafferty thought, I would have punched Seward's lights out. Or murdered him.

'Did you speak to him about what he'd done to your wife?'

Bignall found his voice at last. 'No, of course not. How could I? The evening of the reception was neither the time nor the place for such recriminations. It would have greatly upset my wife if I had brought up such a matter in public. Besides, it was only my wife's word against Seward's. There were no witnesses to the rape. Dorothea was ashamed and had told no one about it, not even her parents. They just assumed she had been careless with some boy, especially when she refused to reveal who the father was.'

'Yet you still attended the reception? Why?'

'I insisted, Inspector,' Dorothea interrupted. 'My husband had several joint business interests with Rufus Seward. Even for my sake, I wouldn't allow him to risk a public falling out that might jeopardise these. Besides, this was a one-off occasion. I thought myself capable of getting through the evening, especially as I knew I was unlikely to have to socialize with Rufus Seward again.'

Was that because she thought it unlikely that Seward would again visit his hometown, Rafferty wondered, or because she knew he was shortly to leave this life?

Bignall again insisted he had said nothing to Seward. 'I intended to speak to him privately the next day. But by then it was too late, of course. The swine got away with what he did and I was never able to force him to confront his guilt.'

It all sounded a little pat to Rafferty. Had Bignall really managed to hold his fury in check all that evening after his wife's tearful confession and the realization that Seward was the reason he had never had the brood of sons his dynastic ambitions had craved?

It seemed increasingly unlikely to Rafferty the more he considered it. But until they had proof that Bignall was lying – and Bignall was saying nothing more, that much was clear – they had no reason to take him into custody.

'Quite a revelation,' Llewellyn commented as the Bignalls' front door closed behind them. A chill and gusty wind had developed and they both hurried to get into the car and out of its path. 'I'm surprised Mrs Bignall told us anything about the rape and its consequences when, on the face of it, it gives both her and her husband a strong reason for wishing Seward dead.'

'True,' Rafferty agreed as he turned the ignition and started the car. With several things still to accomplish before he could go home, he hadn't wanted Llewellyn's cautious driving to delay him more than it had already done, so he had taken the precaution of relieving his partner of the keys.

'Either she hates her husband – I imagine he must sometimes be pretty overbearing – and wouldn't be sorry to see him banged up or she really does love him and doesn't think he did it. Still,' he remarked, once he'd got the car in gear and rolling, 'she can't be sure which way we would jump. And as I said, old I've a Big'un must be a difficult man to live with. It strikes me that he might well blame her as much as Seward for the fact they have no children. He must also wonder why she chose to keep the rape and the rapist's identity a secret. And the timing is strangely coincidental when you consider that Seward was murdered on the evening of the day Bignall finally learned the truth.'

'It looks suspicious, I agree,' said Llewellyn, struggling to strap himself in as the car careered round a bend, 'but I find it difficult to imagine a man like Bignall knifing someone in the back. As he said himself last time we spoke to him, it's such a cowardly way to kill someone. Besides, apart from any other consideration, surely he would want Seward to see his face and understand the reason he wanted him dead?'

'Maybe, maybe not. It could be that Bignall thought a knife in the back was all a man like Seward deserved: a fitting death, given that Bignall must have thought Seward's actions had knifed *him* in the back all those years ago.'

'I still think the psychology of this murder is all wrong for Mr Bignall.'

'Please, not that psychology stuff again,' Rafferty protested. 'Anyway, that angle, on its own, would provide a very good reason for Bignall to kill him that way,' Rafferty pointed out as he moved up the gears after straightening up once past the bend. 'By its very nature, such a cowardly means of murder would serve to make us more dismissive of Bignall as a suspect. You said yourself he's an intelligent man,' Rafferty reminded Llewellyn. 'He'd have to be to have got where he is, with that beautiful house and substantial business interests. To me they're a pointer that he'd be clever enough to work out the most psychologically unlikely way for him to kill someone and then to do it in just that way.'

Honestly, Rafferty thought, sometimes Llewellyn complicated the simplest things. 'Look,' he said, 'if Bignall had
decided to do his best to get away with murder, why would
a guy with his smarts choose to do the deed in a manly, face-
to-face confrontation when he must have realized doing it the
back-stabbing way would speak volumes to coppers like you
and any possible profiler and point you and them in entirely
the wrong direction? It would be the act of a fool.

'And even if he wasn't smart enough to manipulate the
psychological aspect to his advantage, sometimes people just
behave out of character. He'd just had one hell of a shock,
remember. Here was a man whose greatest ambition, after
he'd built his wealth, was to produce a brood of fine sons to
pass it on to. But instead he has no one to inherit it but a
barren wife – a wife who had kept the true reason for her
infertility a secret from him for years. Such discoveries would
enrage any man. Imagine what they would do to a man with
a desire to sire a dynasty.'

Rafferty grimaced as he failed to beat the red at the traffic
lights. He pulled up with a sharpness that caused the car to
judder, and turned to his passenger. 'And then you've got to
question why he agreed to attend the party at all after hearing
such shocking news. Maybe the real reason was not to protect
his business interests at all, as his wife claimed, but to get his
revenge.'

The lights finally changed to green and Rafferty roared
away.

Beside him, Llewellyn got a firm grip on the dashboard.
But although clearly unimpressed by Rafferty's incautious
driving style, he didn't allow it to distract him from putting
forward some more arguments of his own. 'I think Mrs Bignall
told us the truth: that he felt he had no choice when his and
Seward's business interests were so entwined. Besides, he
must have faced and accepted that they were unlikely to have
children some time ago. It was an old wound that might well
have healed with the years. Besides, I gained the distinct
impression that it was Mrs Bignall rather than her husband
who minded the most about their not having a family.'

'Either way, you must see that Bignall accepting a fluke of
nature is one thing but this was something very different.

Maybe we'll find that he attended that party for another reason altogether, as I said, and that was that he had discovered another ambition: getting away with murder.'

Rafferty turned into Bacon Lane, pulled into the rear yard of the police station and parked untidily across two bays. He shrugged as Llewellyn, in a pained voice, pointed this out to him. To himself, he admitted he felt a vague twinge of unease about his own conclusions, because although he didn't doubt that Bignall was clever enough to come up with a method of killing that would point the finger away from him, he was also clever enough to realize that it must, instead, point the finger at less forceful suspects than himself. Would he really be willing for someone else to be convicted and serve a prison term for what he had done? Rafferty wondered whether he was reading him all wrong, or was he, like Llewellyn, creating unnecessary complications when, in reality, it was a possibility that the eminently sane Ivor Bignall had been sent beyond reason into temporary madness? In which case, it was probable that he had given no thought to that aspect at all. Until it was too late.

Irritated by his own contradictory thoughts, Rafferty climbed out of the car, slammed the door and stomped across the yard to the station's back entrance. And then he thought of his brother, hiding out further up the Essex coast, and caught something of Bignall's supposed insanity himself. No brother of his was taking the rap for this crime. If Bignall was guilty, Rafferty was set on proving it. He mightn't like doing it; he mightn't like being the police officer who caged such a big and proud beast as Bignall, especially when the victim had used him so cruelly, but if it came to a toss up between Bignall and Mickey then it was no contest. Still, as he climbed the stairs to his office, Rafferty's heart was heavy because he privately felt that whoever had killed Rufus Seward had done the world a favour.

Fourteen

It had been after nine o'clock by the time they got back to the station. It was a little while later when Rafferty picked up his own car from the car park and headed for his ma's house.

After visiting the Bignalls' beautiful manor house home and seeing again the elegance of the Christmas tree in their sitting room with its subtle silver and gold decorations, the eyeball-searing yuletide gaudiness that met him as he turned into his ma's road on the council estate almost caused him to stall the car. Although not normally one to flinch at such flamboyantly exuberant colours, even Rafferty admitted that the vision before his eyes was completely over the top.

Between his last visit and this one, Ma's next door neighbour had surpassed herself. Still trailing his ma – the proud possessor of twelve grandchildren and one great-grandchild – in the grandmother stakes, she had, it seemed, hit on a way of beating Ma in something. The neighbour's accomplishment really was a blinder in more ways than one because between the flashing, illuminated and mechanical Santa, the reindeer gambolling over the roof, the choir of gold-winged, haloed angels around the crib on the dirty pebbledash beneath, who were in imminent danger of having their heads kicked in by the reindeers' hooves, and the glowing primary-coloured lights that festooned whatever space remained, Ma's neighbour had certainly won the year's vulgarity cup.

But, as she sharply informed him when he went inside to pick up Mickey's clean clothes and was foolish enough to point out her neighbour's feat of one-upmanship, Ma had no desire to win such a trophy.

'Christmas is about the birth of our Saviour,' she told the son who was still considering transferring his allegiance to

139

Old Nick. After she had banged about in the kitchen to make tea and fill another hot water bottle for Mickey, this theme continued. 'It's not meant to be turned into some kind of three-ringed circus with people coming from miles around to watch the show. I'm surprised you could get into the street. Since those monstrosities went up, by this time in the evening the road's usually clogged with cars and gawpers.'

She snorted. 'Her-next-door even comes out every evening around this time to take a bow as if she's done something to be proud of.'

Rafferty didn't doubt that his ma's feelings on the religious front were entirely genuine; she was a regular at St Boniface Catholic Church, but although religious, she also had a strong competitive instinct and liked to be a winner. And in spite of vigorously protesting that she had no desire to match her neighbour's flashy show, she must hate being trumped by a woman who had never bested her in anything before.

This year, of course, Ma had the Mickey problem to contend with. She had confided to Rafferty that with all the anxiety his brother was causing her, she had really had no heart to put up her own Christmas decorations. She wouldn't have bothered at all if it wasn't for the grandchildren, who expected their gran to do Christmas properly. Rafferty could see that, in the circumstances, Her-next-door's blatantly colourful and offensively irreligious decorations must be even harder for her to stomach.

With the trip out to Mickey still to be made, Rafferty cut his visit as short as he could. He left Ma muttering darkly about 'short-circuiting the entire street'. He wasn't sure whether this comment was indicative of worry that the neighbour's Christmas decorations would bring this about or whether his ma was actually plotting some kind of sabotage. He wouldn't put it past her. It was a worry he could do without right now. But, he comforted himself as he left to pick up Mickey's takeaway and other food, she wouldn't have the technical knowledge to bring this about. The comfort this thought brought was soon edged out by the realization that she hadn't had a husband, two sons and other assorted relatives working in various aspects of the building trade for years without having picked up a trick or two . . .

*   *   *

The shops in the High Street were open late, as was usual at this time of year in order to accommodate as many free-spending customers as possible, and were lit up with their entirely commercialized version of Christmas. And unlike the neighbour's innocent if vulgar exuberance, theirs showed their grasping, greedy desire to part their customers from every last penny. This year, he saw as he drove past, they had even gone in for a form of emotional blackmail that he had never noticed in previous years. A sign in one of the larger stores proclaimed in neon-lit letters a foot high: *Why not spend that little bit extra this year and purchase the gifts your loved ones will adore? Surely they're worth it?* Not when the January credit card bills fell on the mat and induced half a year or more of penury, they're not, he thought. But even Rafferty, who had believed himself immune from such blatant cash extraction tricks, found himself imbued with uncomfortable feelings of meanness and guilt as the traffic stalled and allowed them to impart their message over and over again to their captive vehicular audience. Because the sign made him realize that he had yet to find time to buy Abra anything at all.

In previous years, his ma and sisters had sorted out his Christmas list between them without consulting him. But this year, seeing as he was with Abra and their relationship had now been cemented by an engagement, they had taken it for granted that she would assume this mantle. Rafferty had rather assumed it, too. But whether Abra realized this or not, he knew he could hardly expect her to buy her own present.

On an impulse, he indicated left and was just about to try to find a parking space to look in the window of the same jeweller's where he had bought Abra's engagement ring to see if he couldn't get her a pair of matching earrings, when his mobile went. Still without a hands-free phone and guiltily aware that he was breaking the law, he pressed it furtively to his ear and cupped a concealing hand around it.

It was Mickey calling, complaining about something Rafferty couldn't quite catch and demanding his immediate presence.

'I can't hear you,' Rafferty bellowed into the phone, 'you're breaking up.'

'There's . . . storm . . . injured . . . dangerous. Come. . .'
Then the phone went dead.

Rafferty looked up through the windscreen at the night sky.
He could see a few faint stars vainly trying to compete with
the neon glow from Earth and asked himself, Storm? What
storm?

He vaguely recalled hearing snatches of that morning's
weather forecast. He'd had more than enough other worries
and hadn't paid it much heed at the time, but now he remembered that there *had* been a storm warning. Mickey was on a
jutting-out part of the coast so the weather promised from the
east would hit him first.

Rafferty abandoned any further thoughts of browsing for
Abra's Christmas present and finding his way back into her
good books. He would have to get himself out to the caravan
park to see what was happening to his brother. He'd sounded
panicked about something.

The rain started coming down in earnest and he was forced
to switch the wipers to double speed, but they were still having
trouble coping with the downpour. Talk about it never rained
but it poured.

Suddenly, as a hefty gust slewed the car towards the pavement and he had to struggle to correct it, it occurred to him
to wonder what it must be like in a flimsy caravan when the
weather was this windy. Feeling as panicked now as Mickey
had sounded when he had struggled to transfer the word
'injured' over the air waves, Rafferty was finally able to put
his foot down and aqua-planed his way through the puddles,
earning more than a few clenched fist salutes and more
colourful expletives from the soaked pedestrians he passed
that, thankfully for his delicate sensibilities, blew away on the
wind.

But although he mouthed several useless 'sorry's' through
the rain-drenched windows, Mickey's well-being took first
claim. He was now too worried about what might have
happened to his brother to allow himself to be distracted by
his own road-hoggery.

But the anxious dash through the storm turned out to have
been needless. Mickey was perfectly all right, as Rafferty

discovered when he had finally fought his way through the wind and rain. When he approached the caravan, getting thoroughly soaked in the process, it was to find Mickey standing in the doorway, one of their ma's best blankets around his shoulders, peering out at the weather.

When he saw Rafferty, he shouted, '... took your time ... been scared witless ...'

The wind took away most of his brother's words, but the ones remaining were sufficient to tell Rafferty that Mickey was in a foul mood. He hoped he hadn't managed to persuade one of the family to bring him more booze.

Rafferty reached the van, angrily pushed his brother aside and barged past him inside. When Mickey followed him, he turned accusingly. 'What did you have to get me all worried like that for? You're not injured. There's damn all wrong with you as far as I can see. You're not even wet,' he remarked begrudgingly, 'unlike me. And as for the storm—'

This had died down somewhat in the last few minutes. OK, he conceded, it might have been a bit gusty before, but it was quiet enough now.

But they must have been in a lull, for just then the caravan rocked alarmingly from side to side. Rafferty and Mickey looked at one another, then they made a simultaneous dash for the door before the wind could blow the caravan right over. In their rush to escape, they both reached the door together, then promptly got wedged in the opening. The caravan teetered even more violently and threatened to land on top of them.

They fought free of each other's shoulders, waited till the wind, which was thrashing and crashing its way around the park like some unearthly predator, forced the caravan to lean the other way, then they both jumped free to land on the hard-standing. Rafferty turned an ankle. He hobbled, supported by the begrudging Mickey, till they reached the protected lee of the concrete toilet block from where they stood and watched the storm do its worst.

By some miracle, and, it had to be said, to Mickey's bitter regret, when the storm finally died out two hours later and they went to inspect the damage, it was to find that although battered, the hated caravan was still standing and was ready

143

to resume its job of harbouring Mickey's fugitive and reluctant body.

As they tidied up the thrown-about contents, Rafferty asked, 'Why on earth didn't you abandon the bloody thing if you were frightened and take refuge somewhere out of the wind?'

'And where was I meant to go, exactly?' a sullen Mickey demanded. 'You told me to stay inside, out of sight.'

'True, but I didn't mean for you to remain in the van, you idiot,' Rafferty contradicted, 'if you felt you were in imminent danger of being blown out to sea. I assumed I could rely on you to use your common sense.' Why had he made such an assumption? he wondered as he took in his brother's features dimly glowering at him in the gloom. He sighed. 'The storm's over, let's get you bedded down for the night. I was expected home hours ago.'

'Nice to have a home to go to,' Mickey muttered.

Rafferty decided his best response to this was to ignore it. He had little compunction about leaving his ingrate of a brother to his own devices a short time later. In his panic, he had neglected to buy any food; something else about which Mickey wasn't slow to complain. Rafferty retrieved the bag of clean clothes from the boot along with the replacement and, by now, lukewarm hot water bottle. Wordlessly, he thrust them at his brother before heading home, doubtless to listen to the anticipated further complaints from his neglected fiancée.

By the following morning, the night's storm had turned into a penetrating drizzle, which, although light, had an unpleasant way of stealing under the collar and soaking through the soles of one's shoes, causing a miserable dampness of the spirit as well as the body.

When Rafferty had reached home the previous evening, Abra had been in bed with her back turned. And after his other brother, Patrick Sean, had rung to plead that they swap nights on the Mickey mercy run, his memory of such a cool welcome encouraged him to make an early visit the following evening to re-provision his brother so as to be able to get home at a reasonable hour.

Peeved at having to visit Mickey two evenings running, Rafferty splashed his way across the puddle-bestrewn police station car park. Somehow, he got through another day's work on the investigation without once feeling he was even coming close to fingering the murderer and so enabling his brother to regain his freedom. His continuing failure to do that went down even worse than his failure to refill Mickey's food stocks. Rafferty scowled. He seemed to be getting it in the neck from all sides.

That evening, once he'd decreed that work was over for the day, Rafferty stopped off at the twenty-four-hour supermarket on the outskirts of Elmhurst, before heading for the caravan park. He arrived to find a sea of mud to be crossed. He squelched his way across to the caravan from the entrance, being unwilling for his car to get bogged down. He slipped and almost fell in a particularly cloggy spot, while the rain, now not quite as light as it had been and even more penetrating, lashed his unprotected head unmercifully.

Bitterly, Rafferty cursed his brother, the weather and Rufus Seward for landing him with such a mess. He was in no mood for this, especially as he felt Mickey should be thankful it wasn't *him* out in all weathers making grocery deliveries. No, he could stay nicely tucked up in the caravan rather than risk an undignified and impromptu mud bath.

But Mickey, when Rafferty reached the van, didn't seem to share this viewpoint. And rather than being appreciative of Rafferty's efforts on his behalf, he did nothing but complain as soon as Rafferty stuck his dripping head round the door.

After taking in the supermarket carrier bags, he said bitterly, 'I see. I'm to go without a hot meal *again*, am I?' A heavy scowl on his face, Mickey threw himself back down on the banquette and observed, 'I don't know why you bother to bring me food at all if that's the best you can do.'

'Neither do I,' Rafferty retorted, 'when you're such a miserable git, so don't tempt me. I've got plenty of other things I could be doing instead of dancing attendance on you, believe me.' He slammed the carrier bags down on the table with such force that the pull-out leg collapsed and deposited his purchases on the floor where they rolled in the dust of months, the uncut loaf in its flimsy wrapping included.

'I'm not eating that now,' Mickey told him.

Rafferty, not as fussy as his less physically robust brother, said, with the brusque impatience of the rarely sick, 'For God's sake, just give it a dust over with that tea towel Ma sent you and it'll be fine. It'll probably do you some good to get a few germs down your neck. I don't think all Ma's molly-coddling when you were young did you any favours at all.'

He abandoned his brother to do what he could with the soiled loaf and made for the door. 'I've got to get going. I still have a murder to solve, remember?'

He just managed to duck as said loaf came flying towards his head.

Fifteen

Between one thing and another, Rafferty realized he had forgotten to look at the security tapes from Seward's Norfolk home. There had been so many people to check out and question – those who had attended the party, all the acquaintances in the contacts book and Seward's diary – that it was several days before he even remembered their existence.

Normally, he would have delegated such a task to a junior member of the team. But as this was a case in which he already had plenty to conceal, he thought it prudent to do the job himself.

And when he did, it was to make the discovery that 'dear' Nigel had been amongst those who had visited Rufus Seward at his Norfolk estate in the days prior to Seward's death. He had, therefore, had the opportunity to help himself to one of the blank invitations; an opportunity the ever-networking Nigel was unlikely to have denied himself.

Fast-forwarding his way through these tapes, it had been a matter of hours only before Rafferty had observed Nigel's arrival and admission to the house. After that, it had taken even less time to extract an explanation for these events from Canthorpe when he got him on the phone.

As well as helping himself to an invitation, Nigel must also have taken the opportunity when left alone in the office for a short while to access Marcus Canthorpe's computer and enter his name on the official guest list because it was certainly there. How very entrepreneurial, was Rafferty's reluctantly admiring thought at this discovery. He might have felt a greater admiration for his cousin's nerve it if wasn't for the fact that, invariably with Nigel, he generally managed to get someone else to take the rap for him. This time, if he was responsible for the murder, however unlikely this still struck Rafferty as being, his fall guy was *not* going to be Mickey. Even if his brother *was* being a prickly, ungrateful git.

Canthorpe had already identified the majority of the other visitors to Seward's home during the relevant time. Strangely, he had forgotten all about Nigel's visit. But perhaps, because Canthorpe revealed that Nigel had turned up out of the blue and uninvited, that wasn't so strange. With Rafferty jogging his memory, providing a description of Nigel and, from the tape, the date and time of his arrival, Canthorpe recalled Nigel's visit. And with his memory jogged, he recalled the visit with a greater clarity than Nigel would doubtless have liked. Given that his name was now associated with the murder scene *and* the victim's home, he would probably have preferred any memory of his visit to be beyond anyone's recall.

During their telephone conversation, Canthorpe told Rafferty, 'I didn't know this Nigel Blythe at all. He insisted he was a recent business acquaintance of Sir Rufus and that he had an urgent proposition to put to him relevant to previous discussions they had had together. He was very persuasive, as I recall.'

The art of persuading the unwilling and reluctant was Nigel's special métier. 'But surely you would have known about this proposition and what it involved? You were Sir Rufus's assistant, after all.'

Canthorpe had laughed. 'You're right, Inspector. Yes, mostly I did know. But Sir Rufus always had one or two little schemes up his sleeve that he kept to himself until he was ready to reveal them. I just assumed this was one of those. As I told you, this Mr Blythe was very insistent – most of Sir Rufus's visitors are used to getting their own way – and he said that my boss would make my life hell if he missed this golden opportunity because I failed to notify Sir Rufus of his arrival. Though as he had no appointment, I don't quite understand why he was so sure my boss was even at home.'

Rafferty did. The scenario had Nigel's MO all over it: supreme confidence allied with the guile to snatch his opportunity. He had probably watched the gate or paid someone to do it for him to warn him of Seward's arrival, and on the off-chance that he would find his quarry in a benign, agreeable mood. And for all that he was inclined to be lazy and rarely pursued things to the ultimate if they were proving difficult, at the beginning of the chase, Nigel could be persistence itself.

'Did you leave this gentleman alone in your office at all?' Rafferty questioned. He must have done, since Nigel's name didn't get on the computer-compiled guest list all by itself. Rafferty wasn't surprised when Canthorpe replied in the affirmative.

'Well, yes, as a matter of fact I did. I assumed, as someone Sir Rufus was prepared to do business with, that this Mr Blythe must be above petty theft. Besides, at that stage, I had no reason to doubt his credentials as a business acquaintance of Sir Rufus,' Canthorpe said in his defence.

'And later?'

'Oh yes.' Rafferty sensed the wry smile from Canthorpe's end of the phone. 'Later, I certainly had reason to doubt his claims, particularly as Sir Rufus refused to see him. My boss had told me to leave him undisturbed for an hour a short time before this gentleman, Mr Blythe, arrived. Anyway, this Mr Blythe insisted on waiting out the hour. He was perfectly amicable about it. He didn't even attempt to start throwing his weight about at being kept waiting.'

'So what did Sir Rufus say when you told him that Mr Blythe was waiting to see him?' Rafferty asked, pretty sure by now that he could guess the answer.

Canthorpe paused, probably feeling embarrassed as Seward had surely used intemperate language in his rebuff of the importuning Nigel. 'He was pretty rude. Unsurprisingly, I have a vivid recall of his words. He said: "You can tell that f—ing devious excuse for a snake oil salesman to get off my property. I wouldn't do business with that shyster if I was down to my last million and desperate. Get rid of him before I'm forced to come out there and kick his sorry arse out the door myself".'

'And was Mr Blythe likely to have heard what Sir Rufus said?' Rafferty asked.

'Oh yes, I don't doubt it. Sir Rufus was something of a champion shouter when crossed. And Mr Blythe didn't wait for me to relay the message. He took himself off pretty smartly looking decidedly put out.'

Rafferty nodded to himself. Even Nigel, who, as an estate agent, so often tried to impose himself on the unwilling and received the inevitable rebuffs, had a limit to how much rudeness he could swallow. And it sounded as if he might have reached his limit with Seward. But, with the blank invitation clutched in his sticky, thieving paw, he had surely got what he had come for. Anything else would have been a bonus. And even the ever-optimistic Nigel must have known he was chancing his arm in trying to impose himself on a man who clearly considered Nigel not the sort that he wanted to do business with.

'Strange that Mr Blythe said nothing of this when we interviewed him,' Llewellyn commented later when Rafferty recounted the conversation.

'Isn't it?' Rafferty replied. But both Nigel's little stunt and his attempt to conceal it were very much in character. This latest discovery had produced a number of answers and yet more questions, one of which was how 'put out' had Nigel been at the way Seward had dismissed him? Insults were, in Nigel's line, an occupational hazard and accepted as such, but even the Nigels of this world had their limits. And if he had been deeply offended to be so rudely ejected from Seward's home, how likely was it that he had crawled out of the shadows and revenged himself?

Rafferty shook his head. He had already once before considered Nigel in the role of murderer in this investigation. He still couldn't see it, even if Nigel's ejection from Seward's home had upped the anti. Such an upfront murder would never be Nigel's style. Like a creature of the night, which was how Rafferty sometimes thought of his cousin, if Nigel wanted someone dead, he'd employ a sly and subtle poisoning rather than the open thrust of a blade. That way, he wouldn't even need to be around when death occurred.

Llewellyn had been silent while Rafferty brooded on the fact that Nigel appeared to be yet another *unofficial* party guest. But now, Rafferty became conscious of Llewellyn's questioning gaze upon him.

'Mr Blythe seems to be making a habit of popping up in the middle of our investigation,' Llewellyn observed. 'Firstly at the Elmhurst Hotel reception and now we find he also turned up at Sir Rufus's home. Do you think he's aiming for a hat-trick?'

'Search me,' Rafferty replied, 'though I think this is just an unfortunate coincidence. Murder's not Nigel's style – at least not this sort of murder. He hasn't got the bottle for it. Though it makes you wonder, after he'd instructed Canthorpe in no uncertain terms that Nigel was to leave his home, how Seward reacted when Nigel turned up at the party. It doesn't seem likely he'd have given him a warm welcome, yet no one's mentioned any kind of rumpus at his appearance.'

'Mmm,' Llewellyn murmured. 'That strikes me as odd too. I can only surmise that Sir Rufus must have concluded that Mr Blythe was one of the council's invitees. But he had only to ask Ivor Bignall if this was the case, yet, according to Mr Bignall, not only was Mr Blythe not on the council's guest list, Sir Rufus failed to question him about the possibility.'

'Maybe that was because I've a Big'un was giving him the big freeze treatment. Anyway, between one thing and another, Nigel managed to gatecrash the swanky do and get his feet under the table, his nose in the trough and his name nicely networked amongst the town's high flyers without being challenged and thrown out on his ear.'

You have to hand it to him, Rafferty thought, for sheer gall and chutzpah, Nigel's hard to beat.

'I suppose he'd worked out that, between them, the council and Seward wouldn't be sure that the other hadn't slipped a few last-minute guests an invite and each would assume Nigel was the other's guest. And then, of course, on the night, as I said, Bignall was giving Seward the big freeze. Typical of Nigel's luck. He always was a jammy git.'

Llewellyn's thinly handsome face nodded briefly at this as if it was a conclusion which he had also reached. Then he said, 'It will be all the more interesting to discover how he responds to *our* challenge when we ask how exactly he obtained his invitation and why, specifically, he was so determined to attend.'

'Won't it just?' Rafferty stared unseeingly through the window at the chill drizzle of rain falling with that relentlessness that indicated it was in for the day. He hoped it was a challenge that Nigel proved able to meet. If he couldn't,

Rafferty knew he faced the prospect of having *two* close relatives at risk of having their collars felt. Really, he gloomed to himself, the fates had more than upped the anti this time. He was beginning to feel his problems were spiralling out of control. The only hope he had that they didn't do so was that 'dear' Nigel would manage to smarm and cozen his way out of trouble with all his usual skill.

Nigel was in his office at the estate agency he ran, as one of his staff reluctantly confirmed upon Rafferty and Llewellyn's arrival. Like Nigel himself, the estate agency's decor oozed designer styling; in this instance, black leather and more chrome than even B&Q could stock. The place looked more like some fancy knocking shop than the office of an estate agent. The black leather seats were so low that Rafferty thought it likely the elderly, infirm, pregnant or overweight would get out of them only with difficulty. Though he supposed that was the idea: keep your customers captive while you talked them into buying the most expensive property on the books.

Rafferty found both the decor and its 'captivating' style chilling rather than welcoming. Like Nigel himself and others of his ilk, it was yet another example of the modern Britain and its ethos of greed that he so disliked, though it didn't seem to have deterred Nigel's up-market clientele. He could only presume it was an ethos they shared.

Several well-heeled looking couples with more money than taste were seated in the outer office as Rafferty and Llewellyn passed through. They were enthusing about similarly bleakly designed top of the range apartments and converted lofts. More money than taste *or* sense, was Rafferty's conclusion as he entered Nigel's office.

Unsurprisingly, Nigel didn't look pleased to see them. At first, he tried to deny that he had helped himself to the blank invitation after bamboozling Marcus Canthorpe into buzzing him through the security gate and into his office.

Rafferty shook his head and said, 'Don't try to kid a kidder, Nigel. You weren't invited to the party. You invited yourself. You even had the gall to add your own name to the guest list on Canthorpe's computer.'

Nigel clearly took this as praise for his derring-do, for he preened a bit and failed to deny Rafferty's accusation.

'So, come on, how did you know that if you could gain access to Seward's home you'd be able to get your hands on one of those party invites?'

As expected, even when shown a still taken from the security tape from Seward's home, Nigel admitted nothing beyond his innocence, which he proclaimed freely and volubly. But he didn't have to admit anything. Rafferty realized, with a blinding flash of insight, just how his cousin had known about the unsecured invitations to the reception. He had inside knowledge, of course: inside knowledge most likely gained via the Farraday twins.

As a youngster, Nigel, never one to lose out on any chance of holding the aces, had taken the trouble to become the twins' best friend at school. Even then, he had recognized that collectors of potentially lucrative gossip such as the Farraday twins might be worth cultivating.

The determinedly upwardly-mobile Nigel must have been delighted when he learned the twins had gone to work for Sir Rufus Seward. Nigel would have hoped their employment would provide him, too, with an 'in' to Seward's circle. How wrong he had been. All he'd got was a flea in his ear from Seward and one illicit invitation that placed him, like Mickey, as a suspect in a murder inquiry. Rafferty could almost feel sorry for him.

Nigel was still admitting nothing by the time Rafferty and Llewellyn stood up to leave five minutes later. As Llewellyn departed, Rafferty hung back to enquire, 'And how *are* the twins since last I saw them?'

He knew his comment had hit the spot when Nigel began a too-rapid blinking of his eyelashes. His protest of 'I don't know what you mean' was automatic and utterly unconvincing to someone like Rafferty who knew him of old. Even a practised liar like Nigel, who engaged in deceit with the natural aptitude of the born con man, required an audience a little more gullible than his policeman cousin.

'Oh Nigel, dear,' said Rafferty, 'I think you know only too well.' Rafferty's voice hardened and he added, 'I'll tell you what I told your little pals. Information can be dangerous.

And so can lying to the police, especially when you've caught up in a murder investigation. Think about it,' he said, before he followed Llewellyn back through the main office and out to the car.

The only thing he was left to ponder – apart, that is, from whether Nigel might actually turn out to be their killer – was why his twin little friends hadn't taken the invitation for him themselves instead of leaving Nigel to go to the trouble of driving himself all the way to Norwich, talking his way past Canthorpe and helping himself to the invitation. But maybe that was down to the twins' base desire to create mischief. They had probably hoped to get Canthorpe into trouble with the boss. After all, *he* had been the one to buzz Nigel in and give him the opportunity to out-Cinderella Cinders at the council's swanky reception. Doubtless the twins had hoped that Seward would probe till he discovered exactly how Nigel could have acquired the invite. It was the sort of underhand trick the Farradays were famous for.

'So, what now?' Llewellyn asked, reminding him, 'Forensic have come up with nothing incriminating at the scene.'

Rafferty was only too aware of it. He was aware, too, that unless he could find some little chink in the murderer's armour then he was likely to get away with the crime.

Which, of course, would leave Mickey – and the rest of the family – in limbo. But even this was unlikely to last. Mickey was, by the day, becoming more stir-crazy in his damp metal cell. Now, each time he visited his brother, Rafferty expected to find him gone and with all hell let loose in his wake.

But the next problem to rear its head didn't turn out to be Mickey making a bid for freedom. No, the next problem was far more basic. It was also one he should probably have predicted. But, Rafferty told himself consolingly, we can all be wise after the event.

Sixteen

'You told me it would only be for a few days,' Algy Edwards complained down the phone, 'but it's been way more than that. I'm beginning to think you're taking me for a mug and renting my caravan to some punter for your own profit.'

'Don't say that, Algy,' Rafferty was quick to respond. 'If I was smart enough to persuade a punter to pay me money for an unheated caravan in December, I'd give up coppering. I told you, it's just a mate who needs to lie low for a while, that's all. There's some blokes after him.' Ones in dark uniforms with big, shiny buttons . . .

'Why? What's he done? I don't want to get mixed up with violent gangsters. If—'

'It's nothing like that. He's done nothing, I tell you. It's just that some bastard's set him up to take the rap for something that wasn't his fault.'

That was true enough for Rafferty's voice to have the ring of conviction.

But Algy Edwards' suspicions weren't assuaged. Nor was his greed. 'That caravan's on a prime site. I want some rent or you can tell your friend to clear out of there.'

Prime site? On the east coast in a raw December winter? Briefly too gobsmacked to speak, Rafferty could only listen as Algy told him what he considered a fair market rent for his caravan on its 'prime site'.

The figure was shocking enough to loosen Rafferty's tongue. 'Two hundred and fifty quid a week? For that damp tin can? Are you mad?'

'Me? No, sunshine, I'm not mad but I reckon you might be if you think you're taking me for a sucker any longer. Two hundred and fifty smackers or your shy, retiring little friend can find some other bolt-hole to play hide and seek. Got it?'

Rafferty got it all right. He also got the feeling he'd no idea how he was going to explain the withdrawal of such a sum to Abra's satisfaction when they were meant to be saving for their wedding.

'You can meet me tomorrow lunchtime with the money. One o'clock in the Red Lion on the High Street. Don't be late.'

The phone on the other end banged down. Rafferty pulled a face. Thanks Algy, he thought. You're a real pal. But he knew he had no choice but to meet Algy Edwards' demands. Where else was he to stash Mickey where he'd be out of the way? His mugshot had been circulated so Rafferty couldn't risk putting him in a hotel.

Rafferty was beginning to wish now that he'd taken him to Ma's in the first place. But blind panic had scattered his ability to think clearly. No way did he want to risk moving Mickey now. He'd just have to cough up and hope Algy didn't up the ante when Rafferty proved willing to meet his current demand. Algy might well start thinking he'd undercut himself, which was likely to lead him to wondering just what – and who – he had stashed in his caravan. If he took the trouble to get himself up there again and managed to clock Mickey's face, he might think all his paydays had come at once as Seward's sister had put up a handsome reward once she knew what she was down for in the will.

No. Rafferty shook his head. The only thing he could do was play it reluctant on the rental front when he met Algy Edwards. Argue his corner, plead poverty and make it plain that his tenant had merely chosen his bedroom partners unwisely. Or something . . .

Rafferty wasn't sure just how he should play it. All he was sure of was that if he needed to keep Mickey hidden away for a month or even two, his and Abra's joint bank account was going to have a very big, unexplainable hole in it.

Once he had met Algy Edwards and paid him off for the time being, Rafferty was left to ponder on the nature of suspicion. Algy had suspected he and his shy caravan tenant were up to no good. Well, he wasn't far wrong there . . .

Similarly, given the dearth of proof against their murder

suspects and even with the contradictory evidence provided by the two security guards and the hotel's security tape, Rafferty was beginning to think that Bradley *had* seen someone entering Seward's bedroom late on the night of the reception, but he suspected it hadn't been the blonde Bradley had conjured up from a mix of imagination, alcohol blur and short sight. Rather, he thought the blonde had been what Bradley had seen because she was what he had expected – wanted – to see, as it would lower Seward even further in his estimation.

Maybe the super could be encouraged to recall what – who – he had actually seen that night. But when Rafferty remembered who he was dealing with – a bluff, gruff professional Yorkshireman, he realized that suggesting the super should be hypnotized was never likely to be a runner that got off the starting blocks. Trying to persuade Bradley to agree to being hypnotized wasn't the answer and never would be.

No, he'd have to carry on trying to do this the hard way. Think, man, *think*, Rafferty told himself. Go over all the suspects and their likely motives again. You're missing something, something you haven't thought through thoroughly enough.

In the hope that he would be able to see this elusive 'something', when Llewellyn brought in the mid-afternoon mugs of tea, Rafferty collared him and made him go through some 'what if' possibilities. It was something they did on every case. It might seem as though they were clutching possibilities out of the air, but they had had some surprising results in the past, even though Rafferty wasn't sure whether he insisted they went through the routine partly because it gave him the chance to shoot Llewellyn's ideas out of the sky. And if it did indeed have nothing else to recommend it, this role reversal had a certain novelty value. He admitted it was pretty low, morally speaking, and that he mightn't love himself in the morning. But the morning seemed far away and a man had to get his pleasures where life – and the fates – allowed.

Llewellyn, now with his thoughts in order, said, 'OK. I know we've heard from several sources that Idris Khan was puffed up with pride at the honour of becoming mayor—'

'Even if it was just because it was Buggins's turn.'

Llewellyn ignored the interruption and continued. 'What if,

secretly, Khan was actually more concerned with upholding his dignity and reputation as a *man* than he was with that of his mayoral office? That "honour" killing we discussed before seems, to me, still to be a possible.'

Rafferty pursed his lips, then commented, 'As I said before, surely he'd have killed the faithless Mandy too?'

Llewellyn tried again. 'Very well. As you've disposed of that theory, here's another. What if Randy Rawlins decided to pay Seward back for all the years of humiliation?'

'He'd have wanted to stick that chisel up Seward's plump derriere, surely, after what our late and unlamented cadaver had done to him?'

Rafferty could see that his dismissive responses were beginning to annoy Llewellyn. But one thing for Llewellyn, he was a sticker, so he continued doggedly on.

'Here's another scenario then. What if Marcus Canthorpe discovered he wasn't down to receive a legacy in Sir Rufus's will after all the promises of future reward he had been given, and after all the better paying job offers he'd turned down?'

Rafferty raised his eyebrows. 'And how was he going to do that? He lacked the opportunity. Seward always dealt with correspondence to do with the will himself. His solicitor confirmed it. OK, Seward used Canthorpe as a messenger boy to go backwards and forwards between his home and the Norwich solicitors, but any confidential personal documents concerning Seward's various wills were always sealed before he got his hands on them. As were the ones that Seward had him messenger over to the solicitor.

'According to Metcalfe, there was never a sign that any of the envelopes containing Seward's assorted will redrafts or instructions had been tampered with. Besides, can you picture Seward letting one of his staff get away with tampering with his confidential correspondence? He'd blow a gasket, and at such high volume that *all* his staff would hear him, even groundsmen at the far edge of the estate.'

Frustrated, Rafferty swung round in his chair and gazed out the window. The evening was as black as the murderer's soul. It was also still raining; he could hear the icy raindrops clattering against the glass. He watched for a few moments as they cascaded down the pane, then, with a sigh, he swung his chair back again. 'Let's face it, Seward made a point of keeping all his heirs and potential heirs in the dark about his intentions. He liked to play with them, set them one against the other, to promise and then to take away the promise. It was his hobby. An enjoyable, amusing game he liked to play.'

'A dangerous game.'

'Only if his puppets knew his intentions at any stage of the game and whether they were the star of the latest will or consigned to the wings and destitution. And his solicitor himself told us that Seward played the game with great skill and care. Yes, they all probably had reason to wish him dead, but if any one of them killed him or arranged for him to be killed, they would have known they were playing a game of Russian roulette with their financial futures.'

Rafferty, bored with this unprofitable speculation, decided to bring them both back to the real world. 'That's how Seward liked to keep his puppets,' he reminded Llewellyn, 'in ignorance, dancing to his tune, under his control. He teased them, sent them calendars and photos as reminders of where they were going wrong and what they stood to lose if they failed to remain in his good books.'

Rafferty picked his tea up from the desk, leaned his expensive executive chair back as far as it would go and balanced his tea on his chest. He stared into the liquid's dark depths. 'Me, I'd have told him to take his money and stick it up his arse, much like Rawlins should have done with that chisel.'

It was Llewellyn's turn to raise his eyebrows, though in his case, as in everything else, it was a less extravagant, one eyebrow gesture.

But Rafferty still got the message. 'I *would*,' he insisted. Then he grinned. 'I mean, can you see me mixing with the beautiful people, the international jet set?' Before Llewellyn had a chance to try to picture such an unlikely scenario, Rafferty dismissed the idea with a, 'No, nor me. Mind, it was the sort of "up yours, sunshine" gesture that would cost me nothing: it's not as if Rufus bloody Seward had me down to inherit anything.'

His tea slopped over the side of his mug. He frowned and watched as the tea spread over his white shirt and stuck it to his chest. It was an unwelcome reminder of how they had found Seward's body, with the crimson tide spread across his white dress shirt, though the image was of course reversed, as Seward's stain had spread across his back rather than his chest.

Rafferty stared again at the stain and sighed. 'All he left me, the bastard, was the job of finding his murderer.'

Not to mention that other, even more onerous task, of getting his brother, maybe even 'dear' Nigel, out from under. And safeguarding himself, also, and his career. And now he'd lost the one thing he had had going for him – the possibility of being able to play the super like Seward had played his much larger collection of puppets.

For he had, of course, questioned Superintendent Bradley again. He had previously obtained Llewellyn and Mary Carmody's promises to say nothing about Superintendent Bradley's presence at the reception. Llewellyn, for one, had been astonished that Rafferty should seem keen to protect his boss. He even congratulated him for showing the superintendent such sensitive consideration, which made Rafferty feel like the hypocrite he was.

Llewellyn had gone on to caution, 'But you need to be even-handed. And much as I can applaud you for trying to keep the superintendent's presence low-key to protect him, it's important that you don't shy away from questioning him just as you've questioned the other guests.'

Rafferty had nodded and added in as humble a manner as he could manage, 'I know that, Daff. Don't worry. In fact, that's where I'm going now. No stone unturned and all that.'

True to his word, Rafferty had headed up the corridor, conscious that, for once, he had the full-hearted approval of his moral-high-ground sergeant. Shame really that he didn't deserve it.

Superintendent Bradley had clearly been expecting Rafferty, unlike on their previous encounter. On this occasion, he had had time to come up with answers to any awkward questions about the mysterious blonde and her Houdini tendencies.

'I thought I explained, Rafferty,' Bradley began complacently, after he'd graciously permitted Rafferty to question him again, 'I caught merely the briefest glimpse of this woman out of the corner of my eye. Maybe I was mistaken. And from what you say about this woman not showing up on the security footage, it seems that I was. We all make mistakes.'

An admission from Bradley that he was capable of making a mistake was an event in itself. Rafferty rather wished he'd arranged witnesses.

Bradley's tone of voice indicated that if Rafferty pursued the mystery of the disappearing blonde, it would be the biggest mistake of his life. And now that Rafferty knew the tale about how Bradley had been almost forced out of the police service at Seward's instigation and with the help of his friends amongst the brass, he surmised that Bradley had learned a valuable lesson from the experience. Certainly, now he was the one with the power, Rafferty had no reason to doubt Bradley wouldn't attempt to concoct some false case against him should he feel the need. Bradley could stitch him up till he was as well cocooned as a shrouded corpse. And, if the super discovered the identity of Seward's mystery late-night male visitor and Rafferty's part in his disappearance, Bradley wouldn't even need to use his limited imagination to accomplish the task.

And as Bradley had failed to make an official statement – Rafferty had questioned him alone and also failed in the statement-taking front, thinking it prudent to take no notes – there was nothing to prevent the super altering his story. And nothing for him to use as a bargaining counter to help him safeguard Mickey.

Doubtless Bradley had now taken the precaution of writing a statement to cover himself and would produce it should it prove necessary, having 'forgotten' all about his previous verbal statement in the meantime. But even that wouldn't be necessary, Rafferty knew. The super claimed he had merely been 'mistaken' about what he had seen and he was sorry, etc, but . . . blah, blah, blah.

Feeling frustrated and cranky, Rafferty had asked him to write another statement anyway, an official one, just for the records.

Bradley had smiled his large, white-dentured smile. It made him look like a particularly malevolent and overted vulture. 'Leaving out the blonde who never was?'

'Leaving out the blonde who never was, if you wish,' Rafferty tonelessly agreed.

Bradley picked up his glasses and perched them on the end of his nose. It was his signal that the interview was over.

But before Rafferty had reached the door, Bradley raised his head and commented, 'Though, you know, Rafferty, even though this woman doesn't appear on the security camera, I could have sworn I saw her.' He shook his head. 'It must have been a trick of the light. I know my eyes felt dazzled by those enormous chandeliers.' He sounded quite put out that his faculties might be failing him to the extent that they caused him to make such an error. And as he left, Rafferty began to wonder if vanity at failing eyesight had made the super reluctant to admit that he had been wrong about seeing the blonde. Word in the station had it that Bradley had recently been diagnosed with short sight; he could see things close up and was able to read without his glasses, but he needed them to see across a room or to drive. Had he, again for reasons of vanity, decided against wearing the glasses to such a prestigious event as Sir Rufus Seward's reception? It was certainly a possibility. Another possibility was that he would rather say he had made a mistake about the blonde on the official report than have questions asked about his eyesight and the vanity that caused him to try to see without his glasses.

Bradley, in arriving late at Seward's civic recetion, had missed the photographer from the local newspaper who had captured the event, so Rafferty couldn't trawl newsprint to see if the super had been minus his spectacles. Still, it shouldn't be too difficult to find out from another source. Someone must remember. He could ask Randy Rawlins or the waitress Samantha Harman if the 'pompous fat man' they had described had been wearing glasses.

As Rafferty had suspected, Superintendent Bradley's vanity *had* encouraged him to leave his glasses off during the reception. Both Randy Rawlins and Samantha Harman had confirmed it. Rafferty had been able to quell their curiosity about his questions by telling them it was a minor matter and of no significance as far as Seward's murder was concerned.

But the question of whether Bradley *had* actually seen

someone enter Seward's bedroom that night continued to niggle him. Clearly, whoever the super thought he had seen had not been the non-existent mystery blonde, but someone else entirely.

But when Rafferty dared the bull's pen once again, the super was inclined to be hazy in his recollection, whether deliberately or not, and Rafferty was unable to get him to state with any firmness whether he really *had* seen someone and now, with doubts cast on what he had said before, the super proved reluctant to have further doubts cast on what he said now. But with the super showing this inclination to be unnaturally indecisive on the matter, Rafferty, unable to force Bradley to plump more firmly for one or the other, had to let it go and concentrate on other aspects of the investigation.

Rafferty, with these troublesome memories at the forefront of his mind, sighed again, threw what remained of his tea down his throat, and stood up. 'There's nothing doing on the case, Daff. Let's call it a night.'

His new fiancée deserved some quality time and so did he. He needed to get back home in time to be in with a chance of a mellow, sulk-free evening with Abra and a few glasses of Jameson's. Abra would help him to stop thinking and pause the spinning brain, which was the best way he had ever found of loosening up the thought processes so they operated at maximum efficiency. Or as efficiently, at any rate, as his ever managed. Then the whiskey would come into its own in helping his rested brain to think clearly. At least, that was the theory . . .

But this little time of teasing some possibilities out of Llewellyn had given Rafferty an idea or two of his own. If they were any good, he needed to put them aside so they could mature without any interference from him.

He almost stopped off at the garage on his way home, then he thought better of it. Arriving home with flowers was a sure way to persuade Abra that he had done something he shouldn't. OK, in concealing Mickey in the caravan he *had* done something he shouldn't, but Abra, being a woman, would think he had a guilty conscience over some other misdemeanour and was trying to ease both her suspicions and his conscience with

163

the gift of a bouquet of cheap, destined soon-to-wilt blooms. There was no surer way to start the evening with a row and more recriminations, so he abandoned the idea.

Instead, he settled on a non-incriminatory Indian takeaway. He parked on double yellow lines; the inclement weather would, he guessed, keep him safe from prowling traffic wardens. He ran across the pavement to the door of the restaurant through the continuing downpour and as he waited for his takeaway order, he reflected that the flowers would certainly have been a mistake. There was no need to make for himself another hostage to fortune. Between Mickey and Nigel he had enough of those already – more than enough, more than he could handle.

It was unfortunate that his wise non-purchase of the bouquet seemed to make no difference to his reception. For he sensed as soon as he was through the door of the flat, shaking himself free of chilling raindrops, that Abra had built herself up for a row and was determined to have one.

'I'm glad you're home early,' she told him as soon as the meal was dished up and they had sat down. The 'for a change' at the end was clearly understood by both of them and needed no vocalisation. 'I want to talk to you.'

Rafferty, his mouth full of chicken vindaloo and naan bread, made no response other than to place his head at an encouragingly enquiring angle. For some reason this seemed to rub Abra up the wrong way, for she burst out, 'It's not fair, Joe. You seem to think that getting your ring on my finger gives you the right to neglect me. You don't come home till all hours and when you do you're still somewhere else, in your head. You hardly talk to me any more.'

Abra's gaze flashed fire and water; angry and tearful in about equal measures, though perhaps the anger had the edge. 'Are you beginning to regret asking me to marry you already?'

Hastily, Rafferty swallowed his hot curry and bread. He managed not to choke, although his throat felt aflame. He grabbed a glass of water and cooled the flames before he was able to voice a protest. 'No, of course not,' he said. 'It's not that at all.'

'Then what is it? Don't you think I have a right to know?'

That was just it – she did. Trouble was that it wasn't his

secret to tell. It was Mickey's. But it was on a need-to-know basis and Abra didn't need to know. Certainly, neither he nor his brother wanted his unfortunate connection to the victim to be bandied about any more than absolutely necessary. But he had to tell her something.

Stumblingly, he told her part of the truth. She was entitled to that much. 'It's my brother, Mickey. He's in a bit of bother.' If getting yourself suspected of murder could be called 'a bit of bother'. Talk about famous British understatement.

'So what's he done?'

'That's just it: I can't tell you. It's Mickey's business, not mine.' He wished. But now he – and his career – were a very big part of it.

Of course Abra, like all women, having learned a little wanted to know the rest. And when Rafferty failed to come up with the goods, she retired to bed in a huff. He was in the doghouse. Again.

How did other police officers manage to keep their relationships intact? he wondered as he listened to Abra banging and clattering in the bedroom. Perhaps, alongside all the political-correctness and racial-awareness courses the police were forced to attend nowadays there ought to be one on how to keep your partner content? Though, if they were run by the same thought police who ran the other courses . . .

This was a special time in *his* life *and* Abra's. He wished he could attend solely to their own concerns and their future happiness for a while. But then it was a pretty special time in Mickey's life, too. And Ma's, and the rest of the family. Sometimes it was difficult to split himself in so many directions but he would have to continue to do so until he'd caught his murderer. He just wished he felt able to come clean and explain all the ramifications to Abra.

Seventeen

T he next morning was clear and cold. Thankfully, the chill rain had stopped during the night. Rafferty, in order to avoid any more questions or sulks from Abra, was up while it was still as dark as the midnight hour. He didn't even stop for a hot drink in case his clattering about in the kitchen should wake her.

As he had strode from the warmth of his small block of flats and headed across the car park, the stiff, North Sea breeze made his cheeks tingle. Even the eternally argumentative seagulls, who had risen as early or earlier than him, seemed less shrill and merely swooped and circled lazily on the wind like so many aerial ballerinas.

Fanciful, Rafferty, he had smiled to himself. The sea's champion crappers as aerial ballerinas was surely a fancy too far even for him.

And even though, once at work, he still had the problem of Mickey, the sulks of Abra and a murder to solve, the solution of which seemed scarcely closer than it had been at the beginning of the inquiry, he felt inexplicably happy. Nothing was any different from the day before, not really. Yet *he* felt different. Unreasoning optimism had him in its grasp and he could only hope it kept a good hold. Perhaps he should make an early start more often? He was so early that he had beaten the ever early Llewellyn to work. He had even beaten the dawn, though that wasn't difficult since the sun rose so late in December. In fact, he had been at the station for over an hour before either Llewellyn, or the dawn, showed up.

The latter heralded a promising sky, weather-wise, of duck egg blue with wispy clouds. It put new heart into Rafferty. He could bear the cold: it was grey skies day after day that brought his mood spiralling downwards.

But today looked set fair to be one of those glorious days that occurred far more often during the autumn and winter than his grey-sky humours would admit to.

Llewellyn, when he arrived, was, by contrast, in a pensive mood. Before he had even greeted Rafferty, or got the tea in, he made purposefully for one of the many photofit pictures of Mickey that Ivor Bignall and the security guards had put together with the computer artist, and gazed intently at it.

Immediately, Rafferty's joy in the morning died away, sure that Llewellyn had at last made the connection between the photofit and Mickey himself, even though their only previous meeting had been a brief one. He awaited retribution.

Llewellyn glanced across at him and said firmly, 'I know this man. I've met him. We both have, I'm sure of it.'

Rafferty, dismayed at this revelation, sat corpse-like in his chair, awaiting the inevitable upset of his own dark connivings. His relief when Llewellyn frowned and told him, 'But I just can't place him,' was so profound that his entire body slumped. Thankfully, Llewellyn, still intent on the picture, didn't notice his chief's reaction and he brightened a fraction. Perhaps all his joy in the day wasn't about to drain away entirely.

Llewellyn thrust the photofit under his nose. 'Look at it again. Does anyone spring to mind?'

Rafferty looked at the picture for a good thirty seconds, as if he was studying it as intently as Llewellyn had. Then he shrugged. 'Sorry, Daff. As you say, this man looks vaguely familiar, but I can't place him either. In our line of work we meet so many people that sometimes the faces become jumbled.' Rafferty hoped such a comment would provide some sort of defence, should the worst-case scenario unfold. 'The trouble with these computer pictures is that they are often so generalized and rely on witnesses being observant enough to take note of the shape and size of a person's nose, eyes and the rest and most don't, or not accurately enough. But if I *do* know him, it'll come to me sooner or later, I'm sure, particularly if neither of us keeps worrying and staring at it.' You in particular, he added in a silent rejoinder to Llewellyn.

Fortunately, Llewellyn seemed to take his last comment as a hint that he was time-wasting, for he returned to his desk, put the photofit aside, and continued with organizing the allocation of the day's CID duties.

Llewellyn, still convinced that Ivor Bignall was psychologically wrong for the role of back-stabbing murderer, was concentrating his investigatory efforts on those he believed *did* fit such a profile and who were both psychologically capable of the crime and had the means and opportunity to commit it. In this category he had filed the Farraday twins and Randy Rawlins.

Rafferty left him to get on with it, happy that he was, for the moment, concentrating all his energies away from Mickey and the photofit. Not that Llewellyn had much choice about this, because to Rafferty's considerable surprise, the self-imposed form of 'omertà' that Mickey's friends had applied to themselves seemed to be holding. Indeed, several of them, concerned by both the Mickey-inspired photofit and his lengthy and unexplained absence both from his flat and his usual haunts, even rang Rafferty at the station to seek his guidance as to what they should do.

As discreetly as he could, he simply advised them to carry on as they were doing, which was keeping shtum, confident that they would spread the word.

Meanwhile, with Llewellyn engaged in trying to prove which of the three he had selected as most closely matching his profile for Seward's killer was the guilty party, Rafferty concentrated his fire on the rest: Ivor Bignall, Idris Khan and Marcus Canthorpe. The ladies in the case – Mandy Khan, Dorothea Bignall and Samantha Harman, as well as the two security guards who seemed to have had no previous connection with Seward – he would fit in as and when. Certainly the first two ladies had motives in plenty for wishing to kill Rufus Seward and he knew he would need to find time to question them again.

As for the male suspects: Bignall's plans on advancing his family tree had been stymied before his seed could take root, which might or might not provide Bignall with a major motive, depending on how strongly he really felt about carrying his genes forth into the next generation.

Idris Khan, too, could be said to have a strong motive. If,

that was, the Farraday twins could be believed when they claimed to have overheard Mandy Khan being dismissed by Seward as if he considered her nothing more than a gold-digging camp follower.

Although the story about Mandy having an affair with Seward didn't seem to have spread beyond the twins, when he questioned Khan about it in his parlour, Rafferty, from the mayor's determined and furious denials that it was true, got the distinct impression that the opposite was in fact the case.

Maybe Seward had unwisely boasted of his conquest to Mandy's mayoral husband, or maybe Khan had heard about it from some other source? The creeping Farraday twins seemed a distinct probability.

The other possibility was Marcus Canthorpe, he of the legacy expectations that were destined to remain unfulfilled. Rafferty wondered if Canthorpe had yet learned the bad news from Seward's solicitor.

On an impulse, he rang their Norwich offices and managed to speak to Philip Metcalfe. Metcalfe confirmed he had written to all the heirs. Canthorpe must have heard on the Seward family grapevine about these letters and had contacted the solicitor himself when he didn't receive one. Metcalfe told Rafferty that he had already broken the bad news.

'How did Canthorpe take it?' Rafferty asked.

'He was upset at first, but he realized there was little point in arguing about the terms of the will with me. In fact, he seemed to be more annoyed at himself for being gullible enough to take Sir Rufus at his word that he would receive a legacy. I've had Keith Farraday on the phone, too, with the same result. Though he didn't take it on the chin with quite Canthorpe's phlegm and became so abusive that I had to put the phone down on him.'

Rafferty thanked the solicitor and hung up. He sat thoughtfully staring out of the window as the afternoon turned into twilight and the lights in the town came on, one after the other, like so many yellow tiger eyes glowing in the darkness. He wished they could show him the way as easily as they did those *not* on the trail of a murderer.

He had been able to find no connections between Seward's heirs, deposed heirs or those present at the reception and who might, for a consideration, agree to remove the obstacle to their inheritance. Unless, that was, one of the guests bore Seward a grudge on their own account and was in need of funds and prepared to rid the world of Seward in a 'two grudges for the price of one' scenario and had come to some private arrangement.

Bignall's grudge wasn't about money. Neither was Idris Khan's. And Canthorpe couldn't have known before Seward's death that he had reason to bear his employer a grudge. His finances were reasonably healthy considering he had lived in at Seward's expense for the past five years and been able to save quite a little nest egg.

The Farraday twins, too, although presumably, owing to their much shorter employment status, bearing a lesser grudge over the failure of their legacies to materialize, didn't seem short of funds either, if their self-indulgence in drugs, antiques and objets d'art were any indication.

Which left Randy Rawlins, who, in spite of the extensive and expensive wardrobe that took up half his staff bedroom, didn't seem to have any other money put by. His bank account was overdrawn by a grand and his three credit cards were all up to their limit. Shame he had no reason to believe himself down to inherit some much needed money in Seward's will . . .

But, of course, all of them had had the opportunity to murder Seward, whether for reasons of monetary gain or some other motive, so none could be discounted. It was comforting to think that, as a suspect, Mickey was no longer the only contender.

But were any of the other possibles the type to kill in such a manner? he found himself wondering, and realized that Llewellyn had managed to infect him with his psychology angle. And while Rafferty might not have as great a belief in the benefits of psychological assessment or profiling as his educated, intellectual sergeant and thought it just as likely that someone determined to kill would choose the means most likely to be successful and least likely to put them in any physical danger, he didn't, whatever Llewellyn might believe, dismiss the angle completely out of hand.

As with Ivor Bignall and Idris Khan, he simply thought that all three of Seward's employees were either smart enough or sly enough to go in for a bluff in the means they chose to commit murder. Though, in the twins' case, he supposed it would have to be a double bluff, given the cowardly, back-stabbing way the murder was committed. The cowardly behind the back attack had always been their preferred style.

This thought, of course, reminded him that the ghastly Farraday twins weren't the only ones with a yellow streak. Cousin Nigel, he of the devious nature and preference for deceit and working behind people's backs might, after all, turn out to be a stronger candidate for this murder than Rafferty had at first believed likely.

Rafferty sighed and dragged his gaze away from the lights beyond the window before he was mesmerized. Once again, all this thinking had got him nowhere, with or without Llewellyn's psychological approach. What he needed was a pointer to guilt. But so far, even though he had as fine an assortment of suspects as any policeman could wish for, this was the one thing he lacked.

Eighteen

'You and Maureen all sorted for Christmas?' Rafferty asked Llewellyn as they prepared to go home at the end of another frustrating day, still with plenty of suspects and nothing concrete to help them to point the finger at a single one of them.

'Yes. All the preparations are in place. All the presents either under the tree or long since posted.'

It was far more than Rafferty had achieved, but he kept a grip on his envy to ask, 'Your mother coming for the festivities?'

Llewellyn shook his head. 'No. She wanted Maureen and me to have our first Christmas since our marriage on our own. I couldn't dissuade her from the decision.'

With his own not so distant memories of playing gooseberry when the pair were courting, Rafferty murmured with feeling, 'Not always easy, I suppose, to make a third with two lovebirds. Maybe next year?'

'Maybe – I hope so. I don't like to think of her on her own. Christmas should be a time for families to be together.'

Rafferty, unwilling to consider what action his brother might take should he still be incarcerated in the caravan over the festive season, changed the subject. 'So, what have you bought Maureen for Christmas? Something nice, I hope?'

'We thought so. A joint present. We chose it together. We've booked a cruise up the Nile for the end of January with stops at all the ancient sites.'

It sounded a typical Dafyd Llewelyn holiday; both he and his new wife, Maureen were keen on foot-slogging around ancient sites of historical significance. Rafferty, by contrast, while having an interest in history closer to home, was more keen on sun-loungers by the pool than tiring tramps.

'Always supposing we've solved the case by the time your cruise comes round,' Rafferty reminded him.

'Of course. Maureen understands that we may have to cancel if this investigation hasn't been concluded by then.'

'You've got her something to open on the day, I take it? You can't open a holiday cruise.'

'Token gifts only. We're not children.'

Rafferty pulled a face. A 'token' gift didn't sound much fun to him. And while he wouldn't say no to a cruise, Christmas without piles of presents to open held no allure.

'And what about you and Abra?' Llewellyn asked as they retrieved their coats and headed down the corridor. 'Is your Christmas all arranged?'

'I wish. I don't know how Abra's Christmas list is progressing, but I haven't even written mine – nor bought anything for Abra.' Or anyone else. Conscious that he was leaving it late, Rafferty added brightly, 'Still, her engagement ring cost me a packet. Maybe she'll take it as engagement and Christmas present both?'

Beyond questioning this, Llewellyn said nothing more, simply raised an eyebrow. But he didn't need to say anything, Rafferty reflected, as they reached the door to reception. Rafferty didn't actually believe such a reaction from Abra was likely either.

Llewellyn said goodnight and vanished through the outer doors. Rafferty, just about to follow him, was delayed by Bill Beard behind the reception counter.

'Mind the shop for me?' he asked Rafferty. 'I'm bursting and need to go to the bog, only Smales disappeared twenty minutes ago and left me on my own. I haven't seen the idler since. But when I do—' Beard broke off and headed for the door.

Rafferty shouted after Bill's retreating back, 'But don't be too long. I want to get away.'

'Give me five, ten minutes,' the now disembodied voice replied. Bill popped his head back round the door. 'Only the waterworks don't get up the head of steam they once did, so every visit takes a lot longer.'

Once Bill had disappeared on his urgent mission, Rafferty reached his hand under the reception counter and helped himself to Bill's *Daily Mirror* to while away the time, suspecting from previous experience that Bill's 'five or ten minutes' would stretch to half an hour. Rafferty had completed the crossword for the middle-aged constable before Bill returned.

'I was saving that to finish later,' Bill complained.

'Well, now I've saved you the trouble,' Rafferty told him. 'You've never managed to finish the thing yet. Anyway, I'm off. See you tomorrow.' Before Bill could voice any further complaints, Rafferty went out into the night.

The rain had started up again, only now it had thickened to hard hailstones. As Rafferty made his way across the car park to his car, a bitter wind rose up and rushed full at his face, making his eyes water. The wind trailed a number of hailstones, which it threw at his unprotected head as if indulging in a cruel juvenile snowball fight, but using clumps of ice for the balls.

'You play too rough for me,' Rafferty grumbled into the wind as several of the sharp little missiles landed direct hits. And as the size and number of these hard and icy missiles increased, he put his arms over his bare head and ran for the car. He slithered his way out on to the road on a carpet of the white stones, only too aware that the drop in temperature wouldn't have warmed Mickey's cockles one iota.

It had been yet another long day. It was after nine o'clock by the time Rafferty drove away from the station and headed for the coast, stopping to pick up bread, milk and a takeaway for his brother on the way.

The caravan park was as gloomy as ever. And, as Rafferty discovered after he had fought his way through the vicious hail onslaught, so was Mickey. Each time Rafferty saw his brother he appeared more depressed and morose. He wondered how much longer he could persuade Mickey to remain hidden. He wasn't hopeful, as a resigned acceptance to the inevitable seemed to have taken hold of Mickey.

In the hope that it would cheer his brother up, for the first time Rafferty risked a light. He had seen no one on his journey through the park so how risky could it be? Even so, he placed the low light on the floor in order to limit the possibility of its rays being noticed from outside.

To add what he hoped would provide more cheer, he told his morose sibling, 'We've a number of strong possibilities on the case. We've discovered that several of the suspects had reason to hate Seward.'

The news didn't noticeably improve Mickey's demeanour. He just grunted as if he was past caring.

Rafferty tried again. 'Yes, as I said, several of the guests at the party had a very strong motive to want Seward dead. Even better, one of them only found out what damage Seward had done to him on the day of the reception.' He thought better of mentioning the names in case Mickey took it into his head to find them and drag a confession out of them. 'That's why, until I can nail down some proof, it's essential you remain here. If I get taken off the case it will all be out of my hands.'

He stared at his brother's bent head. 'Mickey? Did you hear what I said?'

All Mickey could manage in response was an uninterested shrug.

With a frown, Rafferty decided he'd leave it for now. He dished up the meal. He had hoped some hot food in his brother's stomach would help warm his body *and* his spirit and make him more receptive, but Mickey just picked at his food, pushing it around his plate till it got too cold and inedible to eat.

Rafferty, needing food to give him the stamina necessary to address all his current problems, cleared his plate, wiping it clean with naan bread. He finished his meal, only then realizing that his brother had stirred sufficiently from his listlessness to have come to a conclusion of his own.

He sat opposite Rafferty at the rickety table, his expression set. Rafferty asked, 'What's on your mind?' He feared he already knew the answer. Mickey's next words told him he was right.

'I've been thinking, JAR. Maybe I should give myself up, or perhaps it would look better if you were to take me in. The longer I skulk in this rat trap of a caravan, the more guilty I look – the more guilty we *both* look. Could I be any more miserable in a cell than I am here?'

'You could, believe me,' Rafferty told him vehemently.

'Take my word for it. Maybe if you'd reported Seward's death when you found him, things would be different, but since you didn't—'

Guilt made him break off at this point. Would his brother have come forward even after he had left the scene of the murder if Rafferty hadn't hustled him away from his flat? Rafferty wished he could be sure of the reason why he had persuaded Mickey to allow himself to be stashed in this grim caravan. Had it been for his brother's sake, or his own? A brother as the main suspect in a murder investigation was, as he silently admitted, likely to do little to enhance his career.

At least Mickey didn't start throwing accusations about, which was just as well, as Rafferty's conscience was doing a good enough job on its own. He had done little but think about the case, and to cheer his brother up he told him one of the conclusions he had come to. 'Know what strikes me about this case?'

Mickey barely managed a half-hearted shrug in response, but Rafferty told him anyway.

'What strikes me is that you've been set up. The more I've thought about this case, and the unlikelihood of you receiving an invitation to his civic shindig from Rufus Seward, the more I've come to believe it. Let's face it, you've been as well-framed as the Mona Lisa. Think about it,' he invited Mickey. 'You get an invite to a swanky do from a bloke you hate, one who wouldn't have given you the time of day when he was alive; you arrive to find the host skewered like a lamb kebab. Then you leg it, leaving your prints behind and three people conveniently able to provide us with your description. The whole thing stinks worse than a week-old corpse.'

At least his observations seemed to have stirred Mickey from his lethargy. Now, he was actually sitting up and paying attention.

'You said you received a note with the invitation.' Rafferty, suspecting that Mickey hadn't told the complete – or indeed *any* – of the truth about this conveniently burned note, questioned him further. 'Tell me what it said again.'

Mickey reddened and his lips thinned to a stubborn line of reluctance. But Rafferty wasn't about to let it go. 'Never mind being coy. If your ID's discovered, you're well placed to get charged with murder. It's not as if you'll be able to hide out here indefinitely.' Not at the extortionate price of two hundred and fifty smackers a week that Algy Edwards was charging, he wouldn't. 'You've got a motive. You had the opportunity. Who's to say you didn't also bring the means to kill him with you? You're placed at the scene, bro, or it's likely you soon will be, so come on, out with it. What did that note say? And never mind that "let's be friends" crap you told me before.'

Mickey's entire face seemed screwed up tighter than a pig's tail. But then he suddenly burst out, 'OK, if you must know, it said, "Maybe you" – meaning me – "could do your party piece for the ladies".'

'Party piece?'

'Drop my trousers like that bastard Seward used to do to me. Do I need to spell it out? He said some of those posh bints liked to get down and dirty with a bit of rough. And he did mean *dirty*. He said I'd already had the number two treatment. Maybe it was time I tried the number one one, too, and have some posh bird piss on me.'

Rafferty's eyebrows rose, then as quickly lowered as Mickey was wearing his belligerent face again. But no wonder his brother had decided to take Seward up on his invite. The note would have brought back all the humiliation he'd suffered as a youth, only now he was a man, and a fit and muscular one at that. And with all his own wood-working tools . . .

'You didn't—?' he began as doubt about Mickey's innocence came back to worry him.

'No, I didn't,' Mickey spat out, 'but, by Christ, I might have done if someone hadn't beaten me to it.'

Rafferty nodded and said no more, but if Mickey was telling the truth, and Rafferty believed he was, then *someone* had set him up. And he didn't think that someone was Sir Rufus Seward.

No, Mickey had been set up as a patsy to cover up someone else's loathing and murder. And his brother had taken the proffered bait and plunged into the trap as obligingly as the town bike dropped her drawers for the boys. Rafferty sat back thoughtfully. 'The three people who provided your description were Ivor Bignall and the two security men, Jake Arthur and Andy Watling. You're sure you don't know any of them?'

'No. Don't you think if I'd recognized them I'd have mentioned it before now?'

'OK. Perhaps it's that one or more of them knows you. It's got to be someone who knows what Seward did to you when you were young.'

Mickey sneered at his great detective big brother. 'Well done, Sherlock. Even I can work that much out. But let's face it, it could be anyone. You don't think Seward just *carried out* his ritual humiliations on his victims? He liked everyone to know about them, too.' Mickey leaned his head back against the orange banquette and closed his eyes. Despair was deeply etched into his face as he muttered, 'It could be anyone, I tell you.'

'Actually, that's not strictly true. It had to be someone who attended the party, for one thing, either in receipt of an official invitation or in the position to help themselves to a blank invitation and know what to write that would anger you sufficiently to attend Seward's party looking for a fight. Not quite anyone could do all those things. Presumably, this self-same person offed Seward.'

Rafferty picked up the one remaining piece of naan bread, wiped it round the now congealed vindaloo sauce and stuffed it in his mouth, chewing with every indication of enjoyment while his more fastidious brother made a face.

'You've reason to hope, Mickey. Things are looking brighter than they were at the beginning of the case. We're getting the suspects whittled down nicely and—'

'Whittle a bit faster, can't you,' Mickey interrupted without troubling to open his dark-shadowed eyes, 'or they might just get away with setting me up.'

Rafferty's ears pricked up then. He thought he had heard a noise outside. He shushed the already silent Mickey so he'd remain that way, got up from the hard banquette and edged the thin curtains aside a fraction.

'Shit!' he said. 'Turn that light out. I think I can hear a car. Who on earth . . .?

Rafferty peered with narrowed eyes through a gap at the edge of the not quite wide enough curtains. 'Damn. It *is* a car.' He peered harder and his entire body went stiff. 'Double shit! Mickey, come over here and tell me that car doesn't look the exact double of bloody Nigel's bird-pulling Porsche.'

Mickey, still apparently dejected in spite of Rafferty's determined pep talk, was taking no interest in proceedings. He hadn't even bothered to turn the light out, as Rafferty discovered as he pulled his head back from examining the world outside the caravan.

It was too late now, he realized. Nigel would have spotted the light for sure – not to mention taken note of his own car.

'What the hell's *he* doing here?' Rafferty asked of no one in particular. 'I've never taken him for a likely caravan buyer. Swanky apartments are more in his line.'

'Probably managed to get a look at that photofit picture you've been praying he wouldn't see,' Mickey told him listlessly from his slouched position on the torn banquette. He held out his wrists. 'You might as well put the cuffs on now.'

Rafferty ignored this suggestion.

Mickey shrugged and dropped his hands back in his lap. 'He'll have recognized me straight away if he's seen the photofit, and guessed you'll have stashed me somewhere out of the way. All he had to do was wait his chance, then follow you.'

'Elementary, my dear Watson,' Nigel said as he flung open the ill-fitting caravan door, climbed the steps and entered. He took in the scene at a glance and grinned. 'What a veritable Fagin's den we have here, to be sure.' He paused, but only to direct a sarcastic comment at the dejected Mickey.

'Remarkable that one of your intellect should recognize the keenness of my Holmesian deductions, but you're right, Mickey. When I saw the photofit of you, which I don't doubt Joseph tried to delay in getting to the media, I recognized you immediately. And as I knew my dear cousin was in charge of the investigation into Seward's death; it didn't take one of my wit and perspicacity long to deduce that he'd stashed his brother, the chief suspect, somewhere out of the way. And lo and behold – how right I was, because here you are, you pair of miscreants, up to yet more skulduggery. I heard you while I was outside. I thought I might as well listen to your conspiracy to see if I could learn anything else to my advantage.'

Rafferty sighed. He supposed it *had* only been a matter of time before someone sussed them. And perhaps he'd become a little careless when the days had passed and no one had come forward to identify Mickey. He'd certainly paid for his carelessness now. But why did it have to be bloody Nigel, of all people? That really was a mean trick, he silently informed the Almighty. You'll get yours, one day, God. What goes around, comes around. Maybe Lucifer will manage to stage a successful coup next time. Rafferty surely hoped so. For the Almighty's latest bit of fun in arranging Nigel's arrival could only mean their number was well and truly up. Nigel would at last be in a position to extract the revenge to which his sufferings on a previous case made him feel entitled. It was a revenge which he would undoubtedly feel Rafferty thoroughly deserved. Nigel had waited a long time for this moment and all he would be doing was his public duty.

In the light thrown up from the floor, Nigel's face positively glowed with the unaccustomed self-righteousness of good citizenship.

Nineteen

But Rafferty was wrong about Nigel's intentions, as, much to his surprise, he discovered shortly afterwards. Because Nigel had another agenda entirely, as he was quick to reveal.

Nigel, it seemed, was keen to use his knowledge of Mickey's whereabouts and Rafferty's complicity in his disappearance to do a deal. He would, he told them, trade discretion on his part for a similar favour from Rafferty's ma. Ma's knowledge of Nigel's more underhand doings had got Rafferty out of another problem earlier in the year when she had been able to threaten Nigel should he fail to keep his mouth shut about Rafferty's invidious position as chief suspect during the Made in Heaven murder investigation.

Rafferty knew he should be thankful that his cousin was only too ready to keep his and Mickey's secret. It was a quid pro quo situation, as even Ma, with two of her sons to protect, would agree when he had time to consult her on the matter. Doubtless she would soon manage to ferret out more of Nigel's indiscretions should they have need of them to replace the one that had got away.

Nigel had a bottle of the finest malt – what else? – in his car. After they had struck the deal, he retrieved it and they all took a swig. Although Mickey, who was still nursing more than fond fancies for a warm police cell, wore an expression of rueful regret rather than relief that he was destined to remain in his damp caravan for a while longer. Fortunately this preoccupation meant the 'kept in the dark' Mickey failed to question Rafferty about his own time as chief suspect.

It was some time later when Rafferty backed his car out of the caravan park and edged on to the road, followed by Nigel in his Porsche. Nigel didn't hang about. With a flash of his lights in the park entrance, he put his foot down, waved a triumphant hand in Rafferty's direction and zoomed past. Rather more slowly, pondering what excuse he could come up with for his lateness *this* time, Rafferty drove home to Abra. He rather thought he was going to have to tell her the truth. He had been reluctant to do so before because with every increase in those who knew about Mickey and where he was hidden, the likelihood that the information would get out increased too. As if it wasn't bad enough that all his family and now *Nigel* knew his guilty secret . . .

Rafferty acknowledged that it would have been wiser for him to have told Abra about Mickey earlier. To be the last in the know would gall any woman. He would have lied about this, too, but he'd never been any good at lying and knew she would suss the truth almost immediately. The upsetting advent of Nigel entering the equation now made him reluctant to keep her out of the loop any longer. Besides, he knew he was no longer capable of maintaining this deceit at home as well as at work.

So, it was with a hangdog demeanour that Rafferty let himself into their flat . . .

Abra was still up when Rafferty arrived home. It was an ominous sign. It was clear she'd stayed up deliberately in order to have a serious go at him about his plentiful disappearing acts.

He found her sitting in the living room, her arms folded and her expression worryingly determined. Worse, she reminded him of his ma. *Not* a good sign; it certainly didn't bode well for him or his secret. It was probably just as well that he had finally decided to tell Abra everything. He collapsed, exhausted, into an armchair and waited for the inquisition to start.

'Joseph Rafferty, you're making me think I'm about to shackle myself to the village idiot,' she told him when he finally shuffled out part of the back story.

Rafferty nodded. 'You may be right. Can I use it as a plea in mitigation, Your Honour?'

'No.'

But he'd known the answer before she had said it. He held his hands up. 'OK, Abra, I wouldn't lie to you if I didn't have a family like mine. And it's not even as if I *have* lied to you.'

'Just been economical with the truth? Is that what you're saying?'

He gave a begrudging nod before he launched into his defence. 'Have you any idea what it's like? Any idea how many scrapes I've barely got out of because of them? If it's not Ma, it's some three-times removed eejit from across the water. If it's not them it's "dear" Nigel. And now—'

'And now, I gather, from what you said last time we had this conversation, it's your equally eejit brother?' Abra encouraged.

Rafferty sighed and gave another nod. 'As you say, and now it's my eejit little brother, Mickey.'

To his relief, Abra failed to remind him of his own folly during the Made in Heaven case. This had been before he had met her and, feeling lonely, he had signed up with the dating agency borrowing Nigel's name so his matchmaking ma wouldn't interfere. The ensuing murders had made his life very difficult for a time.

Her expression turned conciliatory. Or perhaps he was just imagining the softening. He brightened when she patted her lap and said, as Rafferty laid his weary head down, 'So, come on, let's have the rest. What's he done, exactly? I want the Full Monty.'

Rafferty nestled into a warm place, took a deep breath, and told her. 'He's only managed to get himself at the top of the suspect list for Sir Rufus bloody Seward's murder. Dozy git.'

'Must run in the family. No wonder I thought that photofit of Seward's suspected murderer looked familiar. That's because he was.'

Rafferty nodded into her lap. Hoping for sympathy and thinking he might be in with a chance of getting some, he added on a plaintive note intended to encourage confirmation, 'Still sure you want to become a Rafferty?'

'Don't tempt me. And don't play the little boy lost card, Joe. I'm not your mother. This is serious. Surely I don't have to tell you that?' She shuffled his head off her lap and forced him to sit up. 'I want to hear the rest. So how – exactly – did he manage to become chief suspect?'

Reluctantly, Rafferty did as he was bidden. But, not totally obedient, he pulled Abra on to *his* lap. 'I can explain why I didn't tell you,' he began.

'You always can.'

Rafferty sighed quietly to himself – he didn't want to encourage more disparaging comments from his fiancée – if she still was his fiancée, that was. He felt sorry for himself even if Abra didn't. Why wasn't I born into a nice, respectable, middle-class family? he asked himself. I might be Chief Constable by now.

'I said I can explain and I will. Only reach for that bottle on the coffee table. I feel the need for some soothing balm hitting the cockles coming on.'

Abra reached, poured, crossed her arms and said, 'Well?'

Rafferty took his medication in one swallow. Then he began. He didn't stop till he'd got to the end. He told her the lot; right back to Seward's and Mickey's schooldays and up to the present.

Abra was quiet for some time. Then, either accidentally or intentionally, giving some pain to Rafferty's nether regions, she edged herself up from his lap and observed, 'The old goat seems to have quite a history, quite a past, of making enemies.'

'Mmm. Thankfully, the numbers of those in a position to have killed him are pretty limited.'

'And your brother's managed to put himself at the head of the list,' Abra unkindly reminded him before she reached for the Jameson's whiskey and poured him a second healthy slug as well as one for herself. 'So tell me about these other enemies and how they could have hit on your brother as the fall guy.'

Once he'd laid out the details of the other suspects and their possible involvement, he was relieved to see that Abra began to show some more sympathy.

'Poor Joe. It's clear to see that the worry about your brother has distracted you from this case.' She picked up her glass and sipped, her expression thoughtful. 'Go through with me what each of the suspects has said to you, what others have said about them and what conclusions you've drawn. I feel between all these you're just not seeing something obvious.'

Rafferty, a bit miffed it had to be said at this slight, put away his wounded pride sufficiently to do as she had asked.

His humility was rewarded, which was more – far more – than he had expected, because Abra helped him see what he had simply taken for granted about one aspect of the case, and it was such an obvious aspect now she had pointed it out. How could he not have realized it for himself before now?

Pouring out the latest confession to Abra had done wonders to concentrate Rafferty's mind; he knew he wouldn't have managed to shake loose some ideas about the murder and who might have committed it without Abra's help. She had encouraged him to think in a more rounded fashion about every aspect of the case. He'd been bogged down and distracted, as she had said – mostly by Mickey's involvement, but also, in the early days, by the sheer quantity of potential suspects.

Her comment as to how – *why* – the murderer had hit on Mickey as the patsy was a significant one – one he should have given greater thought to much earlier. As was her later comment about the *type* of murder it was: committed in the bedroom of a suite still populated with guests, it showed a certain arrogance on the part of the murderer. Even the clearly deliberate and successful attempt to brand Mickey as the fall guy indicated the ability to plan and scheme with a degree of ruthlessness. Given the number of ruthless business types who had been present at the party, that alone hadn't been enough to provide a lead. But now, with the whittling down done and with the suspects still in the frame matched with those who could have known about Mickey and his grudge against the dead man lined up in a row, the list was whittled down even further. To one, in fact. Ironically, this one even managed to encompass Superintendent Bradley's phantom blonde.

There were still several possibilities, of course, none of which he could afford to ignore in case his conclusions on the case were not as sound as he believed them to be. And over the following days, Rafferty examined them all with eyes made clearer by Abra's critical comments until he finally felt able to discount the rest and settle on the prime suspect. Because now, with the rest of the suspects exonerated, it made sense. Everything made sense. How had he not seen it before? he wondered again. He even thought he knew how it had been done. And *why* it had been done. It was a pity that proving it was likely to be the stickler . . .

*   *   *

It was fortunate that he had a bit of luck. Not fortunate for the Farraday twins, of course. But perhaps they, like Rufus Seward, had had it coming for some time. What did they say? What had he taunted God about? What goes around, comes around. That really did say it all, to Rafferty's mind.

It was DI Apsley, the opposite number he had spoken to when he and Llewellyn had visited the Norwich officer's patch who, aware of Rafferty's investigation, repaid his previous courtesy by notifying them about the latest deaths. The Norfolk Police had found the bodies of the twins shortly after they had been called in when one of the late Sir Rufus Seward's staff went to their cottage after they failed to turn up for work and found them both dead.

The twins had overdosed on some seriously pure heroin. Rafferty assumed it was the same stuff that he had read about in the Norwich newspaper. They hadn't even had time to get the needles out of their arms before they died.

After Inspector Apsley had spoken to Rafferty and they had had a mutual exchange of views about the twins' nastier habits as well as Rafferty's belief that someone had helped them to eternity, Apsley and his team had taken the twins' cottage apart. And while they hadn't found any contact details for their drug supplier, they *had* found a stash of heroin, which the forensic laboratory were in the process of testing for purity. They had also found a collection of interesting paperwork, tapes and photographs that confirmed Rafferty's suspicions about how the twins had been able to afford to indulge their various expensive hobbies.

After thanking Inspector Apsley, Rafferty put the phone down and said to Llewellyn, 'Get your coat on. We're off for another trip to Norfolk.'

As they hurried out to the car park, Rafferty filled Llewellyn in about the twins as well as his own conclusions as to the murderer's identity.

'What do you think are the chances of making an arrest?' Llewellyn enquired after he observed an excited Rafferty climb eagerly into the driver's seat and had resignedly walked round to the passenger side.

Rafferty gunned up the gas pedal, grinning to himself as he felt his sergeant wince. 'For the twins' murder, every chance.

Apparently there's a concealed CCTV camera opposite the end of the road where the police discovered the Norwich dealer has his dirty den. With any luck, we'll get a nice picture of our killer to add to our hall of fame. We're also in with a good chance of getting him for Seward's murder, because I think he'll cough once he knows we've got him for the twins' murders. He'll want to get *something* out of all this. I don't think he'll be able to stop himself explaining how cleverly he almost pulled it off.'

Rafferty drove out of the car park at record speed, just avoided colliding with a traffic island, and headed in the direction of the A12.

'Remember I told you what a sneaky pair of lowlifes the Farraday twins always were?' He didn't wait for Llewellyn's reply. 'They had quite a collection of stuff on various of Seward's associates and other assorted enemies, including our boy. Lots of nice little earners, apparently. The Farraday lads were always ones to keep their eyes open and their ears to the ground in search of blackmail booty. According to the Norfolk plods, the twins' cottage had been seriously pulled apart before they got there.

'But our killer didn't find what he was looking for. The Farradays had their blackmail evidence stash too well hidden for anyone but a professional searcher. Thankfully, Norfolk's finest put their backs into it and managed to find the twins' hidey-hole. The twins had each even written and signed witness statements about what they'd seen on the night of Seward's murder. The mad, greedy little bastards were blackmailing Seward's murderer for his inheritance. The one he wasn't even going to get. Adds a nice touch, I thought. I doubt it took him long to figure out who amongst those at the party had played "I Spy", with him as the answer. But as he wasn't down to receive a fat inheritance from Seward at all, they were demanding the one thing he was unable to give them. So, instead, he gave them what he could – death and silence at the end of a needle.'

As Rafferty's racing-driver motoring out of the car park had indicated, he was impatient to get to his destination. They even got to Norwich in one piece, though not without reducing Llewellyn's sallow Welsh colouring to something approaching tallow.

187

But Rafferty had ignored all Llewellyn's cautious warnings on the way, as he ignored all his recriminatory reproaches once they had arrived at the Norwich police station and parked up.

'Quit griping, Daff. Do you want these Norfolk boys to steal all our thunder? Which they will if we don't manage to get there before they find the right piece of CCTV footage.'

They were immediately directed up to the viewing room, which was filled with excited Norwich cops working their way through the pile of tapes and talking about 'compooters' in their Norfolk accents.

There was a roar of laughter as they recognized a well-known national politician gaze furtively to left and right on the tape, before he gained admission to the dealer's house.

'Nice to know we're represented by such pillars of the community,' one officer commented. 'What is it with these politicos? If it's not drugs, its mouthy mistresses or rent boys. Aren't fat pay cheques, very long holidays, free foreign jollies and index-linked pensions enough for the greedy bastards? If this politician and his liking for mind-altering substances is anything to go by, it's no wonder they come up with such naff, ill-thought-through laws that we're expected to make work.'

'Bastards are probably all high as kites, half the time,' another jaded detective commented.

'Mmm,' a third commented. 'God knows how they'd manage if most of them weren't lawyers by trade.'

'Might manage some common sense, for a change,' Apsley offered. 'So whose turn is it to leak it to the press?'

Enthusiastic volunteers clamoured vociferously for the job, but before Apsley could choose his favourite, he held his hand up, asked for hush and added, 'Hang on. We can toss for that pleasure later. For now, take a look at that tousle-haired git.' He turned and gazed at Rafferty. 'Is he our John?'

Rafferty pushed his way nearer to the screen. 'Wind it back,' he tersely instructed. 'I want to take a closer look.'

The Norfolk officer seated before the screen threw a dirty look in his direction, but did as he was told.

Rafferty squinted hard at the grainy tape as the man on the CCTV footage approached the dealer's terraced home and climbed the steps to the door. He checked the date on the tape. Yesterday. Then he grinned and punched the air. 'Yes!'

Because even though Marcus Canthorpe had tried to disguise himself with a scarf pulled around his thin face, there was no disguising his mop of fair hair, which vanity had probably made him reluctant to crush under a concealing hat.

'I didn't have Canthorpe down as a druggie,' Rafferty commented later as he and Llewellyn took advantage of the Norfolk force's canteen facilities to grab a bite of lunch with Inspector Apsley. Canthorpe had been picked up and was safely stashed in the cells and Rafferty had been given permission to join the local officers in questioning him. He was looking forward to that.

'I don't think he is,' said Apsley just before he took a giant bite of his burger in a bun. He was forced to chew hard before he could go on. His dentures flashed brilliant white in contrast to his jowly, mottled, beer and junk food raddled face. Rafferty caught a glimpse of well-chewed burger and bun before he hastily lowered his gaze.

'We've had this backstreet den of iniquity under regular surveillance for some time, and not just via the CCTV. There have been several fatalities since this pure heroin hit the streets over a week ago. The usual waste of space druggies, of course, but also one high-profile media type, which had the Chief Constable pressing all our buttons after the dead media bloke's family had doubtless pressed his. At least he agreed to fund the surveillance, which he mightn't have done without the media mogul's death. Reckon this media type must have slept with someone in high office.'

'Those bastards are all under one another's duvets,' a sour and grizzled uniformed officer offered.

'Anyway,' Apsley went on, 'as I said, your boy hasn't showed up on our surveillance cameras before but this pure heroin has received plenty of publicity locally. Maybe your suspected perp just read the papers like anyone else, put a few feelers out and got the dealer's name. Rocket science it ain't. The doziest new scumbag in town manages to score with hardly any trouble at all. Your suspect must have thought that with his victims already being keen and enthusiastic druggies it was a perfect method of getting rid of the twin dangers to his future without any suspicion landing on him.

'They'd treated themselves to a batch of this pure and deadly stuff and overdosed on it, is what we must have been expected to think. Probably what we *would* have thought if you and I hadn't had our little chat,' he told Rafferty. 'I imagine he waited till they were out of the way, then searched their cottage till he found where they kept their stash and swapped it for this deadly heroin. After all,' he shrugged, 'what could be more likely? What more common than another dead drug addict or two? Devious bastard.'

'Might have got away with it, too, as you said, but for his own vanity and for the fact the twins were well-known for being a pair of grasping little gits,' opined Rafferty as he sipped his tea before reapplying himself to the steaming plateful of chicken curry. 'And,' he added airily, 'if I hadn't already hit on him as chief suspect. But,' he also added, in pursuit of future cooperation, 'I doubt we'd have got him without your help. Thanks, Inspector.'

'You're welcome. Just do the same for me one day.' Apsley turned his red face around on his fat neck and shouted across the canteen. 'Hey, Jenkins, you sorted out yet who's going to leak the news on the druggie politician?'

Before Jenkins had a chance to answer, Apsley added in a voice that brooked no argument, 'We're doing it in order of rank, I take it? None of this Buggins's turn?'

Once he'd gained Jenkins' reluctant agreement that he was top dog in this particular kennel, Apsley turned back and gave Rafferty a self-satisfied smile. He had a piece of burger stuck to his dentures, Rafferty noticed. Saving it for later, probably.

'Why should politicians be the only ones to get the perks?' Apsley asked of no one in particular. 'Bloody shame Guy Fawkes didn't pull it off and manage to blow up that Westminster knocking shop. Still, it's a good job our glorious leader pushed for the surveillance after the media guy turned his toes up. Heard he threw a right hissy fit with the holders of the purse strings till he got his way.'

Rafferty, not usually one to have anything to thank the force's brass for, sent up a silent song of gratitude to the hissy-fitter-in-chief.

The drive back to Elmhurst was a rather more leisurely one than the outward journey had been. Possibly this was down to the fact that Llewellyn had grabbed the car keys and inserted his slim body into the driver's seat in a determined fashion before Rafferty had a chance to object.

Rafferty shrugged. He was in no rush – not now. The Norfolk cops had Marcus Canthorpe safely in custody and although he wasn't singing yet, as Rafferty had already concluded, he didn't think it would be too long before Canthorpe gave in to the temptation to show them how clever he had been.

He had almost done so once already, when Rafferty had sought confirmation as to how Canthorpe had managed to learn that he didn't, after all, feature in Seward's will. But, as Rafferty had finally realized, after Abra had encouraged some logical sideways thought on the problem, Canthorpe was in and out of Seward's solicitors, McCann, Doolittle and Steel, all the time. Doubtless, he had become such a familiar face, that, like himself with Bill Beard's station reception the other evening, Marcus Canthorpe had practically a free run of the place. So, the secretaries had become careless, much as Bill Beard had been when his urgent need to use the gents' toilet had inclined him to leave his post in reception to Rafferty's tender mercies and he'd returned to find his jealously protected *Mirror* crossword had been completed in his absence.

There must have been plenty of opportunities for Canthorpe to help himself to the solicitors' branded envelopes. Once he'd done that, all he had to do was open the envelope containing the latest redrafted will when it arrived, read it and discover what a treacherous, chiselling cur was his boss, reseal it in one of the stolen envelopes and drop it into the outgoing post tray at the solicitor's so that when it was franked it bore their advertising logo.

After that, as Rafferty had remarked to Canthorpe's 'No comment', it had simply been a matter of plotting how best to get his revenge on his employer for his failure to include the generous legacy in his will as he had promised.

Canthorpe's room had been taken apart. They had found a safety deposit key and the box was revealed to contain fifty grand that he had presumably stolen from Seward's safe. He had, it was clear, intended to have his revenge *and* his legacy, even if it was a legacy he had decided to provide for himself.

Alongside his 'No comment', Canthorpe had merely smiled his thin smile when he heard they had found the money earmarked for his R and R in the sun. It was a smile that hadn't reached his eyes. For his eyes glittered with a malevolent fury that his plans had gone awry that Rafferty found more than satisfying. He was confident that Canthorpe, denied everything else that he had hoped for, would want to get *something* out of the last weeks. Even if it was only the reluctant admiration of a bunch of plods.

Rafferty felt that, having endured so much grief and anguish, he had more than earned a reward himself, even if it was just the petty one of being proved right, though he admitted to himself that he was a bit put out that Superintendent Bradley would also gain some satisfaction at the successful conclusion to the case. Because he *had* seen a blond vanish through the door to Seward's bedroom, only it had been the fair mop of hair of the slimly-built Marcus Canthorpe, not that of a young woman at all. Seen from the back with Bradley's limited vision, it was an easy mistake to make, which the super hadn't been slow to point out.

Twenty

I t was the night before Christmas. Rafferty had received an early gift. For Marcus Canthorpe had begun to sing. Fortunately, his chosen airs weren't Christmas carols, but the truth about Seward's murder.

He was pleased that he had been right in his expectation that Canthorpe would tell all sooner rather than later. They had proof enough of his guilt over the twins' deaths, so why should he continue to deprive himself of the satisfaction of explaining just how clever he'd been over the murder of Sir Rufus Seward? He was going to jail whatever happened.

Rafferty and Llewellyn, recalled to Norwich Police Station by DI Apsley for another session with Canthorpe, had hardly entered the interview room before Canthorpe launched into his torrent.

'Shame that old bastard Seward never mentioned that Mickey Rafferty had a police inspector for a brother,' he observed bitterly before he paused and admitted, 'But perhaps I should give him the benefit of the doubt on that. After all, I don't suppose he troubled to keep in contact with his carpenter classmate. It was his wealthy, influential peers he was keen to impress and network with. Over the long years of working for him, I discovered most of the tales about what Seward had done to people in his youth. He used to boast about them. The humiliations, the bullying, the lies. I looked some of these people up when I knew this civic reception in Seward's home-town was in the offing. I thought I might be able to entice one or two of the more gullible amongst his earlier victims along to the reception.'

'So, what made you pick on Mickey to take the rap for Seward's murder?' Rafferty asked.

Canthorpe shrugged. 'Sheer fluke, really. Your brother was

the only one of the unimportant, underachieving nobodies to reply to the invitation and actually turn up. The others of his ilk to whom I had sent invitations contented themselves with sending back rude RSVP responses. Apart from Sir Rufus's local charity cases who all left early, the other invitees who accepted were way too rich and powerful for me to even consider trying to use one of them as a patsy for murder.'

'How did you even know my brother had arrived?' Rafferty questioned. 'He told me he never saw anyone but the security guards and Ivor Bignall.'

'Simple enough, Inspector. All the guests had been requested to report to reception when they arrived. I instructed the duty receptionists to ring through to the suite to advise of each guest's arrival so I could be at the door to welcome them. I was warned when he was on his way up.'

'And Mickey gave his name at reception?' Dumbfounded, Rafferty stared at Canthorpe. If that was the case, how on earth had Mickey's identity remained undiscovered? They had questioned the reception staff closely. None had mentioned a Mickey Rafferty amongst the party guests, so how—?

'Come now, Inspector, surely you've worked *that* one out by now? You've done so well with the rest, after all.'

Canthorpe's patronizing tone annoyed Rafferty, but he did his best not to show it. He frowned, glanced at Llewellyn for inspiration, changed his mind about that and was finally forced to shake his head.

Canthorpe breathed out on a sigh as if Rafferty had disappointed him. 'Let's just say your brother's invitation was couched a little differently to the others. But over the years, even though we've never actually met, I've felt I've come to know him rather well. I thought an invitation inscribed with the name Michael "Browncock" Rafferty likely to stir the memory sufficiently that he would be sure to provide merely a brief flash of his invitation at reception and a garbled name. Few indeed of the other guests that night were of a retiring disposition or given to garbling either their names or their syntax. It wasn't hard to guess that the "Mickey Orr" that the receptionist reported as the latest arrival was the man I was waiting for. You'll understand why I didn't tarry at the door to greet him as I had with the other guests. I had another, more pressing task to perform.

'I had instructed reception to simply text their messages to my mobile. Ringing phones can be *so* annoying, don't you find? And, of course, I took the trouble to get chatty with the hotel staff before Sir Rufus's big night so I could discover who were the laziest amongst the security staff. Easily enough accomplished. I soon learned that both Arthur and Watling were well known for their idleness and inattention to duty, so I specifically asked for them to do door duty that night.'

'But why should you want inattentive security guards for the door? You deliberately set Mickey up and must surely—'

'True, but I felt it would look a little *too* set up if his name was immediately known. Besides, I thought a mystery man would add a certain *piquancy* to your investigation.'

'You could have added another suspect to the mix. Why didn't you draw our attention to the fact that Nigel Blythe had turned up at your boss's Norfolk home? You must have recognized him when he arrived at the reception as he sat in your office for an hour before Seward sent him off with a flea in his ear, but I had to find out his presence there for myself when I viewed your security tape.'

'Let's just say Mr Blythe wasn't convenient for my plans. I already had one patsy, I didn't need another to confuse the issue. It was a mistake, I see that now. I suppose that's what first made you suspect me.'

'You were always a suspect, Mr Canthorpe, so let's just say your failure to mention the interesting Mr Blythe made you even more interesting to cynical policemen than he was, especially when it was you who found your boss's body. It was the second time you came to my attention during the investigation. And when I began to think more clearly about who had the best opportunity to send my brother an invitation, the best opportunity, too, to learn all about the history between him and Seward and who was physically present the night he was murdered, you stood out from the crowd.

'Your failure to reveal you recognized Mr Blythe was curious enough on its own. You now say you didn't need a second patsy in Mr Blythe, so why did you try to point the finger at Ivor Bignall?'

'I didn't feel I had any choice about that. I assumed I hadn't been the only one to notice that Ivor Bignall was decidedly cool towards my boss that night. Better, I thought, to mention it than not. I didn't feel I had a choice, as I said. But Mr Blythe was, I thought, my little secret. The only other person who knew of his presence at the Norfolk estate that day was Sir Rufus. And I knew he wouldn't be saying anything. Why draw your eye from the ball I'd put so neatly in place? Nigel Blythe was a wild card I didn't want or need. I'd already decided on my patsy. Why confuse matters?'

By now, Marcus Canthorpe seemed to have accepted his fate. He was certainly being obligingly chatty about what he had done. Even so, his voice held a certain rueful resentment as he added, 'But if I'd known my patsy had a police inspector for a brother, I'd have done without the piquancy. Imagine how I felt when I learned an Inspector Rafferty was to lead the investigation and enquiries revealed that you were one of the three brothers that Sir Rufus had been at school with?'

Canthorpe gave an arrogant, self-congratulatory smile. 'In the circumstances, I think I showed a quite remarkable sangfroid.'

For once, Rafferty's lack of languages didn't let him down. He recalled Llewellyn using the expression once and he'd looked it up. 'You're right,' he told Canthorpe. 'Your blood *is* cold. A good match for your heart, I imagine.'

Canthorpe simply stared at him for several seconds before he demanded, 'Do you want to hear the rest?' When Rafferty gave a brief, unobliging nod, he continued. 'Anyway, your brother was perfect for my plans. And the sharpened carpenter's wood chisel really was a particularly pleasing touch. And what a stroke of luck for me that it should be the carpenter Rafferty brother who took the invitation bait rather than one of the other possible patsies. It was a case of him being in the wrong place at the wrong time. Nothing personal.'

Nothing personal? Rafferty thought. By Christ, it had *felt* personal!

To restrain his urge to beat Canthorpe to a bloody pulp, he demanded, 'So what would you have done if Mickey hadn't turned up that night?'

'Bided my time, of course, till the next occasion. Seward had a party planned for New Year's Eve at his Norwich estate.

I managed to hook another couple of grudge-bearing losers into accepting invitations for that, much as I did your brother for this reception. All it took was to enclose the celebrity guest list with the invitation. Some people will eat any amount of humble pie when the chance to peer down Jordan's cleavage is dangled in front of them.'

Canthorpe, expecting Mickey's imminent arrival after having arranged with reception to text his mobile when each guest arrived at the hotel, now revealed he had concealed himself in the large walk-in closet down the short hallway leading to Seward's bedroom till he could be sure Mickey had actually reached the penthouse suite. From there, he had been able to see the door to the suite reflected in the large mirror on the wall opposite.

Rafferty could only presume it had been this same mirror via which one of the Farraday twins had spotted Canthorpe's strange behaviour in concealing himself in one of the floor-to-ceiling cupboards lining the passage to Seward's bedroom.

Once sure of his patsy's arrival, and after recognizing the hesitant Mickey from an earlier surveillance at his address, Canthorpe had covered his suit with the long raincoat for added protection from blood splashes and hurried down the short hallway leading to Seward's en suite bedroom. It was just then that Superintendent Bradley had spotted him and mistaken him for a young woman.

Mickey had clearly not been sober, Canthorpe told them, and his expression looked pugnacious; his behaviour had, fortunately, encouraged Ivor Bignall to remember him when he had spoken to him to direct him to Seward's bedroom and so improve Canthorpe's ability to use Mickey as a scapegoat and chief suspect.

Once Canthorpe knew his patsy had arrived, he crept into Seward's bedroom, the sharpened chisel stolen from hotel maintenance ready in his pocket. It was time for Seward's planned despatch.

Canthorpe explained that he knew he couldn't waste any time. 'I approached Seward, who was writing at his desk. As usual, Seward didn't trouble to look up. He was a rude man and invariably ignored underlings and made them wait if they wanted his attention.

'However, I had no intention of waiting this time. Instead, after having helped myself to a large bath towel from Seward's en suite for additional stain protection, I immediately plunged the chisel into Seward's back, having taken the added precaution of keeping the chisel in a plastic bag in my pocket and sliding on a pair of cotton gloves from a plastic bag in my other pocket before I touched the chisel's wooden hilt. I'd already given the chisel a good scouring to remove any traces of the maintenance man, as I didn't want it revealed exactly where it had come from in case you started asking questions of the staff.

'I'd already put on thin rubber gloves so none of my DNA traces would come into direct contact with the cotton gloves. The large towel and charity shop raincoat I'd previously purchased protected my clothing from any blood spurts.'

Having murdered his hated boss, and hearing Mickey question Ivor Bignall about Seward's whereabouts, Canthorpe told them he had quickly concealed himself in Seward's en suite bathroom. With the door ajar a fraction, he witnessed Mickey's horror as he took in Seward's clearly dead body and watched as he left the bedroom and did what he had been sure he *would* do – leave the suite without telling anyone what he had seen.

Satisfied, Canthorpe had waited in the en suite till the main hallway was deserted, re-hung the raincoat in one of the closets and discarded the protective towel in the suite's main bathroom. He had then rejoined the party, confident, given the inebriated state of the remaining guests, that he wouldn't have been missed. But between Mickey's arrival, Seward's murder and Mickey's hasty departure, no more than five minutes had elapsed.

Of course, he hadn't taken the snooping twins into consideration. One or both of them must have seen, in the mirror reflection, him conceal himself in the closet. It would be enough to spark curiosity in anyone, but in people as eternally nosey as the Farraday twins, it was a curiosity that was to prove fatal all round. The twins had brought their own downfall as well as Canthorpe's, as he bitterly commented.

The twins were spying little gits, always had been in Rafferty's fading recollection of their shared schooldays. He had suspected that one day their activities would be the death of them. And so it had proved.

With their predilection for spying on people, their concealed paperwork collection had revealed that they had found Seward's many parties and functions an especially fruitful ground for discovering sordid secrets that they could use to their advantage. Doubtless it was the reason they had taken employment with Seward; they had probably both thought becoming Seward's employees might be a big help in this area.

They'd only been on the staff for a matter of months, so Canthorpe, so much younger than the twins and without the advantage of having gone to school with them, had failed to notice in time their unfortunate tendencies to spy and snitch.

Once they had revealed their suspicions of Canthorpe's guilt and demanded money for their silence, their fate was sealed. With so much at stake, Canthorpe had made use of their greedy love of drugs to help the pair to their own deaths.

Rafferty stood up and, for the tape, said, 'Interview terminated at 3.15 p.m.' As he took the twin tapes from the machine he stared at Canthorpe, was about to add something *not* for the tape, then changed his mind. Marcus Canthorpe had already put him, Mickey and the rest of their family through enough. Mickey had come close to losing his freedom; he'd come close to being suspended, losing his career and having the book thrown at him. In view of all that, he refused to lose his dignity also.

Canthorpe wasn't worth wasting any more of his energy over. He needed every ounce of it to get his Christmas shopping sorted. All of it. And if he chose his shops with care, maybe they'd even wrap the gifts for him, and in a far more attractive manner that his ham-fisted efforts were likely to achieve. He could even co-opt Llewellyn as arbiter of taste for the job. After all, with the investigation concluded, that only left the paperwork to be done. And even Bradley wouldn't demand they complete that chore on Christmas Eve.

As Rafferty told Llewellyn on the drive back to Elmhurst, the shopping successfully and speedily accomplished in the nearest department store which offered beautiful gift-wrapping, in his own way, Marcus Canthorpe had become every bit as callous and ruthless as his boss. 'I suppose he'd spent the last five years watching and studying, in Rufus Seward, a ruthless professional at work. Something was bound to rub off.'

'Rather like your poor spelling has an adverse effect on my own,' Llewellyn murmured.

Rafferty chose not to hear this. 'Even so, imagine deliberately setting up an entirely innocent man, a complete stranger, to take the rap for murder. I'm still having trouble getting my head around that.'

Llewellyn shrugged and commented, 'As you said, he didn't lack an excellent tutor in the ways of evil. He'd spent years watching how his boss operated. It was only too likely some of that behaviour would rub off.'

Rafferty nodded. Poor Mickey, as he had discovered, had merely been a randomly selected patsy for Seward's murder. Canthorpe had sent out a number of invitations to people whom, as he had learned during his long employment with Seward, had reason to bear his boss a grudge. Mickey had been the only lowly such invitee to accept the party invitation. Canthorpe hadn't been quite daring enough to target the not-so-lowly, like Ivor Bignall or Idris Khan. Talk about it's the rich wot gets the pleasure and it's the poor wot gets the blame . . .

As Canthorpe had told Rafferty, it had been 'nothing personal'. But, he reflected again, it had sure *felt* personal to Rafferty, Mickey and the rest of their family.

'By the way,' Llewellyn interrupted Rafferty's musings, 'you never told me what the superintendent said when you rang and told him he was in the clear.'

'Didn't I?'

'I hope he thanked you, at least.'

'Not a bit of it. He bawled me out for even daring to consider him a suspect in the first place. I'd be off his Christmas card list for sure – if, that is, I'd ever been on it.'

Llewellyn gave a heartfelt sigh. 'Bosses. They were ever thus.'

'Ain't that the truth,' Rafferty replied, before it occurred to him that *he* was *Llewellyn*'s boss. He frowned. Was Llewellyn having a sly dig? But I'm nothing like Bradley, he felt like protesting. He wanted to ask his sergeant if he *did* consider him on a par with Bradley, but then he thought better of it. He wasn't altogether convinced he would like Llewellyn's reply.

He wasn't too keen on what Llewellyn said next, either.

'So, are you going to tell me now where it was you hid your brother? I finally remembered a couple of days ago where I'd met him before,' he revealed. 'Or are you going to deny his disappearance was your doing?'

Shocked that Llewellyn had correctly deduced his involvement without once betraying a hint of it, Rafferty was happy to take guidance from his sergeant's remark. I'm going to deny it, damn right I am, he said to himself. Deny, deny, deny. It's much the best way. And he proceeded to do exactly that.

Twenty-One

With Mickey absolved from all suspicion – not to mention a similar absolution for Superintendent Bradley and the others who had made the suspects' list – that evening, Rafferty and his family prepared to celebrate the festive season and Mickey's own absolution in style.

They all felt they had earned it, Rafferty not least. And even the God that Rafferty considered so vengeful wouldn't, this time, he felt sure, dare to stick his almighty nose in and try to cause Rafferty grief as he so often did.

'Because if you do,' Rafferty warned the many stars twinkling innocently in the night sky before he got in the car and drove off to release his brother from his caravan cell preparatory to joining Ma, Abra and all down the pub – even Llewellyn had condescended to join them with his wife Maureen, 'I really will consider giving into the many temptations your oppo puts in my path and sign up for *his* army. Who knows, if he ever has another go at starting a heavenly coup, he might be on to a winner, his army of sinners being surely much bigger than your saintly bunch. So think on, Big Boy.'